APPRENTICE

LEXIE WINSTON

Lexie Winston has been an astronaut, rock star, princess and time traveller. In her dreams. But none of the dreams have lived up to what becoming an author has been like. She gets to live in a world of pure imagination, and her heroines get to do the things she's always wished she could.

When not writing books, Lexie is a mother of two gorgeous teenagers and the wife to a patient and understanding man. They live in Western Australia and are lorded over by a black toy poodle. She loves camping, reading and if her iPad was stolen, her world would explode. (It has the kindle app on it.)

And check out my website at lexiewinston.com

And you can find all my links at
https://linktr.ee/LexieWinston

ALSO BY LEXIE WINSTON

The Collectors Division

(Reverse Harem Series)

Guardian

Guardian's Blood

Guardian Ascending

Neighpalm Industries Collective

(Enemies to Lovers Reverse Harem)

Abandoned Girl

Broken Girl

Tormented Girl

Wanted Girl

Cherished Girl

Loved Girl

Superficial Girl - Jacinta's Story

Seductive Sins Collection

(Reverse Harem Series)

Glorious Gluttony

Gangs, Guns, and Glory

Galaxy Circus

(Sci-Fi Reverse Harem Series)

Apprentice

Stagehand

Whisperer

A Night Most Wicked - Galaxy Circus Novella

Broken Promises

(Dark Poly Romance Series)

Secrets Kept

Lies Untold

M.I.T.H.O.S

(Contemporary RH)

Spies Like Me

Coming 2022

First published by Neighpalm Publishing in 2021

Apprentice: Galaxy Circus Series

Mobi format: 978-0-6489412-6-2
Print: 978-0-6489412-7-9

Cover design by Raven Ink Covers
Edited by Inked Imagination

 Created with Vellum

To everyone I went to school with.

Bet you didn't know I was such a freak ;)

Apprentice is the first Galaxy Circus novel, a fast-burn RH series that contains some adult situations which may be triggering, such as dub-con.

Galaxy Circus will also contain MM and male appendages of a somewhat interesting nature.

CHAPTER ONE

"Miss Jenson, did you hear what I just said to you?" Mr. Ryding, the weaselly-looking lawyer, says to me from behind the large walnut desk. He's fidgeting with the papers in front of him, stacking them, picking them up, tapping them, and then placing them back on the desk in front of himself. While I sit there, waiting for him to say more, he straightens the pens in the holder to the right of him. Given he's done this all at least half a dozen times, it seems like he's doing everything in his power to avoid making eye contact with my very confused self.

"I'm sorry. I'm not sure I understand you. I received a letter from your office saying I have been bequeathed something. I was told that I must present myself in person to sign some papers in order to receive it. Now, you are *also* telling me it was from a grandfather I didn't even know existed, one who obviously didn't want me, as I spent the first eighteen years of my life in foster homes."

He looks up, briefly pausing his fidgeting. "Yes, that's correct. Though it's grandfathers. Plural."

Plural? I puzzle internally. *Never mind, I'll come back to that.*

"John, William, and Eric Adams are your paternal grandfathers, and it wasn't that they didn't want you." His shifty eyes soften briefly before he continues. "They weren't able to find you. Your parents were estranged from them, and they were not notified at the time of your parents' accident. When you were placed in foster care, they weren't in the States, making it even harder for word to come down the appropriate channels." He shuffles his papers again. "When they did eventually find out, John rushed back. Unfortunately, you'd been placed in the system and had your name changed, as per a request in your parents' will, by then. You'd disappeared and were well hidden. Due to the nature of their business, they decided that maybe you were better off. Their job required constant traveling, never settling in one place for very long. It was no place to raise a child, or so they thought. They believed you were safe and loved."

I scoff out loud at that one, hitting my limit of holding my tongue. Though I have to give the man credit. Despite his obvious nerves and my apparent skepticism, he soldiers on. "Otherwise, they would have claimed you immediately," he assures me.

"So, why am I finding out about this now? I'm

assuming they're all dead, so why leave our estrangement until I had no chance of getting to know them?" I'm trying my best to keep my tone under control, but I'm honestly at a loss. There isn't a part of me that can reconcile these strangers leaving their granddaughter at the mercy of the system, name change or not. There had to be something terribly wrong with them, or maybe they thought there was something terribly wrong with me, if they'd chosen to stay away until we lost the chance to ever have a relationship.

The shifty look in his eyes is back, and the fidgeting obviously isn't cutting it since he gets up from his desk and starts to pace behind it. He marches back and forth in front of the big picture window which holds the view of the river his office backs onto. He stops, takes a deep breath, and turns to look at me.

"Well, actually, that's not quite true. Misters Adams have not passed on. They've decided to retire, and the family business may only pass down to a family member. You're the one that was chosen, so they contracted our firm to find you. It has taken quite a while, I can assure you."

"Excuse me?" I gasp. "Are you saying my grandfathers are alive and want to meet me?" As a little girl, I would have dreams of a relative swooping in to rescue me from the never-ending cycle of foster homes. I had finally given up around the age of thirteen. I wasn't one of those kids who were beaten or abused in care; I just never seemed to fit in. I was never really included or felt like I was one of the family. It would've been nice to know there was someone out there who wanted me.

Of course, my very skeptical nature decides this is too good to be true, turning my surprise into anger.

"Why the fuck am I dealing with a lawyer and not them directly? Can they not even be bothered, or are they too fucking chicken to face me themselves?" I can practically feel the steam escaping from my ears. It takes a lot to get me mad, but when I get there, you better watch out. Mr. Ryding swallows nervously and brings a finger up, trying to loosen his collar.

"Ah… but… They're…" he stammers. The man must be good at his job if he was able to track me down, which was apparently quite the feat, but he's horribly unprepared to deal with a woman's anger.

Taking a deep breath, I try to calm down. *Don't take it out on the lawyer, Lila. He's just the messenger.*

"Why me? I'm assuming there are other family members they could turn to?" I rub my eyes, already feeling a headache brewing. They've steadily been getting more frequent, and this meeting is not doing me any favors.

"Yes, well, no. There *are* other family members, but you are their only grandchild, and they've decided that it's time you join the family legacy. You are to be given the opportunity first. All the details are in the package." He sits back down at the desk and gestures to the stack of papers he'd been fidgeting with. "You're required to spend twelve months within the business, learning all the ins and outs. If, at the end of the twelve-month period, you're unwilling to continue, the business and the role of CEO and all it entails will pass on to the next eligible family member. You will carry on with life as if the previous twelve months had never really happened."

I stare at the package like it's a snake that's going to bite me. I just don't know what to think. Do I ignore it, sign it over now, and wash my hands of the whole debacle? Or do I take a leap of faith and at least meet the men that could be the best *or* the worst thing to happen to me?

"Can I have some time to think about this?" I ask. "It's quite a decision I need to make."

Mr. Ryding shakes his head. "I'm sorry, but this decision needs to be made as soon as possible. Our firm has been looking for you for a while, and I'm afraid we're out of time. You need to be on a plane to London in two days' time. We're going to need an answer now."

It's my turn to start pacing. Jumping out of the chair I've been sitting in, I start stalking back and forth across the room. The pounding behind my eyes has intensified, and I rub my temples in an attempt to alleviate it. What to do? It's not like I have anything keeping me here. I don't really have friends, mainly acquaintances. My best friend and roomie is head over heels in love with her partner, so she'd be ok if I left. I have a dead-end job in a bar that pays crappy but keeps me busy. Looking at the facts of my life, as totally unimpressive as they are, I guess there's nothing specifically stopping me from going. I've always dreamed of adventures, feeling sure that there must be something better in store than the life I've been living.

"All right," I tell him, making the decision, "I'm in. Show me where to sign."

He goes to the stack of papers on the table and pulls some out. "You need to sign here, here, and here. One of them is a non-disclosure form. No matter what happens, from here on, you are bound by a confidentiality clause. Even if at the end of twelve months you change your mind, everything you see and do will be confidential, and there are some very harsh consequences if you break the clause. A plane ticket is also in the pack, in your name, with the details of your flight. You'll be met at the airport by a driver who will take you to where you need to be. For your peace of mind, you can tell people where you are going and why, but there is to be no sharing of any other details. It's actually a good thing that you don't have a huge circle of friends." I'm torn between surprise that he knows that fact and being insulted by the comment despite its truth.

"We've been looking for you for so long I wouldn't hesitate to say we know everything about you," he replies to my look, a little more defensively than I expected the nervous guy to manage.

"Yeah, ok, because that's not creepy or rude," I reply sarcastically.

I busy myself with signing papers, and by the time I'm finished, my hand aches and my head throbs incessantly. Gathering my copies of everything, I shove them in my hand bag; I'll read it all when I get home. "So what business have I just signed my life away to?" I ask Mr. Ryding, thinking this is probably something I should have asked *before* signing. Fuck, I'm an idiot. Why didn't I ask that first? I mentally slap my impulsive self.

"Have you heard of the Galaxy Circus?" he asks, slightly distracted with gathering all his copies of the paperwork.

I nod enthusiastically, feeling more upbeat than I have this entire meeting. "Oh yes, isn't that the circus that claims it has aliens as its performers? It pops up throughout the globe and is always sold out even though the schedule is too random for anyone to know where they'll be next. People have been trying to debunk them for years. I remember reading that PETA was trying to gain access to prove that their animals are mistreated." I laugh loudly, remembering how that particular situation worked out. Apparently, the circus claimed their animals were really shifters, a clever gimmick that allowed them some special dispensation and gave PETA no ground to stand on. Hey, if people were gullible enough to believe it, then that was their problem.

He looks at me, a strange glint in his eye. "Are they gullible or just looking to be entertained?" he questions, his words coming oddly close to the thought I hadn't spoken aloud. "Well, whether they're gullible or not is besides the point. It still attracts huge crowds when it does tour. It is one of the most popular circuses around, even outselling

Cirque du Soleil despite having less shows each year."

My heart starts to beat rapidly as Mr. Ryding looks at me with an oily-looking grin, possibly the first time I've seen him smile since I walked in the door. "Miss Jenson, with the papers you signed, you just joined the circus."

# CHAPTER TWO

"What the fuck, Lila! Is this some joke?" my best friend Susie asks as she throws herself down on our couch in the living room.

Shrugging, I pour myself a glass of white wine then join her. "It's just what I said. I have family, and they own a circus. My grandfathers, and there's got to be some kind of story behind the plural part of *that*, want to retire, and they'd like me to run the business." I wish I could offer her more than that, but I'm still trying to process what I'm now entangled with. She just stares at me for a moment, taking her own chance to sort through it all, so I sit patiently and enjoy my wine, the cool tart flavor refreshing on my tastebuds. God, I need it after the day I had.

She pulls herself together quickly. Susie, unlike me, is quick to anger but just as quick to get over it. Both of us are easily adaptable, and I think that's part of why our friendship works. We like to just roll with the flow.

"But doesn't it seem strange that they're contacting you so suddenly and out of the blue?"

"Maybe it does, but you know me. I'm not one to back down from a challenge, and this has got to be the ultimate challenge." I'm starting to feel quite excited, my skin already prickling with goosebumps. "I have only a year to learn both the practical and legal sides of the circus, from being the ringmaster, to rigging the trapeze acts, and training the animals." Wincing, I realize I've just broken the confidentiality clause already. God, I hope that's information I was allowed to share, though I guess there's really no way of them knowing I spilled some of the details.

"So, you're going to run off and join the circus, just like that?" she asks incredulously, her face screwed up in surprise, before she shakes her head. "I don't know why I'm so surprised. You've always wanted adventure. I guess now that you've actually got a chance to do it, I'm a little jealous. Not to mention going to miss you like crazy."

"It's not like I have got much going on in my life," I tell her, looking around our small apartment. It has a little living area where we have the god-awful couch we're sitting on, a small coffee table, and the tv. A tiny kitchen, two small bedrooms, and one bathroom, make up the rest of the space. It's not much, but it's currently ours.

"I have a job that I don't really care for. I mean, I certainly don't want to do that for the rest of my life, but I'm not sure what I want to do. You have Mark, and let's face it, it won't be long before you two are moving in together. After that, what do I have?" I shrug like I don't care, but deep down the answer to that question is terrifying.

"I thought you liked working at the bar, meeting all those people?" she asks, taking a big sip of her own wine. "As for Mark and me, if we did move in together, we'd give you plenty of notice." She looks a bit guilty when saying this, not knowing I overheard her and Mark talking about it a couple of nights ago.

"Don't stress," I tell her, "I knew it had to be coming soon. You two are perfect for each other." They really are a perfect match. She works as a nurse at the local hospital, and he's one of the emergency doctors. I'm secretly quite jealous. I never seem to meet someone who wants more than a one-night stand—the hazards of working in a bar, I guess. For once, it'd be nice to have someone want me as a long-term investment, for lack of better phrasing. Call it residual issues over my foster upbringing or whatever, I don't care, but it'd be nice to date someone who wants to stick around.

Getting up and stretching, I head to the sink where I left the bottle and pour myself another glass of wine. "I'm actually really excited. Working in the bar is getting boring, and I'm sick of fending off drunk losers. I've never really known what to do with my life, like I'm just drifting through it with no purpose or direction. Maybe this is why. Maybe, subconsciously, I knew there was something out there for me? Look at it this way, at least I'll spend the next year doing something really interesting." I put the wine bottle back in the fridge and turn to look at her.

"I owe it to myself to give it the year. If I decide to give it up after that, I can at least say I gave it a go. Who knows what kind of experience I will have gained and where it will take me?"

She curls her legs up on the couch. "Ok, if you feel that way, I support you. If it doesn't work out, you can just come home. Now, tell me more. You said it was called the Galaxy Circus..." She's starting to sound excited now, which is helping to smooth away some of the nerves that were lingering. "Isn't that the one that mysteriously turns up overnight? It has the huge black futuristic circus dome, right?"

Moving back to the couch, I sit back down next to her, feeling a lot less agitated now that she's supporting me. "Yes, that's the one. It's one of the highest-selling circus acts in the world." I grab my phone from the coffee table, pulling up some of the tabs I'd browsed through on the ride home. "I googled it, and there are all sorts of rumors and gossip floating around, but one thing everyone agrees on is that it is quite a show."

"OH!" she exclaims, sitting up straight. "You're going to know all the secrets under the gossip and rumors. I can't wait to hear how it's all done. They say that for the mermaid show, a beam of light shines down and a tank suddenly appears in the middle of the tent. How is it done if it's just set up in a field? There's no way they dig a hole in the field or build a fake floor overnight. People would totally see that!"

I cringe inwardly, putting my phone back down on the coffee table, and turn to look at her. Here it comes... "Actually... I signed a non-disclosure agreement, and I don't want to blow this whole thing before I even start. I *can* tell you that I'm now a part of the circus and that I'm flying to London on Wednesday. But apart from that, no specifics."

"What a load of shit!" she argues, fury flashing in her chocolate-colored eyes. "I'm your person. I need to know everything. How can I know you're being looked after and are safe if you can't give me details? And let's get back to the subject of grandfathers …plural. What the hell? Are they Mormons or something? Am I waving you off with a laugh and a smile when really you're joining some freaky ass cult?" She's worked up now, her arms flying, head shaking, and her corkscrew black curls bouncing all over the place.

"Look," I say, sitting down and wrapping my arms around her, "once I'm settled, I'll send you an itinerary for where we're going. I'm sure I can call you all the time too, and I'll tell you all about my grandfathers. My grandma must have been having a very, very good time. Go her. Maybe I'll take a page out of her book. Get myself a gaggle of men." I wink at her.

She giggles, the sound light now that the tension is gone. "Not a gaggle, a harem! I've read books like that. You lucky bitch, that would be awesome."

"All the circus stuff and imaginary harems aside, maybe I can find out why they were estranged from my parents. I'd really like to know more. Maybe that'll give me something that I just haven't had my whole life, ya know? It won't change what happened, but maybe there was a reason that it all had to go down that way? It'll be fine, you'll see."

I untangle myself from her and get up from the couch. Stretching my arms above my head, I pull down my top as it rides up. "I'm heading to bed. I've had a headache since I met with the lawyer, and I can't seem to shake it. No way I'm going to survive tomorrow if I don't get some sleep. Gotta quit my job and pack all my shit… not that there's much of it." I also want to read through some of the information the lawyer gave me, but I don't want to tell her in case she wants to see it too, confidentiality clause and all.

Walking over to the sink, I wash out my wine glass and leave it to drain on the side. "Night, Susie, I love you. Don't worry. Everything will work out."

She looks at me from the couch, all curled up again, her mouth turned down and eyes glistening with tears. "Don't worry about me," she says. "I'm having a pity party for one. I'm going to miss you so much. I'm going to call Mark before I go to bed and have a little cry to him."

Smiling, I leave her to it. Grabbing my PJs, I move to the bathroom to clean my teeth and get changed, my eyes catching sight of myself in the mirror. *Holy crap, girl, you look like shit.* My usually bright green eyes are dim and sunken, with dark circles underneath them, and my long chestnut hair is in disarray after rubbing my temples all day to help my headache. The turquoise streaks are looking good though. I don't spoil myself too often, can't afford to, really, but the pop of color was a recent splurge. My eyes drift away from my face and further down my body; my usually golden skin has a pallor to it and doesn't look healthy at all. *God*!

In short, I look like I've been dragged backward through a thistle bush. That was what one of my foster moms would say. They were an elderly English couple that tried their hardest but really had nothing in common with a young twelve-year-old girl, though I will forever be grateful to her. She started and encouraged my love of gymnastics by enrolling me in as many local classes as she could find. Once she figured out that I would stay out of trouble if I was kept busy, at least mostly, she also enrolled me in self-defense classes. That home only lasted three years, and then the husband had a heart attack. Once they decided they needed to concentrate on his health, I got moved, *again*.

There's a lot here I can't fix right now, but I can at least get myself feeling a little less of a mess. Once I finish my teeth, I pull a brush through my mid-length hair, putting it up in a loose braid to keep it out of my face while I'm asleep. Reaching into the cupboard under the sink, I grab out two headache pills before walking back into the kitchen to grab a glass of water. I can see that Susie is still talking quietly on the phone to Mark, so I take the medicine and go back to my room. As happy as I am for her, there's just something about Mark that rubs me the wrong way. I can't quite put my finger on it, but it's like he tries too hard to be my friend. I mean, he's Susie's boyfriend; it's *her* he should be trying to impress.

My room isn't very big, and the standard double

bed, chest of drawers, and bedside table with a gaudy lamp I got from the thrift store, barely fit. Grabbing my bag from where I threw it when I got home from seeing the lawyer, I slide out the package of paperwork. I fling back the quilt and climb in, settling down to have a look. *Might as well start with the plane ticket.* It says Los Angeles to London on the twenty-sixth of July, business class. Well, that's nice, traveling in style. Flicking through the papers, I can see most are legal documents regarding the terms of the deal, but it seems there's an envelope underneath the stack of legal jargon. It's thick and fancy-looking, sealed on the back with a purple, black, pink, and blue seal that looks like a G and a C.

My name is on the front, leaving no question that its contents are meant for me. I break the seal and pull out the letter, nervous but impatient to know what it says. The parchment is thick, and the writing is decorative and fancy.

Dear Lila,
You don't understand how thrilled we are that you've been found and will be joining us to claim your birthright. We know you must have thousands of questions, and they'll be answered as soon as you join us. Look for a sign with your name on it when you arrive at Heathrow. There's a car hired to bring you to us. Be brave, Lila, and hold on tight, for this ride is out of this world.
Much love,

Grandfathers J, W, & E

A letter from family, someone who actually wants to get to know me. I swallow to try and shift the lump in my throat even though I know it's not going to work. Putting all the paperwork on the little table next to my bed, I check my phone to make sure the alarm is set, then reach up and turn off the light in my room.

As I lay down on my bed and look up at the ceiling, my eyes trace the galaxy of stars that I stuck up there when we first moved in, glowing like a beacon in the night. An adventure is coming, and I can't wait. In fact, I'm apparently so excited that I wind up tossing and turning for about half an hour before I give up on sleep and turn the light back on.

Well, there's at least one thing that helps me sleep. I grab my latest erotica off my bedside table and open up to one of my favorite scenes. *Nothing like a little tentacle porn and a release of tension to get the job done.* My hand travels under my blanket and into my panties. I circle the hard bud, sliding my finger down between my folds, then, using the evidence of my desire, I drag my finger back to my clit, teasing it. The slick slide intensifies the feeling, and I can't resist moving my finger from my clit to my opening, which is now soaking wet. I push a finger inside my pussy, tight, wet, and hot. After a couple of thrusts, I add a second, my palm rubbing against my clit as I pump in and out, pushing myself up that sweet climb to the orgasm I need. What I wouldn't do for a little more stimulation. Although I know my body and how to get myself off, I've always enjoyed using toys, and my taste is quite… eclectic. I'm a girl who likes some variety—nothing wrong with that.

Reaching into my bedside drawer, I pull out my current favorite. It's from Bad Dragon and not shaped like your usual dildo. This one is blue and shaped like a tentacle, tapering at the top with suckers molded into one side of the toy. I've scared off quite a few men with my unusual tastes, but at least I'll be satisfied until I find one who's interested in sticking around. Lubing it up, I move it back under my blankets then slide the dildo into my pussy, its large size adding a bite of pain as it stretches me out. Thrusting it in and out with just the right rhythm amps up my pleasure until I can feel myself almost plunging over the edge. I drop the book from my other hand, reaching under my top and caressing my breast in a way that sends a tingle of anticipation straight to my core. Pinching my nipple hard, I suck in a quiet breath, enjoying the added bit of pain that sends the orgasm slamming through my body. My hot pussy contracts hard around the dildo, my legs clenching together, while my fingers move slowly across my clit to prolong the sensations.

"Fuuucckkk."

CHAPTER THREE

Once I'd made the decision to go, everything happened rather quickly. Quitting my job was one of the best things I've ever done. My boss had always been such a giant chauvinistic pig, and telling him to kiss my ass was awesome. Relief hit me as soon as I had one foot out the door, that telling me, more than anything else, that I was making the right decision for my future. Whether I stayed with the circus after a year or not, my body knew that I wasn't meant to stay in that damn bar.

I didn't have much in the way of things to pack, and I gave my furniture to Susie to do with what she willed. She might miss me, but she's getting an upgrade out of the situation, for sure. Mark's apartment is bigger and nicer. Definitely won't need much of my crap. If they decide to keep the furniture, that's fine, but if they donate it to Goodwill, I'm not going to be unhappy either.

Before I know it, my two days have flashed by, and I'm walking onto the plane with a heavy heart and too many questions in my mind after a tearful goodbye with Susie at airport security.

"Good morning, miss." The flight attendant with a pleasant smile points me in the direction of my seat. After taking my book out of my carry-on bag, I stow the bag in the overhead compartment before settling into my large window seat. While the plane continues to load passengers, I check out all the buttons on the screen in front of me and pull out the pamphlets from the pocket underneath it.

This is exciting as well as a little nerve wracking. I've never had the opportunity to fly before, and now I'm doing it in style. Talk about being spoiled. Nobody sits in the seat next to mine, which is a bit of a relief. Take-off is thrilling and terrifying all at once, but when we hit cruising altitude, my breathing and heart rate settle. A glass of champagne in my hand, there's nothing left to do but relax and pray that we don't hit turbulence. This flying thing isn't bad so far, but I'm not really looking forward to the prospect of bumping all around.

The flight between L.A. and London is uneventful, and I have no desire to join the mile-high club as a solo passenger, so I swap out my book for the rest of the packet the lawyer gave me. The recirculating air of the plane is giving me a slight headache behind my eyes, but I need to go through the information. It gives me a run down of all the financials and the schedule of stops for the next year, but it's confusing and hard to understand. Lots of words and names I don't know and enough abbreviations that I stock up on several screenshots of terms to Google once I get off the plane. God only knows what language they're in, but it's no form of English that I've ever seen.

I'm not sure whether it's the stress of moving, the puzzle of those crazy words, or what, but my headache only intensifies as time goes by. When the throbbing grows strong enough that not even my book can distract me, I decide to give up. Putting it all back into my carry-on bag, I try to enjoy the facilities that business class has to offer. A good movie, a tasty meal, and a couple of glasses of wine later, God bless you, business class, I fall asleep. Images of tentacles and fangs, fur and claws dominate my dreams, making me restless. Waking just as we land, I feel like I haven't slept at all, and my goddamn headache's still hovering behind my eyes.

The plane touches down in London in the early morning, but the airport is so busy I'm elbowed repeatedly and jostled back and forth as I make my way to the luggage carousel. The smoggy smell of the air is a hit to the senses after being on the plane for hours, so by the time my luggage arrives, I'm more than ready to leave.

Scanning the waiting crowd, I look for a sign with my name on it. As it starts to thin, I find an older gentleman waiting patiently for me dressed in a dark suit, with sunglasses tucked into a jacket pocket. He has a polite professional smile on his ruby-cheeked face as he greets me with an accented, "Welcome to the U.K.,

Miss Jenson. Let me take that for you." He grabs my case from my hands. "If you'll just follow me."

He turns, heading in the opposite direction at a brisk pace, and I have no choice but to scramble to catch up to him. Parked in a waiting bay outside is a long black limo, and after stowing my bag in the trunk, he opens the door for me, another polite smile gracing his face. Thanking him, I slide onto the waiting seat while he gently closes the door behind me. He goes around to the driver's side, the opposite to what I am used to.

Looking around the fancy interior, I start to poke around, but the same accented voice suddenly flows through a speaker. "It's an almost three-hour drive to Somerset, miss. Sit back and relax. There's breakfast in the warmer next to you. They weren't sure what you would like, so they went with pancakes with berries, maple syrup, and cream. If that is not to your liking, I am sure we can find somewhere to stop. There is also your choice of tea or coffee. If you want to speak to me, just push the button in the armrest."

"This is wonderful, thank you. I'm looking forward to watching the countryside on the drive." I'm totally lying my ass off right now since I'm pretty sure my eyes won't stay open, but I don't want to seem rude. "Do you work for my grandfathers?" I ask curiously.

"No, miss, I've just been hired to take you to them." With that, he starts the limo and pulls out into the traffic with a smooth glide.

Okay then, doesn't want to chat. Well, that's ok by me. The traffic is quite heavy as we leave the airport and move into the city. I enjoy the breakfast spread that has been left for me before pouring a cup of coffee and sitting back with it cupped in my hands, enjoying watching the world quietly go by.

As we start to move away from the airport and onto a highway, it thins out considerably. It's summer in England, same as back home, but everything is so green. We make one short stop in Bristol for a bathroom break, but other than that, we keep going. The morning had started out bright and clear when we first left London, but by the time we get close to the Somerset area, it's become overcast. There's a fine layer of fog on the ground, quite eerie. I press the button to lower the privacy screen.

"Wow, the weather sure is strange. I thought it would be a beautiful day. Is it often like this?" I ask the driver.

"No, miss," he says, a hint of disdain in his tone. "It happens every time that godforsaken circus comes to town. They pitch that ruddy demon dome tent in the Glastonbury festival field. Some say it's otherworldly and interferes with the ley lines in the area. Others say it has to do with the small megalith circle, similar to Stonehenge, that is nearby. Who knows?" He shrugs, keeping his eyes on the road. "They stay for a couple of weeks, and we get crowds and crowds of people that come and visit until they disappear overnight and pop up somewhere else in the world a couple of days later. We get all sorts of strange people coming around. The surrounding villages do a roaring trade while the circus is in town, but we're never sorry to see it go. There's something not quite right about it. The performers are polite enough, but they're strange and tend to keep to themselves. When they do show up in town, the youngins get a bit frantic and silly."

He slows the limo down as we go over a small hill, giving me the perfect opportunity to see the black futuristic dome in the distance. There seems to be movement all around it, but from this far away I can't make out any details. For now, it looks like a bunch of ants scurrying around.

As the limo continues driving toward the dome, the driver looks in the rearview mirror at me. "So did you say something about a grandfather? Is he one of the performers? I would have put my money on you being a groupie, hoping to get lucky with one of the performers. They do seem quite popular. Or are you one of those investigative reporters, trying to get the scoop on how they do their tricks? There are always a few each year who try to get hired on as merchandise or concession stand vendors, and they always end up kicked to the curb for poking their noses where they're not wanted. But an actual relative… That's certainly interesting." I can hear the curiosity in his voice, but I don't owe him an explanation. Not to mention, if my bestie didn't get any extra details, they're sure not being shared with this guy who's made his judgment on the circus pretty clear.

I laugh as I vaguely answer, "Something like that. So, tell me, as a local man, what do you think of the rumors? There must be some sort of gossip floating around the villages."

"Who knows," he says. "Some people say they're fairies or witches, and some people say aliens. Goodness knows that dome has an alien look about it. I took the Mrs. once. Some of the things those acts do are quite unbelievable. But then again, David Copperfield managed to make the space shuttle disappear, so who knows?" He shrugs. I smile inwardly, knowing that act had all been set up and the people there were in on it.

We pull up to a gate with a couple of very serious-looking security guards standing at attention. Both are close to seven feet tall, with broad shoulders and pecs you could bounce a quarter off. They're wearing black cargo pants with the requisite tight black security shirt. As one turns around and walks to the gate, it looks like he may have a gun concealed in his waistband. My eyebrows raise at this; they mean business. Why would a circus need armed guards? The other one, this guy holding a clipboard, steps up to the limo and gestures for the driver to wind down the window.

"Name, please," he grunts. Not very chatty, but at least he takes his job seriously.

"Miss Lila Jenson," the driver says to the guard. "Mr. John Adams is expecting her." The guard looks down at his clipboard before giving a curt nod and gesturing to the gate.

"Drive to the door just there at the side of the dome. Unload her luggage, get back in, and drive straight out, please. Someone will come to find you if you take your time, and they won't be happy."

The driver nods to the security guard, winds the window up, and puts the car into gear, driving toward the gate where the other security guard has opened it up. The car slowly inches forward, and my driver is far from the relaxed and more social man he was before. He looks so tense, his face in the rearview mirror is wrinkled, frowny, and definitely stressed. I don't think there will be any issue with him taking his time. I think if he could, he would floor the accelerator, yank the hand brake, slide the limo sideways toward the door, and kick me out on the way past.

When he does stop, I quickly make my way out of the car before the driver jumps out to help to pull my luggage out of the trunk. I'm all ready to go by the time he reaches me, and when he holds out his hand, I grasp it.

"Good luck," he says. "I think you're going to need it." He pushes a business card into my hand. "You look like a nice girl. Don't think it didn't escape my attention that you never told me what you were doing with this lot. If you need a lift or anything, call me."

He looks up at the dome with a shudder before he quickly gets back into the limo and drives off, the limo disappearing in a cloud of dust. One minute, it's there, and then it's through the gate and gone.

My neck stretches as I tip my head back to look all the way to the top of the dome. It really is a sight to see. I walk over to it, reaching out to feel the side, but my hand is stopped by some kind of invisible barrier. *What the fuck?* When I push a little harder, the barrier warms up until my hand is able to pass through it. At the unexpected feel of the material, I pull my hand back, looking between it and the dome in shock. It's weird; it looks like a fabric or canvas tent, like any other circus, but it's not. It's almost as if it's made of a type of metal. Smooth and cold and almost like there's a slight electrical current running through it. It's so strange, and I'm a little wary about what to make of it. To make the situation even odder, there's now no one around. What happened to all the little ants that I'd seen running around in the distance?

Blowing out a breath, I step back from the dome, pacing back and forth while rubbing my hands against my pants. Well, this is it, I'm standing here, expectations high, just like the kids in *Charlie and the Chocolate Factory*. My very own Willy Wonka should be appearing any minute. My heart is beating a million miles an hour, and my breathing has quickened. I cannot wait to start the next part of my big adventure, but taking that final step is hard… freaking hard.

Suddenly, the door in the dome flies open, slamming back against the building. "Well, what are you waiting for, girly? A marching band or a parade?" The gruff voice sounds out from the darkness inside the doorway, surprising me with its normalcy. "Well, you're flat out of luck. Get your ass in gear. We ain't got all day, and the Misters Adams are waiting for you."

CHAPTER FOUR

I've been led into the dome and shown into an empty room that looks like it may be an office or an executive suite. It has a huge picture window that overlooks the whole inside of the arena, and to say I am speechless would be an understatement. There's tiered seating all around the edges of the dome, surrounding what looks like a traditional circus ring on steroids. It's the size of a soccer field! I can't make out what the flooring is made of, but it doesn't look like the traditional sawdust you would expect. My eyes jump up from the floor, following the curve of the walls, to study the setup. Halfway up, I can see some sort of rigging, probably for a trapeze act or something similar. There are also cat walks and a lighting rig that would put a major rock concert to shame. Down on the floor, under the seating, there are doors leading to the backstage area, and one in particular draws my eyes due to its sheer size. This must be how they get their sets or props in and out of the ring. *What else could need to pass through doors that big?*

Generally, the setup is impressive and a bit baffling. They must have a crew of hundreds to get it all set up basically overnight.

The door handle creaks, and I turn around just in time to see three gentlemen walk into the room. They look to be in their mid to late forties, and all are on the tall side with slender builds. Their hair is dark, all styled to various lengths, and one even has it in a man bun. *How hipster.* The coloring is similar to mine, but it's difficult to figure out exactly what the shade is. Two of them are wearing jeans and t-shirts, but one is wearing a suit. They also all have brilliant emerald green eyes that are currently staring at me with varying degrees of excitement. Identical triplets, how the hell am I going to tell them apart? It's lucky they have different hair. *But wait…* Aren't they a little young to be my grandfathers? Just my luck that I'd come all this way to meet them but they send out some strange welcoming committee instead.

"Welcome, welcome." The suited one with the shorter tousled hair steps toward me with his arms stretched wide. I take a little step back, not ready to go there yet, and he stops, looking a little abashed. "Yes, well, I'm John Adams, and this is William—buzz cut— and Eric—man bun. We are so excited to finally meet you, Lila. Why don't we take a seat?" he says, gesturing to the plush couches in the room. "I'm sure you have many questions."

"Yes," says William as he walks to the couches and

sits down, crossing one leg over a knee. "Let's get it all out in the open and out of the way. Then we can see if you'll run screaming or if you've got what it takes to lead the Galaxy Circus." He looks at me, forehead furrowed and eyes squinty like he's sure that it's going to be the former.

Whoa, he's not pulling his punches. Guess they're not all Team Lila.

"Sure, Grandpa," I say, smirking at him, "but I don't scare easily." I stalk to the couch opposite him and sit down, enjoying the way the grandpa comment made him just a little green. Maybe he's not used to being called that. I'm pretty sure Mr. Ryding said I was the only option as far as grandchildren, so it's probably safe to say that he wouldnt be used to it.

"Good, good," says man bun Eric, casually throwing himself onto another couch. "How about we give you the rundown? Anything we miss, you can ask about later."

Looking between the three of them, their serious faces tell me that we're getting straight into this. I nod my agreement, happy that I'm not going to have to do some silly small talk. Really, all I want at the moment is answers.

"So, I'll start. One," John begins, counting off on his fingers, "Galaxy Circus is manned by aliens; that's not a gimmick." My heart skips a beat, but I'm not sure what to think or feel other than that. My mind is starting to come up with a wild idea that these men might be crazy, but I don't see any easy way out of this room. *Looks like I'm hearing them out. For now.*

"Two, Galaxy Circus travels from planet to planet, working as a kind of United Nations. We make deals and trades between various different species." I'm pretty sure my heart has stopped beating now. "Three, we are also used as a bit of a transport service for species who would like to travel the galaxy. You can think of us as a tour service for aliens. They work for us, and they get travel included in their salary."

Now my heartbeat kicks back in at the rate of a freight train. I can practically feel my blood pressure rising, and I'm sure steam is pouring out of my ears like a cartoon character.

"Four, we are not human; therefore, it's safe to say *you're* not human either."

"Stop," I shout, jumping out of my seat, interrupting his little spiel. "Just stop!" I'm just about vibrating with anger. What kind of lunatics fly someone all the way to England for a practical joke? How did I get picked as the hapless orphan who's probably going to end up as some stupid viral sensation? There's got to be cameras somewhere if this is the bullshit they're trying to sell me. How did I get my hopes up for *this*?

"I don't know who you think you are or why you think I'd buy this shit." I look around the room, making eye contact with each of them. "Where are the cameras? Who put you up to this? This is fucked up. I can't believe I quit my job and flew halfway around the world for this shit."

I start walking to the door, grabbing my luggage as I go. Maybe I can catch a lift into town and find someone to take me back to London. Hopefully that damn plane ticket is changeable.

"Stop, Lila," orders William. "I can assure you everything John told you is true, and we can prove it to you." He's still sitting on the couch, legs crossed, looking for all the world like we're not having a conversation regarding aliens. "Prove to me you've got what it takes. Prove to me you aren't a pussy and there's Adams blood flowing through your veins. Sit down, and we'll discuss this in detail."

"John, you dickhead," says Eric from his perch. If he hadn't just spoken, I would have thought he was asleep. Arm resting across his eyes, his body is spread out along the sofa. "If I knew you were going to do it like that, I wouldn't have let you take point. I thought you had it under control."

"Agreed," grunts William. He gets up and walks across to me at the door, keeping enough distance between us until some of the anger softens from my face. "Please," he asks gently. Such a soft word from a previously gruff man makes me pause—call me a sucker, I know. I'm well aware I've got some sort of common sense or self-preservation instinct on the fritz, but I allow him to take my arm and walk me back to the sofa.

"I'm sorry," John mutters, "you aren't the only one who is nervous." He has the grace to look ashamed while he says that, briefly glancing over at me while avoiding the gazes of his brothers. The other two still look a bit disgruntled when their eyes stray to their brother.

Eric picks up a phone from the table next to his sofa. "Yes, can I get a pot of coffee, four cups, and some pastries to the executive suite, please. Thank you." He hangs up and settles back onto the couch. "While we wait, let's start at the beginning. Humans are not the only beings in the world, and Earth is not the only habitable planet. In fact, our home planet Skar is the birthplace of what you would call the human race. Looking for new adventures, a group left our planet many, many eons ago. Their ship suffered catastrophic engine failure, but they were able to safely crash land on Earth. They managed to survive and thrive over the years. Unfortunately, they found out that when they were cut off from Skar and its magical waters, they lost any special abilities they'd once had. The process really happened over the course of generations, so the first of our people on Earth were not immediately bereft of their powers."

Someone knocks on the door before bringing in a tray filled with coffee and pastries, not waiting for an answer. I don't notice who it is, as my attention is completely riveted to Eric.

"Thank you, Max," says John. I turn to look, but the person is already through the door, only his back now visible. *Was that a tail?* I'm staring at the closed door as William takes over the story.

"You see, Skarrians have special abilities that are given to us by the waters of our home planet. It's all very woo, woo magic." He waves his arms around as he says this, earning a skeptical look from me. They expect me to believe this, but they're using terms like 'woo, woo magic'? He turns to Eric. "Will you do the honors of pouring the coffee?" It's been placed on a table at the side of the room.

"Sure," says Eric. He turns, and while still sitting on the couch, gestures to the coffee pot. It floats up and moves toward the cups, steadily tipping over to pour coffee into each one. Out of my control, my mouth drops open. *Holy shit, telekinesis! Or drugs? Could there be some kind of hallucinogenic in the air? That would be some next-level crazy shit.*

"Milk?" he asks me, one eyebrow raised.

"Ye—yes, please," I reply with a gulp. Another little jug floats to one of the cups, and milk pours out. The cup then lifts and floats closely enough that I can reach up and grab it. "Cool!" I exclaim.

"Is that proof enough for you?" William casually asks, leaning back with his arms stretched out along the back of the sofa. "Or would you like a more dramatic demonstration? I'm sure we could come up with something." There's a smirk on his face that fits his younger guy appearance, but it's definitely not an expression I'd expect to see on my *grandfather.*

"Holy shit! I can't believe you can do that. Can all Skarrians? Were my parents Skarrians? Wow, I just …" I start to stammer, the words tripping over themselves as that malfunctioning common sense tries to kick back to life. Surely this can't be real? I look around for invisible wires. I mean, we *are* at a circus. Am I really supposed to take everything they tell me at face value? Instant belief is not really my thing; being skeptical is much more my jam. "I just don't know what to ask first, but I guess it's safe to say that maybe there's more here than I thought there was." My heart rushes with emotion. I'm not sure if it's excitement or terror, but adrenaline is certainly pumping its way through my system.

John gestures to his own cup, making it float over to him. "Let's start with the personal stuff first, and then we'll move on to business and the circus."

I nod in response before taking a sip of my coffee. "What about my parents?" I ask cautiously, hope and curiosity outweighing the terror for the moment. "The lawyer said you were estranged."

"Ah yes, your parents," says John, a sad look on his face. "We'll forever feel like we let them down. When our son married your mother, they were so happy and so were we. She was a lovely girl. Kind and gentle with a streak of fierce protectiveness in her. We couldn't have asked for a better wife for our son, and together they made quite the couple. We didn't have a falling out or anything; they loved being part of the circus. In fact, they were going to take over for us when the time came for us to retire, but running the circus does not come without its fair share of risks. When they became pregnant with you, they decided they didn't want to risk your young life. So, the next time we stopped on Earth, they decided to get off and settle down somewhere. They thought it would be harder for anyone to find them. The plan was to wait until you and any other children they had were older and able to take care of yourselves before they'd join us again."

Why would they be scared? What scared them

enough to give up their lives and move somewhere astronomically different to what they were used to? Who were they hiding from and why?

"Unfortunately, someone must have gotten wind of this plan somehow. Our best guess is that someone used our very own circus as a means to get closer to your parents, traveling with us and taking advantage of our last trip to Earth. They must have waited until we'd left and then gone after your parents." He stops and clears his throat before continuing, his eyes filled with unshed tears. "We're just incredibly lucky that you hadn't been in the car when they had their 'accident' and were staying with a friend of your parents. Whoever did this mustn't have realized you were alive. We've thought about this a lot over the years, but we've never been able to figure it out. We're not even sure if their murderer could be here now, having rejoined the circus after their business was done." By the time he finishes his story, tears are running down my face, my nerves having turned to a heavy lump of sadness in my stomach.

"We really did think it would be safer for you to stay on Earth, away from anyone who may want to hurt you," explains Eric softly. "We desperately wanted you, but not six months earlier we had also lost your grandma, and we were really struggling to hold the circus and ourselves together. We are very sorry, but we are also so very glad you are here with us now."

I wipe at my tears with the bottom of my shirt, sniffling my snotty nose as I try to process everything they just told me.

A tissue floats over, and I pluck it out of the air, blowing my nose loudly. Sorry, if you're looking for dainty, I'm *not* your girl. "Okay, I need to process all of that, so slight subject change. What's with the grandfathers, plural?"

John and Eric shift awkwardly in their seats and look at William. "Pussies," he whispers under his breath, but I still hear him. It brings a smile to my face. "Skarrians are a polyamorous society. We still have traditional one-on-one relationships, like your mom and dad, but multiples are much more common. One of the things that the Skarrian water also does is seal you into a bonded relationship, fully of your choice, of course. Mates are not predestined or anything, but a brand will appear on someone you're attracted to and extremely compatible with and vice versa. You do not necessarily *need* to bond with this person, but it is a good sign that you should get to know one another. If the attraction wanes on either side, the brand disappears. It actually saves a lot of time. If you consummate this relationship five times, you become permanently bound."

"It allows for a little try before you buy," says Eric, winking. Having made the mistake of taking a sip of my coffee as he says this, I manage to splutter it all over the place as I cough. Well, ok then.

"All three of us were bonded to your grandma. Children don't happen for Skarrians unless in a bonded relationship." He starts to look a little uncomfortable, but I appreciate that he pushes through anyway. I'm guessing there's a deadly steep learning curve, and I'm still sitting at the bottom with no idea how to climb up. "And even then, everyone in the bond needs to participate, so to speak, for a child to be conceived. It's a weird side effect of the bond magic, but it means every child is wanted and loved, so it is a good outcome."

Ew, ok, not something you need to know about your grandparents. "Um, ok, let's just move on. My parents though? They were a couple," I push.

"Yes, they were one of the uncommon occurrences of only two people in a relationship. They did love each other very much and had planned on having lots of children to make their family complete. Who knows? Maybe they would have ended up with more in their relationship, but staying on Earth put that on the backburner." John looks quite wistful as he says this, and I imagine I might look the same. I feel a deep loss for the potential family I could have had; I can't imagine what it must feel for all of them to be reliving the memories. I take a moment to breathe deep, compiling a quick list in my head of what's been thrown at me so far.

"So, to recap—not human, telekinetic powers, polyamorous relationships... Is there anything else I need to know?" I laugh.

"Yes," says William, looking very serious, "we also age very slowly, and mates can come from any race you encounter. And yes, it does affect you, Lila. If you drink the water from Skar, your genetic makeup would be triggered, and you'll gain everything a Skarrian has.

It's something you have to think carefully about, but if you decide to, we should do it as soon as possible to give you time to get used to it. "

"Well, fuck."

CHAPTER FIVE

"You know what, it's a lot for me to take in today. Let's just avoid talking about that elephant in the room and move on to the business side of things," I say to my grandfathers. I'm not sure how I feel about this. I'm pretty sure I'll drink the water; I mean, who doesn't want powers? But it's all a bit much at once, and the part of your brain that tells you to be wary is screaming at me. I don't want to make a decision when I have all these conflicting emotions running through my head. A girl's gotta take even five minutes for herself before making a life-changing decision about magical power-giving water. Getting up from the chair, I walk to the big picture window that looks out over the arena.

"Tell me about the circus. What other rumors are true?" I ask as I turn to face the men again, eager to hear the history of the family business.

"We originally started out as just a circus, traveling throughout the galaxy, entertaining the masses with a rotating troupe of performers. We would take on any act that seemed interesting, so our show was always evolving. Eventually, we had visited so many different places that we were becoming well known, and that put a lot of eyes on us. Some of the galaxies that we frequented reached out, their governments seeing us as an opportunity for a source of unbiased negotiation and safe passage. We did this too, and it became quite popular," John explains, pausing to take a sip of his coffee.

"Many races still use us to get from one planet to another, though there are other ways to get to most of those locations. Earth is the most difficult; it's very inaccessible and technologically behind most other planets. They mostly don't acknowledge aliens. Even though there are some government agencies who are aware, they are of the belief that the masses would revolt if they found out, so they've chosen to keep the general population of humans in the dark. In order to preserve that ignorance, travel to and from Earth must be as regulated as possible, and that's left Galaxy Circus as one of the only approved forms of transportation."

Walking over to the table, I grab myself a pastry to go with my coffee then head back to where I was sitting. I get comfortable on the sofa, waiting for more information.

"Earth also really doesn't have much to offer other

planets, so most aliens use it as a holiday destination. Some use it to escape to a new life. In return, Earth governments get options for technology that their countries are well away from creating on their own. They don't realize that they're not even scraping the surface of what our galaxies have been able to achieve." William has continued with the story, smoothly picking up where John left off. I could easily see them doing that stereotypical multiple thing where they would finish each other's sentences. "Governments get to bid on technology, and sometimes even private contractors make a play for what's available. For example, Jobs got the technology for the iPhone from the Telazions."

With another wave of his hand, over floats the coffee pot, filling up his cup again.

"Have you seen the movie *Men in Black*?" asks Eric. I nod in response, I mean, hello, Will Smith. Need I say more? "It's a bit like that… Aliens who want to spend time on Earth have to learn to blend in, and they are policed by that agency."

"I knew it was real!" I interrupt triumphantly. "There are just too many weird and unexplained things that happen."

Eric rolls his eyes goodnaturedly. "If they break the laws or get seen, they're incarcerated until we come back. Then they get shipped home the minute we return, and since many of those offenders are just going to be punished once they return to their own home planets, it's in the best interest of the alien nations to keep their citizens in line. It's one of the reasons we're on Earth quite regularly, while most planets only get a visit once or twice a year. We play somewhere on Earth every couple of months."

"So now, we get to the circus." John rubs his hands together in glee, stealing back control of the conversation. "Our greatest pleasure. The dome is part of a bigger spacecraft. It detaches and lands wherever we are going to perform. Anything we need during the show, the mermaid tank for example, gets transported between the mothership and the dome. It appears in what looks like a flash of light and smoke, but in reality, it's beamed down by a teleporter, 'Scotty' style. Another flash of light, and it's returned to its place on the mothership when it's done."

My mouth drops open in shock, and my nose wrinkles. *Huh, that was not how I thought it would happen. Oh well, it's still freaking exciting.*

Feeling restless and overwhelmed by all the information, I get up and wander to the window. "From the outside, the dome looks like a fabric tent, but when I tried to touch the side, it was like there was a force field stopping me from making contact until I pushed hard enough to make it through. And what's going on with the inside? It's quite obvious it's not a normal circus tent. It's more like an arena. How is it that people think it just appears overnight? I mean, it has a freaking *elevator!* That certainly doesn't happen overnight."

"Ah yes, the dome would have read your DNA before it allowed you through," says John. "The dome has the capacity to appear however we want it to. An illusion, you may say, or a mirage. As for when they come inside, the smoke we use throughout the performance is created to make them forget about those sorts of questions. They only walk out remembering how good the show was. Earth is the only place we actually have to use that smoke." *Holy shit, I didn't really think there were drugs in the air.*

I turn back around to face them, and the surprise on my face must be evident.

"Yes," says William, "you have so much to learn over the coming year. But I think it's time for a break. It's a lot to take in, and I can see you rubbing your temples. Do you have a headache?"

The pounding in my head has returned full force, and I realize he's right. I'm rubbing my temples, and the lingering echo of pressure at my fingertips tells me that I must've been doing it quite hard. I guess the emotions and the revelations have just been too much for me. "Yes, I've gotten them all my life, but they've been getting more and more frequent."

William, Eric, and John frown at each other, eyeing one another like they're having some kind of mental communication. Honestly, they very well could be. Who knows what other tricks they have up their sleeves?

"It is possible your physiology *needs* you to drink the water from Skar. Your mother drank it all through her pregnancy and regularly had supplies delivered when you were first born. It's possible that you've been in withdrawal since her passing, and that could be why you've shown no signs of powers," John muses. "You will need to make a decision soon. Eventually, the headaches will become too much. Your brain could swell, causing you to fall into a coma. In fact I'm surprised it hasn't happened sooner. You've been incredibly lucky." *Well, fuck me, Gramps, way to terrify a girl.*

"For now, let's get you settled in a room. You can freshen up, have a rest, and then join us for dinner in the dining room. Most of our performers and support staff stay on the ground while the show does, so we have bedrooms set up and a communal dining and living area in the dome. The mothership is much larger, with separate suites for everyone as well as various communal areas, so you'll have more privacy once this leg of our tour is done. We spend a lot of time on the ship, and it's large enough that people usually have no problems. As expected, with so many people living together, tensions can get a bit high, but we try to keep the drama at a minimum."

They all stand up, so I follow their lead and walk over to my luggage, grateful for the emotional break. Just as I go to grab the handle, it starts to hover in the air. I turn around to look at my grandfathers, receiving a wink from Eric. "Why work harder when we can work smarter?" he laughs. John opens the door, and we walk out into the corridor with my luggage floating behind us until we reach the elevators I'd used to get up to the executive suite. Stepping in, William takes out a card, swipes it, and hits the button for the first floor.

"All living areas are on the first floor, only accessible with a card. This is a private elevator for staff, but sometimes people get nosy and try to figure out how we do things, so they snoop around. This is to stop them from accessing the first floor and ground floor where all the equipment and tech is kept. If they get on this elevator, it will only take them to the second floor. The public have their own bank of elevators near the entrance to the dome."

The elevator dings right before the doors slide open. Stepping out, we turn left, heading down a corridor with a few people milling about, all of whom seem to pause. My grandpas don't even pay attention, quickly striding off down the corridor. I hurry after them, but my heart is pounding, and I can feel my cheeks heating up with all the extra attention. Holding my head high, I follow them and my floating luggage.

Most people resume what they're doing, but down the corridor a little bit, I notice a man and a woman unabashedly watching us. She has shoulder-length, curly red hair, with freckles and brown eyes and a slender build that I envy. As a 'wannabe gymnast,' I always wanted to be slim, but unfortunately, I ended up all tits and ass. I'm happy now, but my fifteen-year-old self was *devastated*. Like the woman, the man has freckles and curly red hair, but his is cropped short. He's also on the slender side, though part of that could be due to his height. The two of them look similar enough that I would put them as possible siblings, including the fact that neither of them looks thrilled to see me. In fact, I would say they both look angry for some reason. Their foreheads are creased in frowns, and her lips are turned up in a sneer while his purse like he's tasted something sour. My grandpas stop when they get to them, pausing in sync.

"Ah, Phillip and Fiona," John says as William and Eric move to the side to let me through. "I'd like to introduce you to our granddaughter and your cousin. This is Lila Jenson, and she's joined us to learn the ins and outs of the circus." Fiona and Phillip both try to quickly put pleasant looks on their faces, but I've seen the truth already. They don't want me here, I can tell. John turns to me, gesturing at the troublesome twosome. "Phillip and Fiona oversee and perform in one of the animal acts. At the moment, we have dinosaurs from the planet Reccedea with us. Humans believe the act uses animatronics, but in reality, they are living, breathing animals. We've taken care of them at our zoo on Skar, raising them and training them for this show."

I think my eyes are just about popping out of my head at this point.

"Holy shit! Real dinosaurs? That's freaking amazing. Are they similar to the ones from Earth's history?" Phillip and Fiona both get smug looks on their faces, literally looking down at me as if my excitement marks me as a stupid tourist.

"Yes," sneers Fiona in a whiney high-pitched voice, "but better. Your dinosaurs were primitive beings. *Ours* are much more advanced than that."

"Yes, the T-rex allows us to ride on his back," chimes in Phillip.

"Wow, are they kept here or on the ship?" I ask, looking around. They both erupt in peals of laughter.

"Why would they be kept in the staffing accommodations?" asks Phillip. "They're kept in a secure facility on the ship and beamed down at the start of their performance." Fiona sniggers, sharing a nasty side-eye with her brother.

"Imagine if they were kept down here and got free! The humans would be in a huge panic." Looking thoughtful, she shakes her head, turns to me, and says, "You've *so much* to learn." Well, ok then! Pretty sure we're not going to be besties or anything. So much for making a home with my new family. At least the grandpas seem alright so far.

Sensing tension, William interrupts. "Phillip and Fiona are your grandma's sister's grandchildren. This is their first rotation with the circus since they've been living on Skar and training the animals at the zoo. They also help out if any of the other acts need assistants."

Ahhh, so they aren't as experienced as they make out, and they're not part of the actual Adams family line.

"It's very nice to meet you," I lie, using all the skills I'd normally channel when I was the new kid. Got to try and make an effort even if they do rub me the wrong way. They both nod their heads, but their eyes narrow when the grandpas move off down the corridor again.

Still following them, I realize we are steadily moving

around in an arc. *Duh, Lila, you're in a dome. How else would you get around?* John, who is in the lead, stops in front of door number 101. "This is your room while we're in the dome," he says to me. William pulls a card attached to a lanyard out of his pocket and hands it to me. Looking down, I discover it has my name and photo with CEO printed underneath it. *How did they get my photo?*

"This is your pass to everything," he says. "It allows you unlimited access to all our systems. You are the only other person who has a pass like this apart from the three of us. Once people get to know you and see you around, they may come to you to gain access to the teleporter room to go up and down." *Teleporter? Holy crap.* It's like I'm in a movie, and my head feels light for a moment. I slowly reach for the offering, feeling like this is a moment that will change everything. I can't believe they're trusting me with so much so soon. How do they know I'm not going to run off and expose them to the world?

William must be able to see it on my face. "Even though you're family, and we hope that trust is something that will build between all of us, the lanyard has been spelled. The minute you grabbed it, it activated, and now you won't be able to use it for anything that will negatively impact the circus. There was also a gag spell on it, so you will not be able to talk about it with anyone either." A primal rush of indignant anger flows through me but then just as quickly recedes. Of course they need to protect themselves. Blood relation or not, they don't know me from the next human. I nod to him in acceptance, and a look of pride flashes through his eyes.

Eric reaches into his pocket and pulls out a watch-like unit. "This is our communicator. You wear it on your wrist and then say into it who you wish to communicate with. It will dial them directly, and it also allows people access to you. You can use it for regular communication, and there's a meeting mode too. There's no need for anyone to have constant access to you, so just push the button on the side if you do not wish to be interrupted." Again, he winks at me. Ok then, Grandpa, because *that's* not creepy at all. He passes it to me, and I grab it with my other hand. Looking between the two, I can't seem to think of what to say. It's all a little overwhelming.

In the silence, William swipes his own card through the slot on the wall next to the door, and the light on the handle turns green. He opens the door, revealing a fairly large room, and gestures for me to step inside. It has a huge bed that takes up a large amount of space. The comforter on it is purple, pink, black, and blue with silver streaks, with the Galaxy Circus emblem in the middle. On the wall behind the bed, there's a door on either side.

William pushes past me and points to each door. "Bathroom and closet," he explains. Turning, I survey the rest of the room. There's a small desk and chair to one side, and sitting on the desk is what looks like an iPad. William walks over and picks it up. "This is the control for your climate and entertainment unit. It can also work as a communication device, but it gives you a visual as well—similar to Earth's FaceTime. We have also loaded it with all the information on the acts we currently have working with the circus. We're going to have you do time with each of the acts and the tech teams, so we'd like you to familiarize yourself with what is there. We don't want you walking in completely blind."

Eric walks into the already crowded room and pushes William out of the way. "You need to think very carefully about the Skar water," he says to me. "It will benefit you greatly and help you with the ins and outs of the circus. If you decide to take that step, we would like you to drink it at our little celebratory dinner we're having with all the crew to welcome you tonight. We'll also discuss your role further, and you can ask us any questions you need to."

My stomach rolls with nerves at his words. Woah, no pressure or anything, just going to throw me in the deep end and hope that I can swim. Well, lucky for me, I've always been a strong swimmer who can easily adapt to new environments. It comes from living in lots of different foster homes as a kid, and right now, I guess it's going to help me keep my head above water with the aliens. *Never thought I'd think something like that.*

"Okay, I'll think about it while I have a break and freshen up," I promise him. "I'll also have a list of questions about a mile long about everything once my brain catches up. I want to know about possible powers the waters might activate, and a ton of other stuff. Right now, it's just… a lot, so I'm going to take a few minutes for myself." He looks pleased at my response and gives me some space, joining John back in the corridor. I throw the swipe card on the top of the desk as I wander around the room, taking it all in.

"Oh, and Lila," William calls, and I turn to him. "Most of our performers are aliens. We only take performers who have a humanoid form, as it is hard to explain non-humanoid appearances, but some of the performers have three forms—humanoid, their natural form, and half-forms. They'll likely wander about in other forms since this is one of the only places they're free to be out of their humanoid shape, and we want them to be comfortable." His face becomes stern as he cautions me, "I'm warning you now so you can get your game face on. At dinner, there are going to be sights that are out of this world, and we know it might be rough, but they'll be watching for your reaction." With that, he turns and leaves. Before he can shut the door, John pushes past him and bundles me into his arms, his firm hug soothing my emotions almost instantly. I sag against him and bring up my arms to return the embrace. I can't remember the last time someone hugged me or showed me any other kind of affection apart from Susie. Mark tries, but I get this icky feeling every time he touches me. No matter how much she encourages me or how starved for affection I am, I just can't bring myself to allow him to touch me.

"Hang in there, Lila. I know it's so much to take in, and it's going to get worse before it gets better, but the Galaxy Circus is your birthright. This is where you would have been if it weren't for the tragedy that stole your parents from us all." He gives me a kiss on the temple and pulls away, gently closing the door behind him, leaving me feeling like a wrung-out sponge. I'm not sure I've got any emotions left to feel. I've certainly run the gauntlet of them all today.

I flop backward onto the bed, controller in hand, a big breath escaping my lungs.

I'm an alien. Well, fuck my life.

CHAPTER SIX

S ince I have the communication device in my
hand, I decide to give Susie a call to let her know
I've arrived safely. It doesn't take long for it to power
up with a big Galaxy Circus logo appearing on the
home screen, needing only the push of one button. It's
the same logo that was on the wax seal on my letter
and in the middle of the comforter on the bed.
Pressing the phone icon, I dial Susie's number.

"Lila! It's about time, bitch!" Susie shouts after she
answers on the first ring. She must have been sitting on
the phone. "I've been so worried about you."

"Hello to you too," I sigh, holding the device away
from myself. She's so dramatic. "It hasn't been that
long. Stop getting your panties in a twist. It's not like I
could've teleported here." Whoops, probably shouldn't
use that word. I'm going to have to be very careful
what I say around her.

"I'm sorry. I just miss you so much already," she

whines. "You'll be too busy to miss me." I roll my eyes at her antics.

"You have to pack up the apartment and move all your shit into Mark's. Does he really know what he's getting into with asking you to move in? Does he know you have more clothes and shit in storage?" I ask, hoping to distract her. It seems to work, as the frown starts to look a little guilty.

"Ah no," she says, "I'm going to move all my stuff from here and then slowly, day by day, empty the storage unit. He'll never even notice, and if he does, I'm just going to tell him it's yours."

Laughing, I shake my head at her. "I'm not sure that will work, but hey, no harm in trying. Look, I just wanted to check in and let you know I'm okay. I have some reading I need to do before dinner tonight, so I'll call you later in the week and give you all the deets then." Knowing what that crinkle between her eyes means—there's an argument coming—I interrupt before she can speak. "Love you, miss you, talk soon!" I hit the end button on the device. *Phew, that was close.* I may have to do a voice-only call next time. If she asks something I can't answer, she'd take one look at my face and know I'm lying through my teeth.

Throwing the device on the bed, I get up and walk through the door on the left. I know William had told me what they were, but he didn't say which was which, meaning I accidentally walk into the closet instead of the bathroom. Well, might as well be productive while I'm here. Going back out, I grab my suitcase and carry it into the closet, opening it up and shoving my clothes into the built-in drawers. When that's done, I store the suitcase on a shelf above a clothing rail that already has outfits hanging on it. *I guess they wouldn't put me in here if I wasn't free to poke around.* That in mind, I browse through the clothes and find some very space age-looking black jumpsuits with the Galaxy Circus logo on them. How very *Star Trek*, I hope they have size tits and ass. Shaking my head, I ignore my self-consciousness, sure not all the performers are tall and lean like the grandpas, Phillip, and Fiona. Although I didn't really pay attention to what anyone looked like as we walked down the corridor, nothing stood out as different. Which is strange because the grandpas gave me that warning. Maybe all the people I saw were Skarrians like my family members? It's probably a good thing that I didn't see anything too crazy because I might not have gotten the poker face in place quickly enough.

I keep flicking through the hangers, realizing feathers, sequins, satin, and lace dominate the space. A huge grin crosses my face; this is a little girl's dress up fantasy. A squeal leaves my mouth when one particularly mind-blowing costume catches my attention. On the hanger sits a ruby red corset top that has boning and lacing, guaranteed to push my boobs to the sky. Over it, hangs a black and white-striped jacket with tails. There's a pair of black hot pants and a pair of fishnet stockings hanging over the corset. Underneath, a pair of black knee-high boots with gold embellishments up the front and a four-inch platform heel round out the ensemble.

Holy guacamole, I would look *hot* in that. I flick a

little further and see the same outfit in different color combinations, so it seems a safe bet that this'll be the "uniform" for one of the roles I'm supposed to undertake. Probably the ringmaster if any of the human circuses I've attended are to be trusted. There are also some other costumes on the rack, but I don't stop to take a good look. I don't really have the time, so I wander past the rack to a set of cubby holes. In the first one, I come to a ruby red suede top hat, and lying next to it is a black cane with a luminescent, opal-like oval jewel sitting in the handle, stamped with the Galaxy Circus logo. The other cubbies contain the matching top hats to the other color combinations.

With a sigh, I move away from the treasure trove and back into the main bedroom, choosing the bathroom door this time. To the right of the doorway, there's a mirror with a sink and cabinet below it. Directly in front of me is a huge shower big enough for four. I would like to live in that shower. There's no bath, but I guess the jets in the wall of the shower will make up for it. *Where does a spaceship get its water from?* On the wall next to the shower setup is a panel, and when I look a little closer, I realize the shower has a few functions. Score!

There's another door to the left, which I open to reveal a separate toilet, but then the reality of my thoughts just hits me. *Spaceship! Holy fuck.* I sink down onto the closed lid of the toilet as the situation finally catches up to me. Aliens, spaceships, traveling through the galaxy. My grandpas aren't human, and neither am I. *I'm not human.*

Blowing out a deep breath, I try to get my racing heart under control and make sense of my chaotic thoughts. Finally, I go to the sink and turn on the cold water, cupping my hands under the cold stream. The water pools in my hands before I splash it onto my face. Grabbing the towel off the railings next to the shower, I pat my face dry. I hadn't bothered with makeup for the flight, so that is going to be as good as it gets for now. Hanging the towel up, I walk back into the bedroom, pull the door to the bathroom closed behind me, and flop down on the bed.

Looking around the room but not really taking in anything, I think about all I've learned. Why am I so ok with all of this? Why haven't the panic and worry set in? I should be running, *screaming* in the opposite direction, yet I sit here, fairly relaxed. Is it because the few vague memories I have of my parents make this feel familiar? That the bedtime stories they used to tell me prepared me for a future of aliens and outer space? Pulling myself onto the bed, my body sinks down into the softness. I can feel my eyes closing, jet lag catching up with me. *I'll just shut my eyes for ten minutes then get up and read the rundown on the circus.* My eyes become heavier and heavier until darkness descends.

The next thing I know, someone is repeatedly pressing the buzzer on my door. Oh, fuck! Shit! It's seven in the evening; I must've overslept, and I haven't read any of the information. I fell asleep before

I even climbed under the covers. Major failure on the first ever job that my grandpas have asked me to do. Moving off the bed, I walk over to the door and press the intercom to see who it is. Of course it's William. I can see him looking at the camera in the door, his lips moving like he's shouting. *Hmm, the rooms must be sound-proofed, good to know.* I push the handle and open the door, rubbing my eyes at the same time.

"William." I smile at him sheepishly. "How nice of you to come and get me. I'm afraid I must have fallen asleep. Jet lag and all that."

His face softens marginally. "Yes, well, it's dinner-time," he grunts. Ahh, back to grunting. "Come along then."

Just as I step through the doorway, I'm forced to backtrack, grabbing my swipe card before putting it around my neck and walking out the door. I follow William further down the corridor. I wasn't paying much attention when they first brought me to my room, but now that I have the opportunity to look around, I notice there are numbered doors on either side of the corridor.

"Are these all bedrooms?" I ask as we continue along the same path.

"Yes, all of the performers have bedrooms here. The tech department and crew have rooms down to the right of the elevator. The corridors both lead around in a circle to the dining and entertainment areas. We have a small theater, library, and games-style room. The dining room isn't much more than a big cafeteria, but it gets the job done. We don't have chefs;

the food is all created through the dining replicator, a very nifty piece of technology. Because we have different species, they can program in what they need." Now that I'm in less of an awkward state of shock, I can hear some noise coming from some double doors just a bit up the hall.

William stops abruptly and turns to face me. "Lila, did you get to read *any* of the information provided on the circus and the species involved?" he asks seriously.

I shuffle my feet back and forth and avoid looking at him. "I'm afraid I fell asleep before I got a chance to," I tell him quietly.

"Hmm, well, nevermind," he says with a frown. "Can't be helped now. Be prepared for some interesting sights and try to keep your face neutral. You can insult some of these people if you flinch, not to mention lose their respect, and you will need that in order to run this show effectively." He puts his hand to my back, pushes the door in, and we step through.

HOLY SHIT. What was previously a noisy bustling room grinds to a silent halt. Everyone turns to look at us in the doorway, and I struggle to keep a smile on my face instead of allowing my mouth to drop open. I can see fur, fangs, tails, and tentacles. They weren't fucking around when they said some of the aliens like to relax in their half-form. William doesn't let us pause for long before he leads me to a table at the top of the room. The noise resumes, albeit at less of a dull roar than before, but I'm sure more than one pair of ears is focused on our table and whatever I might say.

Sitting there with Fiona and Phillip are John and

Eric, who both stand as we approach. John pulls out a chair in the center of the long table and says, "Sit here, Lila, as our guest of honor." I smile at everyone at the table and take a seat, letting John push in my chair before he sits down on my left. William is on my right as a buffer between Fiona and Phillip, I'm sure, and Eric is next to John. We look out at what seems like a sea of tables. William is right; it does look like a standard cafeteria except for a wall of what looks like ATMs, with keyboards and a big hatch, along the left side of the room.

Eric stands and clinks a fork against the glass he is holding aloft. The noise dies down, and he clears his throat. "Everyone, it is a momentous day for our family as our granddaughter has been returned to us." There is quiet murmuring around the room, but it's all too soft and muddled to get any idea of what sentiment lies behind the conversation. "I would like you all to join us in welcoming Lila to the circus. We know we can trust you all to make her very welcome. To Lila!" He raises his glass, and everyone joins in. "To Lila!"

I smile and nervously raise my hand, waving at everyone and hoping I don't look like an idiot. By the time he sits back down, conversation starts back up. "Lila, did you decide to embrace your birthright and drink the water from Skar?" he asks, getting right to the difficult question.

Crap, I haven't really had any time to think about it, but my gut is telling me to do it. If Mom and Dad had survived, none of this would be new to me. I would have been drinking the water and known about all of this. *Not to mention that the idea of a brain-swelling coma doesn't give me much leeway for planning my future.* I think it's that thought that tips me over the edge—that, and the excitement of the unknown. My life really has not been fun or exciting up until now, so the thought of this new adventure has my blood racing in both nerves and anticipation, and that far outweighs the niggle of negativity in my mind. Swallowing nervously, I nod. "Yes, I'm ready. What will happen?"

"We're not actually sure," replies John, a cautious note to his voice that isn't exactly encouraging. "Most are drinking it from birth and have never gone through such a long period without it. Maybe nothing will happen at all, and you'll have lost all powers." I can see Phillip and Fiona smirking and whispering furiously to each other after that, no doubt liking those odds since it would probably increase the likelihood of the circus passing to them instead of me.

"That's why we've decided not to make it a big deal. We're going to let you drink it here with no announcement. We'll monitor you afterward, just to make sure that there are no side effects or shows of power that require intervention. We don't want to lose you right after we've found you."

Eric had disappeared while John was talking, but he returns quickly, holding a ceremonial-looking pewter goblet. He hands it to me and says, "No matter what happens, we love you and will find a way for you to be with the circus." *Because that doesn't sound ominous.* Oh well, c'est la vie. I grab the glass and chug down the contents, refusing to give my mind a chance to second guess the decision. The water is sweet, cool, and has an effervescent buzz to it, tasting like nothing I've ever had before. There's none of the typical chemically treated taste that our tap water has or even that fresh sterile taste of bottled water. I can't even point out anything it might be similar to. Placing the goblet back on the table, I look up to find everyone at the main table is staring at me.

"Well, that was anticlimactic," I say, wiping my mouth with the back of my hand "I was expecting …" And that is as far as I get. My whole body starts to tingle like a fine current of electricity is running through it, and I can feel my hair rising as if I've suddenly stepped into an anti-gravity chamber. My body soon joins it, levitating toward the ceiling, with lightning crackling and wind blowing all around me. I bet I look like Storm from X-men, which would be much cooler if this wasn't such a clusterfuck.

"Aghhh! A little help here," I scream in panic, throwing my arms out for balance. A bolt of lightning flies from my outstretched fingertips, and when I look to see where it goes, I realize it hit someone in the ass. Squeals and growls sound out through the dining room. Oops! Suddenly, all the energy drains out of me, which would ordinarily be a great thing. At this point, looking down at the floor ten feet below me, not so much. I start to drop just as darkness descends.

"Oh, fuck."

CHAPTER SEVEN

As I struggle my way out of the darkness, the first thing I hear is shouting. A warm, cozy feeling surrounds me, and I feel myself carefully being placed on the ground. My eyes shoot open, and I look up into a pair of magenta eyes surrounded by long, thick black eyelashes that any girl would be envious of.

Blinking a couple of times, I realize the person in front of me is paler than anyone I know, almost corpse-like, but he also has a vibrancy to him that's entirely unexpected for a person that could pass for dead. Okay, I've never seen a corpse, but I bet they don't look like him. He has flawless bone structure that any super-model would be envious of, with a thin nose and full lips. He studies me as deeply as I study him, and when I unconsciously reach up a hand to touch his face, he flashes a grin that exposes pointy fangs. When I reflex-ively pull away, his grin turns to a smirk as he breaks our staredown.

"She awakes." His voice is deep and gravelly, not what I had expected from such a refined-looking specimen. The magenta-eyed honey backs away from me, and the grandpas crowd in, all with various expressions on their faces. John looks concerned, William has a devious, calculating look on his face, and Eric, well, his is plainly gleeful. He speaks first.

"Holy shit, you were like Storm from X-men!" *Huh, I knew it.* Holding up my hand, I offer him a fist to bump, which he does enthusiastically. Creepy grandpa is cool!

"Shut up, Eric," says John. "She could have been badly injured. Thank god for Saxon, with his speed and quick thinking. I can't believe he caught her as she fell." He's anxiously rubbing his hands all over my arms and legs, probably checking for injuries. "How are you feeling? Are you ok? Just sit up slowly. Where's Link? I want him to check her over for damage."

"I'm ok, I think," I say as I follow his direction. The slight tingling is still running throughout my body, almost making my muscles itch to move. Maybe that will help dissipate the feeling? I bring my hand up to my face to push away my hair, and as I do, John, who is sitting in front of me, slowly rises off the ground.

"Arghh!" I shout, flinging my hand back down.

He drops like a sack of bricks, letting out a grunt when he hits the floor. Okay, maybe that was accidentally a bit more violent than intended.

"Help! What do I do? How can I turn it off?" I turn to William as Eric continues to cackle with glee.

"Take a deep breath then let it out. You're just

worked up, so it's happening involuntarily. Once you calm down, it will settle." William scowls at Eric, giving him a not so gentle smack to the back of the head. "You sound like a hyena. Give the girl a break and get her a glass of water."

"No!" I shout, but I manage to keep my hands still.

"Hush," he admonishes, "it'll be fine. Only the first time should have such a big reaction. Granted, I don't know that any of us were expecting *that*." He says that last part in a mumble, probably not realizing he's still close enough that I can catch his final words. With that, he stands up and starts to shoo away everyone who is crowded around, watching the drama unfold. "Give Lila some room."

As people start to move, my eyes catch on the one pushing himself to the front. My head aches, but I can still recognize male perfection at its best. He has a shimmer to his skin tone as if he isn't quite real, and his hair is a silver I've never seen on a human unless it came out of a bottle. It's perfectly styled, with a sexy tousled look to the longer fringe. My eyes scan him when he stops to speak to William. He's wearing a uniform similar to the ones that were in my closet, so I can see all the sleek lines of his body, streamlined like a swimmer, with nice shoulders and a trim waist. They both turn to look at me, so I quickly stop my perusal and drop my eyes down to my lap. I'm supposed to be shocked and possibly in pain, not totally perving on the stranger.

They both approach me and crouch down. "Lila, this is Link. He's the ship's doctor, and he's going to scan you to make sure you're not injured anywhere. Humans are a bit more delicate than most of us, and we can't have any sneaky internal injuries going without treatment," William explains gently.

"No, it's fine. I'm okay," I argue, shaking my head. I'm not sure if I'm ready to be examined by an alien doctor. What if there's probing… *Hang on, sign me up.*

"Let me be the judge of that." His voice is low and gentle, and when I look up, his eyes are the same silver as his hair. When it comes to his hair, it's this cool silver fox look even though he appears young enough, but those silver eyes are just mesmerizing. As they meet mine, one of them does something weird. It's like the pupil twirls and then begins to glow. He starts to run his eyes along my whole length. If it was any other guy, I would think he was checking me out, but I don't think this is the case this time. The scan is too slow, and it looks like he's taking in *everything*, not just my tits and ass.

I look at William, and though he stays silent, he gives me a simple but encouraging nod.

Reaching for my hand, Link picks it up, simply holding it in his. His thumb comes over and brushes across it before I feel a pinching in the middle of my palm. Gasping, I glance down. There's a drop of blood welling and a needle-like probe retracting back into his skin. He puts his index finger over my blood, and I watch, completely amazed, as the blood sinks into his skin and disappears.

A moment later, he pushes back the sleeve of his uniform, revealing a forearm that's weirdly attractive.

Have forearms always been attractive, or did the water do something to my libido? His shimmery skin gives way to a screen. Its setup seems similar to an iPad, but it looks way more advanced. I mean, how could it not? It's in the middle of his goddamn arm! His fingers fly across the screen, his poker face not giving anything away.

"Body scan is normal. No broken bones or any damage to her internally. Blood tests also look normal, but I would need her back in my lab to do extensive tests for DNA and things. She is slightly dehydrated, exhausted, and.." He breaks off, and a blush crosses his cheeks. The silver of his skin is now tinted with a delicate hint of pink, and somehow, it's almost kind of adorable.

"What? What else?" John asks from where he's still sitting next to me.

"Horny," the doctor says dryly, recovering from his embarrassment, and now it's my turn to blush.

"Agh, well, yes, okay, I didn't need to know that." John scrambles to his feet, not waiting for Link to check him over. He holds out a hand to me as Eric joins us, another glass of water in his hand. "Thank you, Link, for coming so quickly."

"No problem, boss. I was already having dinner." He reaches down and helps me up. His skin against mine feels cooler than normal human temperature, and it's a lot smoother too. *I wonder how cold other parts of him are...* He helps me slowly get to my feet. "It was nice to meet you, Lila. I hope to see you around. Maybe next time it won't be as a patient."

"Actually, she needs to have the galactic translator

implanted. Can we get you to do that for her tomorrow?" William asks. What? Hang on now. I didn't sign up for *implants*. My poker face is definitely not in place because I don't even voice my objection before William is sharing a counterargument. "Lila, not everyone in the circus speaks English. Yes, it's the Skarrian language so most of our performers somewhat speak it, but there are many languages spoken throughout the galaxy, and you need to know them. It's only a little chip that gets placed behind your ear. Everyone has them, and all it does is translate; no other surprises, I promise."

"Okay, fine," I grumble, now feeling tired and getting grumpy because of it.

"Of course, come and see me whenever." Link smiles at me before gently dropping my hand and walking away. My eyes follow him as he rejoins a table across the room and starts chatting with the occupants before he looks up, those eyes meeting mine again. He shoots me a cheeky wink, and I almost fan myself. Damn him, I can't believe he could tell how turned on I was.

I grab hold of John as he moves back toward the table. "What is he?" I whisper, not sure how good Link's hearing might be.

"Link is from the planet Cybartronian, and he's a cyborg—half man and half machine. They are technological geniuses, and their species is responsible for creating the pleasure bots that are used in a lot of the brothels around the galaxy. Their creation decreased abductions and sex trafficking exponentially. Not to mention they're responsible for so many other technical advances."

Pleasure bots and brothels? "Sex robots? You mean sex robots!" I shout, and he shushes me as he guides me over to the table so we can sit back down.

Slowly, I sip the water, my mind whirling at the thought of sex robots and cyborg doctors. Tapping a finger on my hand to get my attention, William begins speaking. "Tomorrow, we'll work on your powers in the morning. Then get you familiar with the dome in the afternoon and the show tomorrow night. Let's not get too worried tonight." I smile at his no-nonsense attitude. *Suck it up, Lila, he's trying to distract you.* He turns to the room and raises his voice.

"We would like to introduce all the acts to Lila one at a time. Please start your dinner, and we'll bring you up in order of appearance." He sits back down, and beings start to make their way over to the ATM machines. Ahhh, they must be the food replicators. William turns to John and mutters across me. "I found her fast asleep when I went and got her. She hasn't had a chance to read anything."

"Oh," says John, becoming a bit pale. "Well, this should be interesting." He looks at me. "A typical circus would start off by easing people in with acts that build up to a grand finale, but we're a bit different. Every one of our acts is a grand finale," he proudly states.

"The ringmaster will start by welcoming everyone, and then he will introduce each act before they come out. Maybe a little banter in between if a set needs to be changed, and we have other strategies to draw the audience's eye somewhere else. The first act in our show is a juggling act made up of a troupe of jugglers who use all sorts of things, including balls, batons, and swords. What makes this so interesting and puts a spin on the act are the creatures who are doing it." He speaks across me to Phillip. "Can you get Caspian and Dylan?" Phillip frowns but does as he is asked.

As he walks away, John says to me, "Caspian and Dylan are shifters from the planet Fluxx. Somewhere along the evolutionary chain, they changed, developing two forms, and most can do a half shift. Dylan is a dragon shifter, and he uses his ability to breathe fire, lighting things up mid-juggle. Guests believe he is just using fluid and a light. Caspian..." He pauses and frowns at the two people heading toward us. "Well, you'll see. It looks like he's going for full shock factor tonight."

I turn to where he's looking, and I can't stop it this time. My mouth drops open. Heading toward me are two men. Well, one looks like a man. He is stockily built with dark ebony skin and close-cropped black hair. It's his eyes that draw my attention though. Those reptilian eyes are yellow and green, and I can see shiny black scales shimmering back and forth across his exposed arms and neck.

The other being is all man… from the waist up. If men came in a mottled blue and purple, that is. He isn't wearing a shirt, so his washboard stomach and rounded pecs are on display, both nipples adorned with rings. His arms are covered with what looks like nauti-cal-themed tattoos. I look up into a face that's just as eye-catching as the rest of him, particularly those piercing stormy blue eyes and challenging smirk. His hair is shaved on both sides, with a tousled vivid purple mid-section that drapes down over one eye. From the waist down, he is a writhing mass of shimmering blue and purple tentacles. Holy fuck! An octoman. He could be related to Ursula from *The Little Mermaid*. I close my mouth just as they get to me, but I'm more than sure they saw my reaction. Lila, 0. Aliens, 1.

William stands up, a proud smile on his face. "Dylan, Caspian, this is our granddaughter Lila. We're hoping she'll allow us to retire from performing in a year's time when she takes over as ringmaster. Lila," he turns to me, "this is Dylan and Caspian, the leaders of the first act. They have a few people who work with them, but they're the ones you need to meet. Caspian starts the act in his human form and will shift to half-form midway through the act. The viewers' minds are blown when he starts juggling with all eight tentacles!"

My mind immediately shifts to the gutter, wondering what else he could do with his eight tentacles. Phew, is it getting hot in here? I start to fan my face before I catch myself and stand up, reaching out my hand to Dylan. "It's a pleasure to meet you," I say. He smiles at me—is that a glimpse of fang I see?—and grasps my hand, shaking it in return. His palm shimmers with scales before it returns to normal. He's warmer than the average human, and the scales are a lot smoother than I thought they would be.

Switching to Caspian, I tentatively reach out a hand to him, wondering how he'll react. Instead of returning the handshake, he gets a wicked gleam in his eye and reaches out a tentacle. *I bet he thinks I'll freak out, but I'll show him.* I grasp the tentacle in my hand, marveling at how thick it is. The thing's gotta be pure muscle. It wraps around my arm, some of the suckers attaching themselves to me, and I can't help the giggle that escapes with the tickling sensation they're causing. He frowns, his suckers detach, and he removes his tentacle.

"Welcome to the freak show. It's nice to meet you," he says to me in a growly rumble. Goosebumps erupt across my flesh, imagining what that voice would sound like when he's balls... er, *tentacles* deep inside me. I'm such a dirty bitch.

"Oh," I say, winking at him, "the pleasure's all mine." He stumbles backwards on his tentacles in what could only be described as shock. His eyes switch from human to cephalopod, the pupil elongating horizontally and the stormy blue bleeding out to cover the entire white part of his iris. He shakes his head, and they switch back before he turns and undulates off in the direction he had come from.

Did I just commit some massive alien faux pas? Is it some kind of workplace harassment to flirt with the performers? That's really something the grandpas should have warned me about. Dylan bursts out laughing. "Wow!" he says. "I've never seen anyone get the best of Caspian. You really knocked the chip from his shoulder, sister." *Ping! There goes my gaydar.* "I think you and I are going to be fabulous friends."

"Actually, Dylan, that would be lovely. Would you

like to join us?" I turn to ask William if he can, but he's already moved down a spot and is making Phillip and Fiona move too.

I can hear them grumbling, proving that prejudiced assholes aren't exclusive to Earth. "Freaking fag," mutters Phillip. I'm really starting to dislike those two. Didn't the grandpas say Skarrians were open to all sorts of relationships? Wonder what their problem is...

"I could really use help getting to know everything about the circus," I say to him as he takes a seat.

"Well, I'm the dragon for you," he chirps. "We've been with the circus for a while now. We just change the act every time we do a new go around. You should see the different things we juggle and set fire to. After we have warmed the audience up, it's time to cool them down, literally. The set changes, and it starts to snow in the dome."

"Yes," says William, taking over, "now as ringmaster, you also take a role in this act and become the 'lion tamer.'"

Dylan laughs. "Lion tamer? Really? That's what you're going to compare them to? Yes, if a lion looked like a saber-toothed tiger and could shoot lightning from its mouth and tail."

William shoots Dylan a dirty look. "We call them ice tigers, and yes, they are similar to saber-toothed tigers. The audience thinks they're animatronics, an assumption we wholeheartedly endorse, since so many countries don't allow the use of animals in circuses any more. If PETA or one of those associations come looking, we've got some animatronics in the equipment area to stop them from snooping too much. In reality, they are a species of aliens that shifts, similar to the shifters from Fluxx, but they are from the planet Iceeen. They have a humanoid-ish form and their animal form. They live in matriarchal family groups, and there are a lot more males born than females, so a female will often mate with more than one. The males are very protective, not sure why, as their females are vicious beasts. The group we have performing with us is not a family group. They are young adults doing some traveling, seeing the galaxy before they go back to Iceeen, form family groups, and settle down. Once they mate, they don't tend to leave the planet. You need their respect, or they will not perform for you. Here come two of them now." He raises an eyebrow then growls at me under his breath, "Be nice."

I scowl at him, not sure why he would think I would be anything other than nice, responsible, and totally capable of taking over the circus. Sure, my mouth dropped open a little bit when I saw the other guys. And, okay, I might have hit someone in the ass with a lightning bolt. And if aliens believed in sexual harassment—*do* they believe in sexual harassment?—I might have already harassed their doctor. Plus, there is the matter of falling asleep instead of actually doing the research they asked me to do. *Okay, you know what, maybe this does make a tiny bit more sense.*

Walking toward us are two beings, both covered in a fine sheen of fur that looks similar to a mink blanket. They vary in color; the male-looking one is dark aqua, the color becoming an ombre as it travels down his body, ending in a snowy white on the lower part of his legs. He has black markings across his shoulders, chest, and arms, like a tiger, but they're not stripes. These almost look like tattoos. The male has a broad chest and well-defined arms. His torso tapers down into his waist, where the fur stops, and there is a naked patch across the front of his body from just above his nipples to as far as his groin. There looks to be plenty of muscle definition. He has a loin cloth covering where his genitals are. Damn! He's stunning, his beauty undimmed by the very unwelcoming frown that's currently on his face.

The female is lighter all over, her entire body a very pale blue, and she has a mane of black long hair running down her back. She has defined breasts, with a slender, toned body leading down into a lean backside and legs. She's covered by a toga-style dress, so I can't see if she has hairy titties. God, I'm bad. I'm *so* going to get myself into trouble.

Both are currently in humanoid-shaped bodies. Their faces have angular high cheekbones, and they have cat ears on top of their head that twitch, likely following the sounds in the room. Their eyes are feline in shape and pupil, and they have fangs sticking out over their bottom lips. Not huge saber-tooth fangs, these look more like vampire fangs.

I can see that both have tails that are moving back and forth in agitation. I've probably been staring for too long, but at least I haven't blurted out any stupid questions. This could totally be going much worse than it is right now.

They reach the table, and Dylan stands up, holding his hand out to the male. "Maxsim, man, good to see you." He turns to the woman and air kisses her on the cheek. "Natalia, beautiful as always." He turns, gesturing to me. "This is Lila, as you probably heard."

Neither look impressed to see me, and I can hear a quiet growling sound as I say, "So happy to meet you. I hear we are going to be in an act together."

Maxsim crosses his arms and just continues to stare at me. Natalia looks me up and down, the growling stops, and she sneers at me with what sounds similar to a Russian accent but is much growlier—probably due to the teeth. "That remains to be seen." She turns to William, dismissing me. "We will not work with this *bistich*." The unfamiliar word sounds more like a sneeze than anything else, but the tone she's using is speaking perfectly clearly. "You insult us if you think that she, a human, can handle us." Right, this must have been why he warned me to be nice. Bitch has attitude.

She turns to Maxsim and lets out a barrage of words in another language, arms flying, tail twitching. He listens and responds in the same language before she turns to me and growls, exposing those fangs, then storms off. I can see a burnt patch of fur just at the bottom of her dress. I snort in amusement as I realize just who got hit by my stray lightning bolt.

Maxsim turns to William and says, in a voice just as heavily accented, "I am sorry."

No-nonsense William is immediately back as he straightens his spine and stares the tigerman in the eye. "Deal with it. Fix it, Maxsim, or you are all out. I can and will find another act. Lila is taking over. Last time we were on Iceeen, the Sensee matriarch mentioned that some of her children would like the opportunity to travel, so I've no worries about being able to replace you." Maxsim nods, throws a scowl in my direction, and follows Natalia. I appreciate the support, but I really don't know how that's going to make them respect me.

"Whoa," I say, leaning back in my chair. "Is everyone so intense?" Not waiting for an answer, I direct my next comment to Dylan. "And what's with all the beautiful creatures? Seriously, when the grandpas told me aliens, I was thinking slimy little green men, but that was definitely *not* a little green man. You could bounce a quarter off of his ass. Even your friend with all the tentacles was smoking hot, and you, you're sex on legs. How is a girl supposed to cope with all of this sexiness around?" I wave in the direction Maxsim had gone, realizing that Dylan's eyes are on said ass.

"Honey, you are not wrong. That is one fine specimen of male tiger, but most of them are." He turns back to me and laughs at the way I'm furiously fanning my face. Hey, you have to find the silver linings. Right now, I've struck out on a first impression with at least one out of two acts, so I'll take the positive where I can.

"I'm not sure I can cope with much more. Not only is all of this so unexpected, but I can feel everyone's eyes on me. Like I'm on display and they're waiting for me to freak out or something. I know that's what Caspian had hoped for. People have been watching all that's been going on and seeing all my reactions. I haven't been popular so far." All of this spews out of my mouth in a rush, and the grandpas exchange a glance. John and William are frowning at their employees, but Eric just stands up and stretches.

"Let's call it a night."

"But she hasn't met everyone yet," John complains.

Eric turns to him and frowns, gesturing to me. "Look at her, she's exhausted and overwhelmed. She can sit and watch the show tomorrow night to get a feel for it."

"I agree," says William, "but we do have that one thing she needs to know."

"That's my cue to leave," says Dylan, getting up. "Lila, it was lovely meeting you. I'll see you tomorrow." He grabs my hand, places a kiss on it, and then walks away.

"So, what was so important that you had to chase him away?" I grumble to the grandpas.

"Not here," says William, glancing at Phillip and Fiona, the two failing in their attempt to look like they're not hanging on every word. "Let's walk you back to your room."

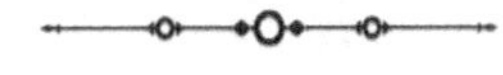

B ack in my room, the grandpas crowd in and shut the door. They all have a serious look on their faces, and William takes the lead. He comes across as the hardass of the group, but not one of them stands out as 'the leader.' They seem content with being on equal footing with one another, so it looks like they almost take turns with who's in charge of what.

"Although we have shared much of what the circus does, there is one thing we haven't shared yet. The most important and most secret thing the Galaxy Circus does is guard the Orb of Power." Well, okay then, that sounds like something out of a movie, but I'm coming to realize my life is much more amazing than a movie could ever be. *Or at least a lot crazier.*

"The Orb of Power was created by the Unas, a now extinct race, as a clean source of energy that could power planets across the galaxy, but it was taken and harnessed in a more destructive way by a race hell-bent on total galaxy domination. The Aaz'ax are a brutal and violent race, or at least their leaders were, and they needed to be stopped. The Unas decided that the bad far outweighed the good and wanted to destroy it and the knowledge. But when they realized destroying the orb would cause millions of worlds to collapse in on themselves, they found a way to hide that object away, never to see the light of day again. By then, the Unas were all but extinct, wiped out by the Aaz'ax, but the Aaz'ax weren't doing so well themselves. Their women had been infected by a mystery virus. Having no women to create mate bonds with meant no children were being born, so their race started to wither too. The war that they had waged against one another had done nothing but bring them both to the brink of species annihilation."

William breaks off with a sigh. Heading to a wall, he pushes his hand against the surface and a door pops open. When he reaches in and pulls out a bottle of water, I realize it's a fridge. He opens the bottle and takes a sip before continuing his story. The other two brothers watch on in quiet solidarity, content to let him handle this.

"In a last bid attempt to keep the orb out of the hands of the Aaz'ax, the Unas roamed the galaxy in search of a soul pure enough to be responsible for it. They landed on Skar and stumbled across an Adams ancestor. Although he wasn't as pure as they had hoped, they'd run out of time, and he was a good, kind, and just man, who would defend his family to the death if needed, so they decided that was good enough. The group combined their power and linked his blood with the orb, making it so that it could only be controlled by someone from his bloodline. They then instructed him to create some kind of cover that would allow him to covertly move through the universe, helping people in need. For the orb is so much more than a source of power. It also heals, both living beings and lands. No one but the Unas and our ancestor knew for sure where the orb ended up, and alien races have been searching for it for ages."

He puts down his bottle of water and grabs hold of my hands as if to emphasize the seriousness of the situation. "If you choose to take over, you will be required to make a blood sacrifice to the orb, and it will become *your* responsibility. We are the current guardians of the orb and the circus, and you are the last of the Adams bloodline. If you choose not to do this, it will become our responsibility to search for a new family bloodline to carry this burden, and like the Unas before us, we will have to sacrifice ourselves to pass this on."

"What do you mean by *sacrifice*?" I ask, a lump of worry in my throat. Nothing sounds good about that word.

"The orb will absorb us just like it did the remaining members of the Unas. We would cease to exist." The lump in my throat grows at the thought of these men no longer existing. I've only just found them; to lose them again so soon would bring me no joy.

The silence is heavy when William finishes his story, and I don't know if I can take any more surprise revelations. After a few beats, the grandpas sigh.

John takes over. "Because of this, you are always going to be in danger. All the performers have sworn an unbreakable loyalty pledge to us, and they will protect you if needed. They believe it is protection for the circus and the tasks that we perform for the various nations throughout the galaxy, whether that be trade or negotiations. Nobody but the four of us know about the orb. Your parents and our wife also knew, but you cannot tell anyone. Once you take a mate and seal the mating bond, then you can share the information. From now on, you will need to be alert to the people you are surrounded with. Although all people who perform with the circus are vetted, you never know who you're going to stumble across when off world."

Eric chimes in, speaking for the first time in a while. Maybe he's just more comfortable letting the other two take charge. "It's a good thing you became friends with Dylan. He will protect you if needed, even more readily than the others might. Get some rest, and we will see you in the morning for training." Eric leaves with William trailing behind him, but once again, John stops and pulls me into a hug.

"I'm so sorry that you have had all of this information dumped on you. I'm sorry that your parents weren't able to share all of it with you themselves. Even though we don't know each other well, I can tell you they would've been so proud of you. You've handled all the surprises with dignity while so many people would be curled up, rocking in a fetal position. You're a brave girl, Lila, and we couldn't be prouder that you are our granddaughter." He kisses my cheek then leaves the room, perhaps sensing that I've justifiably hit and surpassed my limit for the day.

I throw myself backward onto the bed, looking at the ceiling, my mind a haze of information overload with one thought repeating over and over again.

Fuck!

CHAPTER EIGHT

The next morning, it's a struggle to get out of bed. The overload of emotions and influx of questions had made me toss and turn for ages before my mind finally succumbed to exhaustion. There were so many that I couldn't possibly remember them all. I had to make myself a note to write down everything when I got a chance. Maybe it will be easier to sort through it all if I have a tangible list.

The ringing of my door has me stumbling toward it, hair in my face, wearing only the tank and panties I fell asleep in last night. Not bothering to check the monitor, I fling it open and growl at the person on the other side.

A chuckle has me pushing my hair out of my eyes and grinning sheepishly when I see it's Dylan, not one of the grandpas.

"Sorry about that. I didn't sleep so great last night."

He smiles widely and shrugs. "Lila, I'm a dragon. A little bit of growling doesn't scare me." I wave him inside my room and go back to my bed, burrowing under the covers and pulling the pillow over my head. For some reason, I feel completely comfortable with Dylan despite how smoking hot he is. Must be because I know nothing is going to happen there.

"Hey, none of that." I feel him sit on the bed and shake me. "William sent me to bring you to your first lesson in possible powers." He pulls the blankets off and wiggles his fingers in a woo, woo jazz fingers kind of motion. "Aren't you excited to give it a try?"

Another growl escapes my mouth, and I must be seeing things because I could swear a flame appears in his eyes for a moment. The reptilian green flashes with fire before going back to normal, or normal for him. I sit up, looking my fill. He's wearing a Galaxy Circus t-shirt and black jeans. No sign of his fangs like last night, but his skin ripples with scales before they settle back down again into smooth ebony skin. He is black like no person on Earth is though, so I'm not sure how they could mistake him for human. There's an other-worldly glow to him that I guess could be misconstrued as being in good health.

"Sorry if this is rude, but are your eyes always like that? Can you appear more human?" My curiosity is getting the better of me, so now I'm hoping he won't eat me. He just chuckles again, and his eyes turn from the full vivid green to a green pupil surrounded by a white outline.

"I'm not offended at all. I understand your curiosity, but I warn you not everyone will. William said to bring the tablet so you can read up on all the races whenever you get a free moment." His smile turns down for a moment, and he won't meet my eyes with his next question. "Does how I look upset you? I can hold this, but it *is* uncomfortable."

"Oh god no, D." I reach forward, grabbing hold of his hand to make him look at me. He seems surprised by the nickname, or maybe it's the unexpected contact. I probably shouldn't just touch people without getting to know them better first. Man, I fucking suck at people-ing. "I'm sorry, please don't be uncomfortable on my behalf. I think you're hot the other way! I was just wondering if you can leave the ship or if you're stuck inside when on Earth." The glamour fades away, and his eyes return to normal when he smiles again, those slight fangs and rippling scales visible again. *Are his scales affected by his emotions?*

He rolls over me and stretches out on the other side of the bed, getting comfortable. "I can and have done it, but to be honest, Earth is not all that great. It's primitive, and the people are small minded and intolerant."

I bristle at the words, insulted on behalf of the place that has been my home for so long now. "Not all of them... Some humans are capable of the greatest compassion and love. More so than the horrible ones."

"I guess there are horrible people everywhere, but human beings seem hellbent on destroying the planet they live on. Nowhere else in the galaxy is there a race so unconcerned with preserving their planet. Most races take care of their worlds. And what makes it worse is Earthlings don't even know that there are other options out there."

His words resonate with me; the world has always been so wrapped up in the turmoil of whatever political agendas are loudest, while the general state of our world and our environment tends to get forgotten about in the midst of that chaos. Establishing better ways to dispose of our garbage and finding cleaner energy should be the priority, but they're unfortunately not as entertaining as the latest scandals. In any case, I'm sure he didn't mean to send me off in a tangent inside my head, so I try to focus back on him.

We're both quiet for a moment before he claps his hands. "Come on, lazy, get that sweet ass moving. Otherwise, we'll both be in trouble with the boss men." He shoves at me unexpectedly, and I'm not able to brace myself before rolling off the bed.

Omph. I hit the ground hard to the soundtrack of Dylan's chuckles echoing through my room. Getting myself up, I place my hands on my hips and stare down at him. "You'll keep! Payback is a bitch." As I turn to go to the bathroom, I swear I see his eyes flame again, but when I look back, he's not paying any attention to me. He's grabbed my tablet off the bedside table and is doing something to it.

"I programmed my number in here. My room is quite a distance from here, so if you need me, now all you'll have to do is call. I've also programmed it into your watch," he calls out through the door while I pee and brush my hair, wash my face, and clean my teeth.

Thank goodness I wasn't trying to impress him because I almost screamed in fright when I caught sight of myself in the mirror. My hair was everywhere, and I hadn't taken off my eye makeup before bed, so mascara and eyeliner were smeared around my eyes, making me look like a raccoon. After a quick spray of deodorant, I call it good. From my first step out of the bathroom, then back around the bed to the closet on the other side of the room, I can feel Dylan's eyes on me the whole time.

"Are you going to give me the inside scoop on all the gossip? Everything I need to know that isn't in that tablet of my grandfathers'?" I call out to him as I search through my drawers for something to wear. When I shoved all my clothes in there last night, I noticed a few Galaxy Circus shirts like Dylan is wearing.

"Girl, I have all the knowledge you need and more," he calls back as I pull my tank off and put on a clean pair of undies and bra.

Grabbing one of the Galaxy shirts, a favorite pair of jeans, and some socks, I head back out. *Almost ready.* Throwing my clothes on the bed, I start with the socks. "So, if you don't mind, can we go through the different races who work for the circus first? Then you can tell me about the actual people that are from each one. Start with you and Mr. Grumpy. Grandpa John said you guys were shifters from the planet Flux."

Once I pull my socks on, I grab my jeans and put them on too, waiting for Dylan to start, but he doesn't.

When I look up, he's casually resting with his hands behind his head, watching me with wide eyes.

"You okay?" I ask him, and he sort of shakes his head and nods.

"Ah, yeah, sorry. Yes, we're shifters. Just about any animal you can name would exist on our planet. In fact, I think the Earth legends of dragons and unicorns and things come from Fluxxians not being careful when they've been on your planet."

After I button my jeans and pull the zipper up, I throw myself down next to him and impatiently wait for him to tell me more. But again, it's almost like he's mesmerized by the globes of my tits, almost spilling out of the top of my bra, his eyes locked onto them. *Poor guy, I must be making him uncomfortable.* I guess I just thought a gay dragon wouldn't be all that bothered by breasts. I quickly grab my top and pull it on, which breaks his staredown with the girls.

"Ah, right, where were we? Yes, shifters. Our race has three forms. We have a humanoid form which is what you're looking at now." He gestures to his body. "That also has the ability to glamour as I showed you before. We have our full animal form which I can't show you in here because my dragon is about the same size as your room. And then we have our hybrid form which is what you saw Caspian wearing last night. It's a half-form." He sits up and slides off the bed. "You want to see?"

I bounce up and down like a kid at Christmas. "Fuck yes!"

He smiles widely at my enthusiasm. "You are a real

treat, Lila. I never would have guessed a human would be so excited. The usual reaction is terror and aggression, and then we need to make them forget everything they've seen." He pulls off his shirt, and I basically *need* to admire his body now that it's right there in front of me. I mean, it would be rude not to. The guy is ripped, practically all muscle, no body fat whatsoever, but not with that overly bulked up look like so many of the musclebound bodybuilders that used to frequent the bar I worked in. He's sleek and elegant and… A throat clearing has me looking up to find him smirking at me.

"Ready?" he asks, and I nod, discreetly wiping my mouth in case there was drool. *Girl, get with the program. You've looked your fill. Just be happy with that. He's probably got a boyfriend, and goodness knows we don't want to upset someone with otherworldly power. Not until we can at least get a handle on our own to defend ourselves. For all I know, Caspian and him could be a thing.* My mind goes straight to the gutter, and my panties get damp as I imagine them entangled within all of Caspian's tentacles, bodies writhing, practically a scene straight out of my alien porn books made real.

Again, he clears his throat, so I shake my head to clear the image and sit up straighter, paying attention. His chest moves as if he just inhaled deeply, those eyes of his lighting up in flames. This time, I'm not imagining it because they stay like that. I'm transfixed as he grows slightly taller, his body becoming bigger. His jeans must be magicked because they grow with him. Wings explode from his back, and the scales don't just ripple across his body this time; they ripple and stay there like he's covered in armor. His cheekbones sharpen, and his nose flattens out a bit, the fangs in his mouth lengthening. He shimmers like there's silver glitter sprinkled all over him, the flames in his eyes glinting with that shine.

But there's still a wary look on his face and a blatantly obvious tension to his body like his fight or flight response is ready to act. Like he's waiting for me to freak out. But I don't. I didn't think he could get any sexier than he was, but this… this is, excuse the pun, out of this world. My vagina practically weeps in dismay that this sexy being can never be ours.

"Lila! Are you okay?" I can hear the caution in his question, so I shake myself out of my mesmerized state of lust. Hopping off the bed, I walk toward him and reach up to touch his face, stopping before I make contact.

"Sorry, that was rude. May I?" I ask him, and he grabs hold of my hand and puts it against his cheek. Slowly, I run my fingers across the sharp ridges of his cheeks. His cheekbones are sharp, and his face is scale free. I trail down to his lips and prick my fingers against his sharp fangs, both of us gasping loudly as I pull away. He licks the drop of blood I left behind, and maybe, just maybe, I could be imagining the shudder that follows that action.

"Wow, D, this is awesome! But which one is the most comfortable for you?" He shrugs and steps back from me, his wings tightly tucked against his back.

"This is the form I assume whenever we are off Earth, and apart from my beast, it's the one most familiar to me. The one you saw me in before was really done for just you. I didn't want to frighten you, but it does take a lot of concentration." While he talks, I circle him to get a closer look at his wings. Unlike the scales covering his arms, his wings look like leather with bony protrusions spaced between the membranes for support. They flutter ever so slightly under my gaze, and I reach out a finger to touch them, finding the surface is smooth and warm. A shiver flows over Dylan's whole body at my touch, and I quickly pull my finger away.

"Sorry," I say to him as I finish my inspection and step back toward the bed. "Okay, I'm starving. How about you escort me back to the dining hall? I want to grab something to eat since I missed dinner last night, what with everything that happened."

Grabbing my tablet off the bed, I slip my feet into my sneakers and walk to the door. As I pass Dylan, I notice he's got his eyes closed and is breathing deeply. I leave him be, figuring all of this must be just as overwhelming for him as it is me. Either that or maybe touching his wings was a mistake on my behalf. Maybe it just isn't done? I'll have to add that to my questions that need to be answered.

Pushing open the door, I slip out into the hallway which is bustling with people. All of them look human-like to me, so I guess that these people must be Skarrians like the grandpas and, I guess, me, or a race somewhat similar.

A few cautious smiles are thrown in my direction, but I'm mostly ignored. That is, I *was* until Dylan steps out of my room, seemingly in control of himself again. The hallway falls into silence, and people stop and stare.

"What did we do?" I whisper to him out of the side of my mouth as he pulls my door closed and puts his hand on my back, guiding me in the right direction.

"Ignore them. They're looking for something that isn't there," he instructs me, and I just shrug and follow his suggestion. Who am I to care if they stare or gossip about me? I'm sure it won't be the first time since I arrived, and it definitely won't be the last.

I link my arm with Dylan's, appreciating the comforting contact with him. "Come on, tall, dark, and sexy, feed me. The way to this woman's heart is through her stomach. Well, one of the ways." I stop there, figuring it might be in bad taste to talk to an actual alien about my gigantic alien dildo. We might need to get to know each other better first.

He chuckles, and the tension drains from his body. Did he think I was going to reject him in front of the crowd of people? Perhaps the Skarrians are just as judgmental as humans when something is perceived as different.

Maybe the rest of the galaxy isn't as enlightened as I had thought.

CHAPTER NINE

Unlike last night's entrance, nobody pays much attention when we enter the dining hall for breakfast. It's a noisy cacophony of sound, and as we make our way to the head table, I try to take in as much of it as I can.

All three of my grandpas are already sitting down, eating their breakfast, but all stand as we arrive.

"Ah, Lila, there you are. I was wondering if Dylan had managed to wake you or not." John is smiling broadly as he looks between the two of us. He puts on an aura of calm, but his hair is tousled like he's been running his hand through it in agitation. What's upset him? "Grab yourself some breakfast, and then we will get to work on establishing what powers you may have. I also want you to make sure you take time to read up on all the races and acts in the circus. We've got lots to go over during the next few days before we start getting into the practical side of things."

"You also need to drink more water. It's going to be an everyday thing from now on," Eric says, gesturing to the glass sitting in front of an empty space. "All Skarrians in the circus drink at least one a day. You should probably drink it at every meal for the next month or so since you've been without it for so long." The grandpas all sit and continue with their food, William not saying a word to me, though he does shoo me in the direction of the replicators.

"Dylan, can you show her how to use them? No tricks." He growls the last bit, but Dylan shrugs it off.

"I wouldn't do that to her, unlike some," he promises, receiving a grunt and nod in thanks. *Maybe he's not a morning person. Alien? Maybe he's not a morning alien. Is that the most politically correct thing to say?*

Putting his hand on my back, he leads me over to the ATM-looking machines. He gestures to the keyboard once he stops us in front of an empty one. "Press this button here and give it your name. It will have access to all your information and will select the right menu for your race. Then you just swipe through the options until you find what you want and double tap on your choice. The machine will automatically produce it for you." He gives a demonstration, and as he swipes, I see many different human options scroll across the screen. "Instead of saying your name, you can also say the name of the planet you're interested in eating food from, but I'd recommend sticking with what you know until you get a better knowledge of the options."

I scroll through the appropriate screen and order

coffee and a chocolate donut. I don't want too much in my stomach in case I end up flying around the room. Projectile vomit is *not* a good look. Plus, I think the sugar might help settle the butterflies that are also making themselves known.

Once I make my selection, Dylan grabs my hand and puts it over the activation screen. One slight humming sound later, my food appears in the empty space.

"Whoa, that's wicked cool." Chuckling at my enthusiasm, Dylan pulls the plate out and carries it back to the table for me, placing it in my space. He turns to go, but I grab hold of his arm. "Are you coming back?" His smile softens as he nods.

"Of course I am. I have all the important gossip to share with you." Feeling relieved, I let go of his arm and take a sip of my coffee as I watch him get his own breakfast.

"You look to be getting along well." I turn to Eric, rolling my eyes once I see his ridiculous eyebrow waggling. Surely he knows Dylan's gay; he's been with the circus for years. "He showed you his normal form, and you didn't freak out." Eric offers me another fist bump, which I reciprocate, and this time he blows it up at the end. This grandpa is a hoot.

"He's great. He's going to help me catch up on all the information that's in here." I wiggle my tablet at them. "I learn better if I can talk about things as well as read them, so it should hopefully be quicker. I want my new friends to be comfortable around me to be able to do that, so I figure I need to deal with their differences."

"That's good." John sounds pleased, which, in turn, pleases me. Not sure how I've known them for practically no time yet I already want to impress them. Maybe this is just what it feels like when you're around your real family? "The quicker you learn, the less chance you have of insulting or upsetting someone."

"Wow, don't sugarcoat it or anything." The sarcasm just slips out of my mouth as Dylan sits down next to me again like he did last night.

"Not going to baby you, Lila. It can be life or death if you insult someone, and if they demand death as compensation, there is not much we can do about it." William doesn't sound like he's joking.

"Are you kidding?" I ask, now just a bit scared, and he shakes his head.

"No! It shouldn't come to that out of respect for us, but an ass whooping isn't out of the question, and I'm pretty sure your combat skills are not up to par."

I look around the table, noting there are no smiles even from Dylan, who reaches out and pats me on the hand.

"Don't stress, Lila. We'll get you sorted," he reassures me.

"But it wouldn't hurt for you to have some self-defense lessons too. I'll talk to Saxon, ask him if he'll give you some lessons. He's one of our most lethal fighters." With William's suggestion, Eric rubs his hands together in glee.

"Yeah, I want to be in the audience for that, please."

I roll my eyes, all too ready to burst their bubble. I might be a novice in aliens, but I can most definitely defend myself. "I'm a black belt in both Krav Maga and Muay Thai. I think I'll be alright." The grandpas all snort in amusement, so I ignore them and try to concentrate on my coffee and donut, but Dylan's meal has me staring.

He has what looks like bacon, but it's green, and the eggs are blue with what looks like a black yolk. Then he has some blood-red sausages and possibly some kind of vegetable mash, but I couldn't tell you what it is.

John chuckles when he notices where I'm looking. "It's basically bacon and eggs, but the animals they get them from are different to your Earth ones, hence the different colors. Skar and Fluxx are basically twin planets. The animals are the same, but the magic works differently on the inhabitants."

Shaking my head, I concentrate on my food while conversation goes on around me. John, William, and Eric are discussing circus business while both Dylan and I remain fixed on our food.

"Where are Phillip and Fiona?" I ask, noticing they aren't at the table.

"They got an early start and are probably back up at the main ship, taking care of their animals," John tells me.

"That's something you will hopefully learn today," William grumbles.

"Drink your water, Lila," Eric reminds me. He turns to the other grandpas, directing his next comment to them. "I think Lila should have one more day of drinking the water before we work on her powers. Let it settle into her system."

John and William nod their acceptance to the suggestion, the former offering another plan. "Well, in that case, how about I take her to see Link for her translator? Dylan can meet her in the conference room afterward, get comfy and drill her."

We all blink in astonishment, my eyes opening wide when Eric snickers. "That's what he said."

William rolls his eyes. "Jesus, Eric, he means drill her with the information. You need to get laid. This is getting ridiculous."

Eww, no, that's not a thought that needs to be in my brain this early in the morning.

We finish up the rest of the meal in relative silence, thank god. My eyes keep flitting about the room, drinking in everything around me, but I don't linger too long. I don't want to upset anyone or get challenged on my first morning here.

Once Dylan and I have plans set, John escorts me to the medical bay before taking off to do whatever it is alien grandpas do. Right as I walk in, the guy behind the receptionist's desk walks out without even acknowledging me. *Okay then.* There are a couple of chairs, so I take a seat in the empty waiting room and wait for him to return.

After ten minutes, I get sick of waiting, pushing my way through the doors that separate this room from the other. On the other side sits Doctor Link, engrossed in whatever is written on the large monitor in front of him. Clearing my throat, he startles slightly before his face lights up at the sight of me. "Lila, hey." He looks behind me and frowns. "Where's Josa?"

"Hi, Doc. Is that the guy out in the reception area?" I ask him.

"Yes, he's my nurse," he tells me, gesturing me over to the examination bed.

"He left as I walked in, about ten minutes ago. I'm sorry about interrupting you. I got tired of waiting, and I have somewhere I need to be in an hour." His frown deepens as I explain, and I almost have the strange urge to brush my fingers over his cheek to smooth it out. *Why in the world do I keep wanting to touch people? Jesus, Lila.*

"That's weird. He's supposed to be working all day." I shrug and jump up on the bed, ready to get this taken care of.

"Okay, never mind, let's do this." He moves over to a nearby cabinet and starts pulling things out, setting up a tray of tools before bringing it back over to me.

"Okay, let's just check your vitals before we do this." He places the tray down on a table next to the bed before pushing my knees apart and stepping into them.

Whoa, none of my doctors have ever been this close before. With his hands on my knees, his eyes change again, swirling before he scans my body. I can feel the cool touch of his hands through my pants, and a little tingle of awareness tickles my core even though he's being very professional.

He clears his throat softly and steps back from me. *Damn it, he can probably tell that he's turned me on again.* "Right, everything looks good. Dehydration and exhaustion from yesterday seem to have been corrected." I'm glad he doesn't mention the horniness because we both know that that's not changed. "I just need to inject the translation chip behind your ear." He steps away and grabs something from the tray on the table.

"Is this going to hurt, Doc?" I ask him, trying to distract myself from what's about to happen.

"Call me Link, and just a slight pinch." He moves around behind me, and I feel him brush my hair to one side, his hand tickling my neck as he does. Goosebumps erupt across my skin, and it's not from fear. "Just shuffle back a bit, please." I do, shifting until my back is flush with his front. He wraps an arm around my waist and holds me tightly against him. "Try not to move," he whispers in my ear as his grip tightens and he puts the instrument against the skin behind my ear.

There's a small whooshing sound and a quick stab of pain, but all I can do is flinch since he's got me held so tightly I can't move. We stay in the position for a moment, our breath syncing together, and I can feel his chest rising and falling in time with mine. After a moment, the pain disappears, and his grip loosens as he coos in my ear one more time. "Good girl."

He moves away from me, and I shudder from the loss of his body warmth and maybe somewhat from the words. There's nothing sexier than hearing a hot man praise you in low tones. Even though his skin is cooler than mine, it was comforting. Without his body pressed against me, the air of the room feels cold. A warm burn on both my shoulders has me gasping, but as quickly as it arrives, it disappears. Must be a side effect of the implant.

He stumbles slightly, a look of shock crossing his face, before moving back around to face me, placing the instrument on the table, and gesturing for me to shuffle forward once more. When I do so, he steps between my legs again, getting in close, and says something to me in another language that I don't understand.

Frowning, I shake my head at him. "I didn't understand, sorry."

He pushes back his sleeve and fiddles with the monitor on his arm again. "What about now? Did you understand this time?"

"Yes, I did. Are you speaking another language?"

"Yes, I was speaking the native tongue of my home planet. Alright, it looks like you are all done."

I wait for him to move once he tugs down the sleeve of his shirt, but he doesn't. Instead, he crowds in closer and puts his hands back on my thighs. His tongue comes out and wets his bottom lip, drawing my eyes to them. Plump and a raspberry red, it's hard to believe that this man is not all flesh and blood. "Lila, if you would like to get rid of that other problem, I'm happy to help you out with that. All cyborgs are programmed with the same systems the pleasure bots from our planet are so famous for."

Did he just offer to take care of my horniness problem? Is that legal here?

"Of course, from a purely medical point of view, it would be better for your concentration and well-being if this problem was rectified, so you could think of it as the doctor's orders."

God, I would love to say yes to this, but I'm really not sure. I mean, I've just met this man… cyborg… and I'm not sure if I'm technically his boss. Maybe there's something in the tablet that'll clear this up for me. God knows I don't want to ask the grandpas about this one.

.

"I can tell that you are unsure. Humans have such hang-ups about sexuality, but you'll find that most of the rest of the galaxy doesn't. There are no strings attached, nor is there anything expected in return. This is me just helping you out as a friend. I'd like for us to be friends, Lila." He can't hide the sparkle in his eyes no matter how professional he tries to keep his face. His interest in me seems genuine, though I can't for the life of me figure out why. I guess that doesn't really matter though since there are a lot more important questions pushing to the front of my mind.

I want to know all about this man's make up. Is he more machine than organic organism? How are they born? Are they made like this, or do they grow? Is his dick metal or flesh? And what would it feel like sliding into my hot pussy? "Well, when you put it that way…" I break off, and he grins, starting to undo the button on my jeans, but before he can go any further, the medical room door opens.

In walks the nurse from before. "Dr. Tesla." *Huh, I wonder if that's a coincidence.* "Did you call me?" He waltzes into the room even though every single one of us knows he hasn't called him. He's a slender, effeminate thing that has the same type of shimmer to his skin as Link. His hair is a metallic shimmery green, and his eyes match, though those eyes are looking at me with incredibly blatant disgust. Do they have enhanced hearing too? It's the only reason I can think of for him coming in here. He must have heard what he offered me.

A small quiet growl escapes Link's lips before he shakes his head. "No, Nurse Spears, I didn't."

"Oh, well, I could have sworn you did. Dylan is out in the waiting room, says he's here for *her*." He puts on this air of flightiness, but when I look at him, there's a smooth calculation in his eyes.

As much as I'm cursing him internally, maybe it's for the best. Though I *will* be searching out Dr. Link Tesla as soon as I can in a nonprofessional capacity. Purely for data-gathering purposes, of course.

He squeezes my thighs and steps away from me so that I can jump down from the bed.

"Let me know if you have any problems with the implant, but you shouldn't."

I make my way to the exit, calling back to him before I reach the door. "Thanks, Link. I hope to see you around."

"You can count on it."

I push open the door to find Dylan on the other side, waiting, so I guess he wasn't lying about that part at least. "Everything okay?" he asks, frowning as he looks between me and the door that has closed behind me.

"Everything's great. Let's get going." I link my arm with his and drag him out of there as the nurse exits the exam room and watches us go, arms crossed, eyes narrowed. *Yikes, way to go, Lila. Making friends everywhere you go.* First Natalia, now this one. God, I hope everyone in this circus isn't bitchy.

LINK

I watch in disappointment as Lila gets dragged away by that manwhore of a dragon. God, of all people to be taking her under their wing, why the fuck are her grandpas letting it be him? Of course it didn't take him long to get his hooks into her. Not only is she gorgeous, she will be so very politically powerful if not personally powerful once she takes control of the circus. For her sake, I hope that the friendship is genuine, but in case it's not, I plan on being there to pick up the pieces.

There's just something about the girl, something special. I knew it from the moment I put my hands on her. I was completely shocked when I felt her bond mark appear on my shoulder. I'm not even sure if she knows what it means; she certainly didn't show much reaction. It's the reason I offered to take care of her little problem. Despite the ridiculous excuse I gave her, I never would have offered the same to just anyone. I could see in her eyes that she wasn't buying it and braced myself for yet another rejection, but then she said yes. Regardless of how embarrassing it would have been, I just about came in my pants. Imagine, a cyborg with pleasure bot capabilities finishing before he's even given one ounce of pleasure to his woman. What a disgrace.

But could I really blame myself? Who would have thought a human-raised woman would be interested in a cyborg? I mean, we are known throughout the galaxy for being well-versed in the pleasure arts, but she doesn't know that. For all she knows, I haven't even got a working dick. I *am* part machine after all. Lucky for me, and hopefully Lila, that's not a problem for cyborgs. Being made from nano-technology, all parts of us are virtually organic. Our "biology" allows for cell regeneration and manipulation, making our bodies virtually indestructible while also allowing for me to change certain parts at will. Not only do I have a dick, but it can do things that will make her scream.

A throat clearing behind me has me swinging to find my nurse, arms crossed, tapping his foot in annoyance. When did he become so damn annoying? He's new to this rotation, and he definitely isn't an improvement on the last one. He's acting awfully territorial, which is one of the most common drawbacks to working with a receptionist from my home planet. Working with another cyborg is something that's hard for me to trust. They always know who I am, who my family is, and their eagerness and interest in me just muddies the waters. There's no way of knowing whether they're here for an honest job or if my mother manipulated them into applying, trying to secure herself the cyborg-in-law of her dreams. God knows she wants me to return home and take my place at the head of the company, but I have never had any interest in business. Dad put his foot down and said that my investment in our company could develop naturally or not at all, and it didn't. Hence me ending up a doctor. Galaxy Circus is a good fit for me, and I would never want to be forced away from this place I love.

"What is it, Josa? Where were you earlier? Lila said you just up and walked out." I return back into my examination room with Josa trailing behind me.

"Pfft, I can't believe they allowed a human to join the circus, and they're grooming *her* to take over." He crosses her arms and leans against the wall, watching me clean up instead of actually doing his job. If that weren't bad enough, the disgust in his voice when he speaks about Lila is enough to set my gears on edge.

"She's not human. She's Skarrian," I argue. The logical side of me knows that Josa's bigotry won't likely be fixed by anything I say in this moment, but my short exposure to Lila has created some kind of connection between us. I can't just let someone speak ill of her without at least trying to say something in her defense.

"Yeah right, she's practically human. Now the brothers have her mainlining Skarrian water in the hope it will kickstart something. I say they're panicking. You did a body scan. Are there any signs of powers?" He pushes a sly look on his face, and I can feel myself scowl.

No, unfortunately. Apart from the initial burst, I could see nothing on her physiology to suggest she has powers. Skarrians usually have a ball of energy inside their chest that represents their power, but Lila's was missing. I push the scowl off my face, not wanting to tell this annoying cyborg that. Before you know it, the gossip would be spread around the circus like Lycic fleas in a Restolan brothel.

"You know that's covered by patient-doctor confidentiality," I tell him, and I see his eyes slide toward the computer. Not getting what he wanted from me right now, he must decide to choose another topic to fight about. His eyes return to me, and this time, he's fuming.

"How dare you protect her! I heard you offer to take care of that needy bitch's horniness, throwing away your professionalism and reputation! Don't you care how that reflects on you? Actually, forget you. Don't you care how that reflects on *me*? Your mother promised me your hand in marriage, and I will not have you lowering yourself to those standards. 'Taking care of' a Skarrian would be at least some step up. But a *human*? What would everyone at home say?"

I pause, not believing the words that have just come out of his mouth. Surely that can't be right. But then I think about it some more, and a wave of fury at my mother flows through my body. She's done things like this before. Why wouldn't it be true this time too? But this time, instead of throwing a woman at me, she tries the opposite sex in the hope that I might bite. Most cyborgs aren't picky, and especially with my skills and desire to give and receive pleasure, I'm not too picky myself. But I will never, under any circumstance, get pleasure or give it to one of my mother's plants.

Beneath the weight of my anger, the tray of instruments buckles in my hand. The sounds of crushing metal create a sharp echo through my normally tranquil exam room. Flinging it to the side, I whirl on the nurse, my anger only rising thanks to the smug look on his face. "My mother had no right to offer you that. And just what is she getting out of this deal? I know she didn't offer my hand out of the goodness of her heart."

"Never you mind what your mother's deal is. When I find out the information she wants to know, you will be leaving the circus and returning home with me to your rightful place. There will be no argument."

I snort with amusement. "And how do you think you are going to make me do that?" I ask him. Short of him reprogramming me, there is no way that I would voluntarily do that.

"She said she would give me access to your source code."

I stagger with horror as dread hits me. "No, she can't. She hasn't got it." When a cyborg is born, their source code, the very foundation of their being, is imprinted on a data chip. The doctor at birth gives it to the Caretaker, who hides it away so that no cyborg can corrupt another. He is the only one who knows where they are hidden and is fiercely protective of them. There are many rumors floating around about other dimensions or secret vaults on an asteroid, and not even the cyborg's parents have access to it. How could she have gotten hold of mine? "She's lying."

"Are you sure about that? Are you willing to risk it? It's no skin off my nose. I can just make you leave when the time comes. You're under some measure of protection while I'm stuck here as part of this miserable circus, but once your mother gives me that tool, their protection won't matter. Hear this, Link, you *will* be mine." With that, he turns and leaves as I sink down onto a chair.

That smug cunt thinks he holds all the cards, but I'm not about to let him fuck anything up between me and Lila. I want to explore the attraction between us, and no blackmail attempt is going to stop that. I will be contacting my father though, to see if he knows anything about my mother's threats. Then I'll be talking to the warlock. Xavier may know a way to help me. We've been friends since we both started at the circus around the same time. He is much like me, happy to keep to ourselves and a small select group of friends who care nothing about status or powers. He's the type of friend who would help cover up a murder... which it may come to if what Josa says is right. My mother having access to my source code is a nightmare waiting to happen. Forget forcing me to come home. She could just rewrite my whole being. No, she can't possibly have it… Can she? Fuck.

I push a button on my screen to connect me to my father. Hopefully he has some answers for me.

⋅—◦⋅ ⋅•◦•⋅ ⋅◦•⋅ ⋅—⋅

LILA

Dylan flirted his way through the corridors, leaving everyone with a smile on their faces after that single interaction with him, while I stayed quiet and just observed. People were cautious but kind, and quite a few said hi and wished me good luck with all I had to learn. Before long, Dylan is directing me into a plush chair back in the same room I met the grandpas in yesterday. He flops down onto the sofa next to me, wings tucked in behind him, a huge sigh leaving his mouth. "I'm not really sure where to start. I haven't ever had to teach anyone any of this before, and there's just so much."

"God, I don't know," I tell him just as something out the huge picture window catches my eye. The big arena is filled with a water tank, a group of people standing off to the side. It seems like the people are all wearing pastel-colored bodysuits or wetsuits, but as I try to get a closer look, one of them spins.

Whoops, nope, not bodysuits. That's a penis flying around. They're all naked, and that's their skin color.

Standing up, I make my way over to the window and rest my hands on the cool glass as I watch what's going on, trying to get a better look.… at the act, not the naked penises.

"Tell me about them… *that*." I wave in the direction of the action, and Dylan gets up, joining me at the glass.

"What do you know about that part of the act here

on Earth?" he asks, leaning his back against the glass, ignoring the action.

"It's a dolphin show, similar to what SeaWorld has, but the trainers swim with fake mermaid tails."

"Hmm, okay. So, *not* fake tails. These guys come from the planet Aquilia, which is almost 75% water. Not only are they not fake tails, they're not separate entities. The dolphins and the mermaids are one and the same. They shift, similar to what I do, and as you can see, they also have a form with legs. Unlike Earth dolphins, these ones are multicolored. This shows in the tails when they are in half-form and their skin when in human form. They aren't allowed to leave the dome when on Earth unless they can get a glamour from one of the warlocks."

"Warlocks?" I spin away from the window and the sight below before marching back to the sofa. Honestly, I'm definitely owed a dramatic moment or two here, so I throw myself on it and grab a pillow, squishing it over my head. "Agghhh, it's all too much."

My brain is just about fried, and we haven't even been talking for ten minutes! How am I ever going to get a handle on all this?

A set of hands pulls the pillow away from my face, and Dylan is grinning at me. "Sweetie, that's why I'm here. We're going to go through that tablet, and by the end of it, you are going to be an expert on all things Galaxy Circus." His manner brings a sense of calm to me, and I'm able to breathe again. God, it's nice to have a friend to help navigate the very choppy waters that make up the Galaxy Circus. I think without his help I'd be feeling even more lost than I am.

"Okay, I guess we better get to it. Let's start with the warlocks. What do they do for the circus?"

"Not warlocks plural. There's only one in the circus, and he's one of the most powerful of them all. He's the crown prince of the warlock race, but his parents are still strong, healthy, and the ultimate power, so there's not much chance he's going to be needed anytime soon. Lucky for him, he likes to play, and this is what he chooses to do. If he stays home, he fights off potential suitors left and right, with everyone wanting to be the partner of one of the most powerful people in the world. Here, he gets to just be part of the show. Warlocks are fearsome fighters who have magic like nothing you've seen. They can make things manifest out of nothing, and their control over the mind is incredible. You shouldn't look a warlock in the eye for too long, lest they capture your soul."

My mouth drops open, and he laughs. Even though my mind is telling me to be cautious, experience has taught me that I want to trust him and believe that he's telling me the truth. I definitely need someone on my side, so I don't want to be skeptical of Dylan. I might eat those words later, but I think I'm just going to take the leap of trusting his word for now. Worst case scenario, I'll just look like a dumbass when I meet this warlock if I take bad advice and avoid looking him in the eye.

"Well, maybe nothing that dramatic, but they *can* mind control you if they can get a link. Unlike the rest of us who need the transporters, they can also teleport without the use of a machine. Xavier's a cool guy; he takes care of all the magic the show needs, from the mind-fogging gas that we use on the humans to glamours for the Aquilians. He's quiet and keeps to himself, especially since the aura of power he radiates can be too much for some people. Occasionally, they'll add an illusion act in the circus, and he does that, but that's not every night. I'll introduce you to him. I think you'll like him." Dylan can't meet my eyes when he tells me this, and I get the feeling there may be a bit of a crush happening there.

"Can't wait to meet your friend," I assure him. "So, mermaid act, you juggle, saber-toothed tigers, and a dinosaur act is what I know about already. What else is there?" I prompt him, wanting to know more.

"There's one more animal act, and that's the larnuk show. They're an animal from Rilu. Rilu is a desert planet with oasis-like settlements spread far across the land. The Rilu are a nomadic race, so their clans move as they need to. Rilu also has gem mines deep within caves spread across the whole planet, and it's the main product in their trade with other planets. The larnuk are similar to Earth's pegasus myth but are fiercely protective. They spit fire and can grow to the size of a dragon when in defense mode, and they eat diamonds. The Rilu use them for transport and defense, and they raise herds amongst their tribes. The larnuk come in green, purple, red, and gold. Beautiful creatures, but deadly unless they bond to you. Our larnuk mistress is bonded to the five that perform in the show."

Dylan gets up from the couch and makes his way back over to the glass window, watching over the large water tank. I really want to join him, but I think it's important to see the show in its entirety to get a feel for it before I have all the pieces broken down. Instead, I flick through the pages of my tablet and pull up the one I'm most interested in. It appeals to the gymnast in me.

"Tell me about this act." I hold up the tablet and show him the picture of the familiar magenta eyes from last night. Superimposed over the picture is a flying trapeze. "The person who belongs to these eyes caught me last night. I want to know who I should thank."

Dylan frowns and sighs. "Out of all the acts here, they're probably the most dangerous for you, so of course you're the most interested in the seductive bastards."

There's a hint of something in his voice, but I'm not sure if it's malice or jealousy. "Saxon, the person who caught you last night, is where the Earth legend of vampires comes from. Blood drinkers who can move so fast you can't even see them. They avoid sunlight, not because it does anything to them, but because their planet Vilax has only five hours of sunlight a day. They are the acrobat and trapeze act. There are five in the show, and they cannot take your blood without permission, but be careful. They're tricksters, and words can often be twisted so that you end up giving blood without realizing it. They don't kill their donors, but they can make it as pleasurable or as painful as they like. It's not up to you which sensation you'll get."

I've always loved vampire stories, and the thought of being bitten turns me on enough that I squirm in my seat at the thought. Dylan stops talking and sniffs the air, a scowl crossing his face.

"One thing you need to know is that although all of us may have a human-like form, we are far from it. Underneath our clothes, things may not be what you expect. Be aware of this if you decide to pursue any kind of physical relationship with anyone." He gets up and starts pacing the room, refusing to look at me despite my questioning sound in response. "You need to talk to your grandpas about Skarrian physiology too before you do anything like that. Educate yourself before you get into trouble." He growls the last bit before throwing open the door and disappearing.

What the fuck did I do to upset him so much? Could he tell that I was turned on? It's the only thing that could explain such an abrupt change of topic, but what explains the anger?

CHAPTER TEN

My brain was so busy that I went to bed without going to the dining room for dinner. John came looking for me to make sure I was okay, and when he realized I was wiped, he arranged for dinner to be delivered to me along with my mug of Skarrian water.

The water still feels like it has a buzz to it when I drink it, so I guess that's just its make up, but it makes me feel better than I have all day, instantly revitalizing me and wiping away any residual tiredness.

"Lila, anytime it gets too much for you, just have a glass of the water," John recommends. "It can't replace sleep, but it can wipe away that fuzzy feeling that comes from being tired, both emotionally and physically." He pats me on the shoulder. "We recognize and appreciate how hard you're working, but we don't want you to get overwhelmed. We need to work on those powers, and that's going to bring its own kind of strain."

"What powers?" I grumble, glad that he brought it up. "Apart from that first overload, I've noticed nothing." Except there was that funny reaction to my chip implant, but that can't have been my powers, can it? Nah. Why would I feel my powers in my shoulder?

His eyes widen slightly. "Really? Not even any random telekinesis?"

I shake my head, and his frown deepens. "That *is* unusual. That's the one most people have. Never mind. Get a good night's sleep, and between the three of us, we will get you sorted tomorrow."

The following day, I make my way to breakfast on my own, not having seen Dylan around again for the rest of yesterday. As much as I'd like to see him, I don't have time to track down moody dragon shifters. Now the grandpas have cleared out the arena for us to use, and while I stand there dwarfed by the empty space and the power of their combined attention, my nerves kick in. My stomach is officially in my throat even though they've banned everyone for the morning so I can work on whatever I need to with no pressure or scrutiny. The last thing I need is for everyone to realize I'm a dud who has no right to inherit the circus from these men.

"Lila! Lila!" William must have been trying to get my attention because he looks exasperated.

"Sorry! What did you say?"

"You told John that you haven't experienced any more surges of any power. Is that right?"

"No, nothing. I don't feel any different to what I felt before I drank the water. Though I haven't been getting headaches, so if that's the only thing that happens, I'm still happy with that." I tried to go for reassurance, but we all know I'm lying. I'm going to be gutted if I don't get at least something. What's the point of finally having family, of having a legacy, if all I do is let them down?

"Okay, from the looks of what happened the first night, you may have some kind of elemental manipulation, but we might as well start out with the easiest. Let's try speed." Eric rubs his hands together and takes a step forward, literally zooming across the arena. His body just becomes a blur of motion that stops on the other side, only needing mere seconds to cross the distance.

"Now, don't be upset if you can't go that fast," John cautions me. "Eric is unusually fast. Neither Will nor I can replicate his speed, though we are faster than an average human."

"Okay, ready, Lila? Go!" William shouts, and I run as fast as I can toward Eric, but before I get far, I slow and stop.

"I know that was no different to how fast I was before," I complain with frustration, fighting the urge to stomp my foot like a disgruntled little kid.

Both John and William are frowning, and I can hear Eric cackling on the other side, which totally doesn't help. "No, that really wasn't fast," John agrees, him and William exchanging a glance.

"Come back, Eric," William calls. With a blink, Eric is back beside me.

"Never mind, I'm sure it will come." He pats me on the shoulder, not even breathing heavily. "Let's try some telekinesis. All of us have that one, and it's strong."

Eric and John take a seat on a nearby barrel while William steps up in front of me. "I've never had to teach this, so it's going to be a bit of a learning experience for both of us. Skarrian babies just have the instinctual knowledge, so I'm hoping that we can trigger yours. The last time we spoke to your mom and dad, they said that you had been using telekinesis to move your favorite toys around. You also liked to telekinetically throw them when you wanted something." The grandpas all smile, and a lurch inside my chest triggers a long-hidden memory. A stuffed purple winged animal flying above my head, the sound of echoing laughter in the background.

"I remember something!" The lurch turns to a thrill of excitement, and William latches on to it.

"Remember the feeling." He grabs a bucket of balls and holds one out in his palm. "Throw this at Eric!"

"Hey!" Eric complains in the background, but I block it out as my focus zeros in on the ball. Practically staring holes in it, I concentrate, desperately trying to move it with my mind. Breathing in and out, I try with everything that I am to move it, but nothing happens. The ball remains stationary in William's hand.

A feeling of lightheadedness rolls over me, and I

stumble. Eric dashes over and catches me before I can fall to the ground.

"Damn it. Why can't I do it?" I yell to nobody in particular.

"There, there." Eric pats me on the shoulder. "We knew there was a possibility it would take some time."

"Come on, princess! Get up. Let's try again," William says, probably hoping to goad me. Maybe he's trying to trigger something because I can feel my anger start to rise as I flip him off, though he just chuckles.

"Let's keep practicing. Something might just happen," John suggests, trying to ease the tension.

Eric steps away now that I'm stable again, and the three of them line up, facing me. Each holding a ball in their hand. Over and over, I try to make one of them move until sweat is dripping down my face and my hair is plastered to my skin, but nothing happens.

"Okay, let's take five," Eric says an hour later. All three had repeatedly demonstrated how to do it, but I picked up on nothing. No tingling feeling, no electricity in the air, nothing to show me *how* they were doing it.

John grabs some bottles of water out of a nearby tub and hands us all one. "Lila, have you ever meditated?"

"I've tried, but I always have so much going on in my head that I find it hard to switch off," I tell him, taking a long sip of my water before holding the cold bottle against my overheated face.

"Why don't you go over there and just take ten minutes to clear your mind?" John points to a spot in the center of the ring. "While you do that, we will discuss our plan of attack."

Sighing, I do as he asks while the grandpas huddle, whispers floating over the open space but not loudly enough for me to make out the words.

Settling down, I sit cross legged and put my bottle to the side. I close my eyes and try to calm my mind, but it's virtually impossible. All the details I'd learned about the various planets and races cycle through my mind like a neverending carousel of information. Shaking my head, I take some deep breaths, hoping to slow the flow and help it float away, leaving my mind clear.

Breathe in and out… In and out. Clear my mind of everything.

Oh! I should probably call Susie! But what will I tell her? There's not much I can share. Maybe I'll tell her about Dylan and what a great friend he's been.

Focus, Lila! Breathe in and out.

In and out.

. . . . . .

I cannot believe they have vampires in the circus. Fucking bloodsucking vampires!! I don't know whether to pee my pants in excitement or with terror.

Shit, Lila, get it together.

"Stop, just stop. God, it's so painful just watching you. Do you ever sit still?" William's groan has me opening my eyes to see all three grandpas watching me with disbelief.

"You didn't once stop moving. You played with your hair and twitched your fingers. I could practically see your eyeballs moving under your eyelids." John sounds astounded, but Eric is once again smirking.

"Relax, Lila is obviously a doer. I get it. I am too. I hate sitting still." Well, that's nice of him. "So I have another idea. Stand up just in that spot right there." I shuffle to where he points. "Perfect, just perfect."

They turn as one, and when they face me again, they all have the rubber balls in their hands.

"Come on! What makes you think it's going to work this time? My mind didn't clear or anything…" I break off at the look in their eyes. Gone are the concerned grandpas, replaced with the formidable men they must be to protect the orb.

"Sorry, Lila, but sometimes you need to take drastic action." With those words, Eric hurls the first ball at me. Shocked, I'm unable to stop it before it hits me in the middle of the chest and falls back to the ground.

"Hey!" Before I can voice any more complaints, the balls come flying. One after another, they hit me like some deranged game of dodgeball. I abandon the idea of staying in one spot, jumping around, but they're deadshots. And they never run out. One of them uses their own telekinesis to retrieve the balls when they get low.

Finally, everything stops, and I put my hands on my knees as I try to draw more breath into my lungs than I'm capable of at the moment.

"Let's step it up a bit. It's obviously not enough to trigger an automatic response," William suggests, and I watch as they paw around the props before John stands up, some long shiny metal things in his hands. *Oh fuck.*

"Look, Caspian's swords! I'm sure he won't mind if we use these."

A squeak of fright escapes my mouth. When I think about Caspian's swords, pointy metal ones that might cut me are *not* what comes to mind.

"What the fuck?" My voice echoes around the arena while the grandpas load up on whatever else they can find to throw at me. "Come on, this is ridiculous! I can't do it, so scaring me isn't going to help," I plead, but the whistle of a blade past my face and the sharp sting of pain, followed by a trickle of warmth, on my cheek tells me they're not listening at all.

"You are fucking crazy!" I scream at them and start running. Screw this! They can fuck right off. Nothing else hits me as I race out of the arena, but the echo of their laughter trails after me.

"Assholes!" I scream. They just chuckle louder, but at least I'm out of range. That's all that matters. I slide to a stop in front of the elevator, planning to go back to my room. I need a nap and some alcohol. I wonder if I can get me some of each and not necessarily in that order.

Pushing at the button, I feel someone slide to a stop next to me then realize it's Eric.

"You suck," I tell him blandly. He simply hands me a tissue while gesturing to the cut on my face. I dab at it, hoping the bleeding will stop soon.

"Yeah, I'm sorry, but it was worth a try. Don't worry, Lila. It will come eventually, and if it doesn't, well, we will figure something else out. Prince Xavier might have some ideas. There's not much about magic and woo woo shit he doesn't know, and if he doesn't, his mom or dad can help us."

I scoff at him and try not to engage since I'm done with them today. The elevator doors slide open, and I step in, holding my hand out before Eric can join me. "Ah, I don't think so, Gramps. You can wait for the other chuckles and get the next ride or whatever. If you step in here right now, I might just kick your ass, powers or no powers."

He takes a step back, looking all too amused by what's a very realistic threat. "Lila, take a break. We'll come and get you a little later. It's time to start the circus stuff anyway."

A thrill of excitement runs through me on the tail end of all the adrenaline that I just used, making me feel both woozy and stimulated at the same time.

"Can't wait." I salute him as the door closes, leaving me to try to reel in all the emotions again. I'm pretty sure this is a losing battle; my emotions are going to be in a constant state of flux for at least a while.

The sight of my room almost brings a tear to my eye, and as I run my key through the scanner, I breathe a sigh of relief when the door pops open. Heading straight to the wall where I saw Gramps get a drink the other day, I put my hand up, searching for the opening. I must hit the right spot because there's a pop and a hiss before a door swings open, showing me the inside of a refrigerated cabinet. The only thing I recognize are the bottles of water, which I now know is Skarrian water, and the rest is an interesting array of cans and bottled liquids.

Grabbing out a pink bottle, I try to read the label, but of course it's in a whole other language that is unrecognizable. I wonder if my translator is not working? *If it's on the fritz, does that mean I can go see Link again?* I close the fridge and take the bottle over to my bedside table, activating the universal translator in my tablet to see what the heck I'm about to drink. *Rilaxious, from the planet Rilu. This fermented berry juice is made from the Rilax berries which grow in the bottom of the gem mines away from all sunlight. It gets its pink color from being exposed to sunlight during the brewing process. The flavor is said to taste like a cross between an Earth strawberry and pineapple.*

Well, sign me up. It sounds freaking delicious. I push away the tablet and crack open the top. The bottle hisses, but it doesn't bubble up like cider or beer. Taking a cautious sip, the texture surprises me as it flows across my tongue. It's thicker than soda, more the consistency of a thick shake, and it has a slight bubble to it. I can feel the alcoholic kick it has almost instantly.

"Whoa, new favorite thing about all of this."

Climbing up on my bed, I drink the beverage while flicking through more information on the circus. I think I have a handle on all the acts now, but I would really like to see them firsthand and experience everything. Next, I need to work out the layout of this pod. Where everything is and how everything is run. Apparently, everything is automated, but there are always a few crew on hand for set-up and take down and to watch over the flight/control deck in case there's a malfunction mid-show.

My mind skips away from the technical stuff and

back to the disappointment from before. What's the point of learning all of this if I might not ever be able to inherit the circus? What if I'm a dud? Nobody is going to respect me if I'm practically human. I tried so hard, and the lack of results is completely bumming me. I consider trying one of the other drinks in the fridge, having a complete pity bender, but I know they'll be coming for me later. If I can't prove to them I have what it takes as far as special powers go, I can at least prove I've got the determination and sheer stubbornness that make me the right person for the job.

My eyes grow heavier as I continue to read while the drink in my hand empties in a steady correlation. Too tired to enjoy any more of them, I close my eyes and let sleep carry me away in the hope that when I wake next, there may be some sign of powers. Because let's face it, are they really going to trust me with the responsibility over the orb of tremendous power if I can't even get shit right in my own life?

CHAPTER ELEVEN

Over the next week, my mind is completely blown. I'm kept so busy I barely have time to breathe, let alone worry about some ball of energy that I could possibly be killed over. The reality of that important fact hasn't quite registered in my mind yet. Every morning, I have lessons with the grandpas to learn to control telekinesis, and it is *not* going well. Abort, abort, turn around, run away. Let's just leave it at that for now. William is going to introduce me to the warlock tomorrow if things haven't happened by then.

Each afternoon, the grandpas show me around the dome. I've seen the control room which presides over all aspects of the show—from teleporting each act down from the mothership to the lights and special effects inside the dome, such as the snow during the ice tiger show. I've seen the flight deck, and I almost peed my pants. I was so excited! It was like something out of *Star Trek*. The teleportation room was also pretty awesome, while the room that holds the tech department's animatronics was honestly a bit creepy. There's nothing like lifeless robots to give you that little chill down your spine. And even though I've been kept so busy I can barely breathe, I've had a nagging thought about Dylan in the back of my mind. I still don't know what was up with his over the top reaction the other day. I really need to make an effort to search him out and check that we're okay, but when the hell am I supposed to do that?

I collapse into bed every night after the grandpas have dinner sent to me. I'm not sure if it's because I'm still not showing any signs of powers or if they truly understand how freaking tired I am. As it is, I've avoided interaction with anyone due to my embarrassment. The one time I went to dinner, Phillip and Fiona grilled me on my abilities, wanting me to perform like I was one of the circus acts. John quickly put a stop to that, but we decided it might be better to not broadcast my lack of powers.

Tonight, I plan to not only stay awake, but I will see the show. I still haven't managed to do that yet, but it's the last night in this location, and there's nothing left for me to learn. Well, there is, but I have all the technical knowledge either in my brain or in my trusty tablet. Now I need to put all that knowledge into practice.

Once the curtains close on tonight's show, we move from the UK to the US. Nevada, I think they said, to the salt flats that were used for the Burning Man festival. It also means I get to see the mothership. I've been told it has cloaking abilities and sits in the upper atmosphere, not visible to any of Earth's space sensors. Could you imagine the panic if they actually could sense the ship?

I cannot wait! I get to be on the flight deck. *Will I get to sit in the captain's chair?* Although the grandpas are in charge of the whole thing, there's a captain who pilots the crafts to and from the mothership. Just like how Jean Luc doesn't drive the actual Enterprise. That's Captain Lester's job.

After eating dinner in my room and taking a shower, I grab my lanyard and pass then walk toward the elevator. As I walk down the corridor, I get that itchy feeling on the back of my neck. You know, when there's someone watching you and your body tries to give you a heads up. Finding no one there when I try to stealthily peek around, I shrug. For all I know, there's an alien species with invisibility, some jerk laughing his ass off because I look like an idiot. Might as well hop in the elevator and see if the feeling goes away.

Once the elevator arrives, I step inside, needing to get down to the ground level for my ringside seats. That in itself is pretty exciting; I haven't really had the kind of life where I got those kinds of treats very often —if ever. A brush of wind goes past me, bringing a rush of what smells like salty sea air and a hint of coconut like being at the beach in summer time. I swing around quickly, but no one is in the elevator. Weird! Even weirder, when I move to hit the ground-level button, I realize my invisible companion has already hit a different one. Looks like I'm going up first.

With nothing else to do and no invisible admirer revealing themselves, I stare into the reflective walls of the elevator. My ass looks amazing in my pin-up-style tight skirt, its hem falling just below my knees. It has a slit up the back to allow me to walk in it, thank god, because I need a little leverage considering the heels I'm wearing. The long-sleeved, low-cut black top I'm wearing makes my tits look perky and playful, so the only element slightly out of place is my hair. I'm messing around with it, trying to neaten it up, when I see a ripple in the air behind me out of the corner of my eye.

Before I know what's happening, I'm spun around and shoved up against the wall by a man with stormy blue eyes. "Look what we have here. Come out to socialize with the freaks, have you?" he whispers in my ear, and a shiver of desire runs through my body. I'm not afraid of a little roughness, and I've always appreciated someone who can take charge when I'm ready to give up some control. I'm not sure if he thinks he's intimidating me, but he's going to be sorely disappointed.

He has me pinned between himself and the unforgiving wall, our bodies pressed closely together enough that I can feel he's *all* man today. Or at least the parts of him that I can see at the moment. Suddenly, I feel the smooth slide of a tentacle up the inside of my calf, the suckers placing gentle kisses on my soft skin, each little burst of suction sending white-hot heat straight to my core. Holy shit!

"Have you finally decided to slum it with the performers?"

"Where did you come from?" I ask breathlessly, trying not to show how much I'm enjoying having his hard body pushed up against me or the tentacle slowly inching its way up my leg. By now, my core is tingling. Fucking tingling. No man has ever given me fucking *tingles*.

He steps back from me, much to my disappointment, and when I look down, there's no sign of tentacles. As he does, his whole-body ripples, changing to match the surroundings around him. Clothes and all. *Huh, he camouflages.* "My beast is a very good mimic, and the power carries over to me when I'm in human form. I can blend into all surfaces." He reappears, looking quite smug when he says this, probably pleased he was able to get the drop on me.

I can't let these people think they can get one over on me if I'm going to be their boss, so I walk over to him, batting my eyelashes and simpering. "That is *so* amazing, like a real octopus." I have him backed up against the wall this time, running my hands up and over his chest. I can feel his nipple piercings through his shirt. I would love to get my mouth on those, not that I'm going to let him know that. "Does that mean that you'll have sex once and then die a couple of weeks later? Are you a virgin? You poor, poor man, never to have experienced the wonder of a woman." Thank you, Animal Planet and David Attenborough for the random animal facts I have stored in my brain.

I know this kind of sounds bitchy, but damn it, the man has been so fucking agressive toward me while I have no idea what I did to him. Yeah, I might have gaped when I first saw him, but I'm also sure he was going for some kind of reaction. So sue me for not wanting to take any of his shit.

His face turns from smug to shocked, and he starts to sputter, storming from the elevator the moment the doors open. Before he steps out, he delivers a final parting shot, accompanied by what I think might be his ever-present scowl. "This isn't finished, and I'm *not* an octopus. I'm the kraken." He bares his sharp teeth at me in what's probably supposed to be a threatening manner, but I just laugh at him.

"I hoped you wouldn't give up so easily. This is going to be so much fun," I say to him with a wiggle of my fingers, waving goodbye as the elevator doors close behind him. Caspian- 0, Lila- 2. I have a little giggle and fan my face. That man is smoking hot sex on *lots* of legs. Pity he's an asshole. But what's provoked all this animosity? Is it humans in general, me as a woman, or me personally? I may have to hit Dylan up for some gossip. God, I hope everyone isn't going to be as aggressive as him and the cats were. Granted, in the cats' case, I lit one of their asses on fire. That's a fair enough reason for a bad first impression. Caspian, well, who knows what crawled up his ass.

As the elevator starts to descend, I get a message that the grandpas are waiting for me in the lobby. Two of them will sit with me and explain anything I have questions about while the third will be the evening's ringmaster. John takes more of a backstage role since he's not interested in performing, so he'll probably be sitting by my side.

While I wait for the elevator to continue downward, a warm feeling starts to heat both sides of my shoulders. It gradually becomes hotter and hotter until it feels like it's burning. Ripping off my shirt, I turn to look at my shoulders in the reflection of the doors. On the right side is a small faded black circle with what looks like two black angel wings with extremely long feathers at the bottom. On the other, there are two marks. One is a faded blue circle with a sideways figure eight, and the other one kind of looks like the medical symbol on Earth. There are two snakes entwined around a staff, but instead of wings at the top, there's a cog. What the fuck is going on? By the time the elevator dings, its doors slowly opening, I'm still standing there in just my bra and skirt. The horrified look on my face only becomes comically worse when I realize that the three grandpas are waiting for me in all of my half-naked glory.

"What the fuck just happened?" I wobble out of the elevator, pointing at my shoulder blades. "What are these things that just appeared on my shoulders?" I yell at them. They turn me around and take a look at the marks that have appeared, and Eric's smothered laugh is most definitely *not* a welcome sound in the middle of my very reasonable freakout. "Explain, please," I demand.

John takes me by the arm and walks me away from the crowd of onlookers that have migrated toward the elevators with all the commotion. "Calm down, dear. Why don't you put your top back on so we can have a nice quiet conversation?" He's managing me, but I don't call him out on it. I wasn't expecting so much of the public to be milling around in the lobby when I flashed them all a look at the girls. *Though they do look great tonight.* I quickly shrug back into my shirt and take a look around, realizing he's led me to an alcove that's out of the crowd's view. William and Eric have followed, the latter still sniggering. That grandpa is going to get my foot up his ass if he isn't careful.

"Seriously, Mutley, what is your problem?" I snarl at him. Since he's still chuckling, useless at answering my question, I turn to William. "Please explain?"

William gets an uncomfortable look on his face again. "Well, ah, yes," he stumbles.

"Oh, for crying out loud!" I snap at him. "Get it together, man."

Eric is just about rolling on the floor in laughter, while John looks uneasy. Eric gets himself together and says, "Try before you buy, Lila." I just blink at him and turn to William for a bigger explanation.

"Huh?"

"Yes, well, the right shoulder is your bonding mark. It looks like you've picked up the Norse symbol for protector. Quite apt, I might say, if you decide to take on your role with the circus."

"Ok then. My bonding mark! You said that it would show up on men that I'm interested in and will stay there unless I lose interest, right?" I question. After he nods, I think about it for a moment. "It's pretty. I'm ok with that."

Looking relieved that I'm not freaking out as much anymore, he adds, "The mark will intensify and merge with the partner's mark if you fully consummate the bond. Right now, as you can see, the coloring of the marks is faded, but it won't stay that way if someone becomes your permanent partner."

"And that takes five rounds of sex?" I question again.

"Yes, in most cases." *Most* cases? Do I delve further into this, or do I just let it go for now? I mean, haven't I already got enough on my plate? Head in the sand, it is.

"Well, ok then, no having sex with anyone more than five times if they have my mark. Nice and easy. I certainly don't need a husband at the moment." I'm pacing back and forth, repeatedly running my hands down my skirt until William steps into my path to stop me.

"Lila honey," he says to me softly, like he doesn't want to startle me further. "Don't forget it could be husbands, *plural*. Don't close your mind to it just because what you are used to is monogamy. Nobody here will judge you. In fact, it might make others even more open to you if they see you embracing more of our culture. Either way, it's an important decision that deserves your fully informed choice. Remember, anyone you do mate with will gain any abilities you have and vice versa. You could end up with other powers, ones that you're certainly not expecting. Now, your grandma was Skarrian and had the same powers as us, but we know of many matings that have resulted in different species partners gaining new abilities."

It brings a tear to my eye that he's being so gentle with me. Honestly, his care feels less like management and more like genuine care for my feelings. It's kind of sweet… but then I think twice. He's never soft and gentle. What's going on?

Silly me, I ask the question I've been dreading but secretly know the answer to. "What do the other marks mean?" He flinches before he straightens up and looks me in the eye. "The left shoulder will contain the marks of the man or men who return your interest." My heart is pounding so hard I feel like it's going to jump out of my chest. "A mark won't appear if the interest is not mutual."

"So what are you saying?" I ask cautiously, bracing myself for the answer.

"Those are the marks of whoever you find yourself attracted to, so long as they return the attraction."

"The interest has to be mutual for the mark to show?" I need to check, already feeling like my world is about to be rocked.

"Yes," he says, setting my mind whirling. There are plenty of men that I've found attractive so far. If I had to guess, one is the doctor. But who could the other one be?

"Was there anyone in the elevator with you? That's when you felt it, yes?" Eric asks, his eyes still laughing even though he's calmed down.

"Caspian was in it for a while, but he's the only one."

"Well, there you go. It would be safe to assume he's one of them. I guess he's not as grumpy as you thought."

Showing remarkable class and self-control, I very maturely ignore the temptation to make that whole foot/ass situation into reality. Caspian!?

"Well, fuck!"

CASPIAN

The elevator doors close, leaving me with an impression of sexy as fuck Lila wiggling her fingers at me burned into my retinas, and my anger fades away. She really isn't disgusted by me. In fact, if the scent that drifted to my nose as my tentacle caressed her leg is anything to go by, she was turned on. I shake my head when I realize I was so flustered that I got off at the top floor even though I needed to get out on the performers' level. I push the button to call it back while I contemplate the conundrum that is Lila.

The minute I saw her in the cafeteria that first night, my kraken tried to come out. He smelled her and thought *mate*, but I couldn't stand the thought of being rejected again. I pushed him down and brought out my asshole self, but she didn't even flinch. Sure, her mouth dropped open, but she'd quickly recovered and greeted me like I was *normal.* Then gave back as good as I dished out.

But of course Dylan wormed his way into a seat at the head table. Sure, the guy's my buddy and we've been performing together for a while now, but he doesn't hide the fact that he has big goals. And yes, we've been lovers on and off for a while now, but it's nothing serious. I know that my kraken would never consider him a compatible mate, and let's face it the guy's a manwhore. I'm certainly not the only person he's sleeping with. Thankfully, there's an inoculation for alien STIs.

My mind is a whirl of chaotic thoughts on the ride back down. Once I'm on the right floor, I find Dylan already dressed for the performance.

"Cas! Where have you been? Come on, man, you need to get ready." He drags me to our dressing room without waiting for me to answer.

He throws himself onto our couch as I pull off my clothes and replace them with the leather pants I wear for the performance. Moving over to the nearby makeup table, I start to apply the show makeup, using a ridiculous amount so that we can be seen from the top rows.

I'm staring off into space as I apply it, only meeting Dylan's eyes in the mirror after he clears his throat to get my attention. "What's wrong with you? You're all spacey. Where were you?" I can't help but roll my eyes at the suspicion in his voice. God, he's a jealous asshole. He can fuck anything that walks, but the minute I do something out of the ordinary, he assumes there's something else going on.

"I was talking to Lila in the elevator." His face wrinkles into a frown, and there's a flash of his dragon's presence in his eyes.

"Why? I thought you didn't like her. You certainly were an asshole the first day."

"Yeah, but that was when I thought she would be repulsed by me. Now that I talked to her again, I don't think she is." Even to my own ears I sound amazed.

He scoffs. "You don't have a crush on her, do you? Because I think she's a fangbanger. She got all turned on when I was talking about Saxon the other day. You haven't got a chance, bro."

I narrow my eyes at him, which makes putting on eyeliner a little tricky. "I thought you were all Team Lila. Sure seemed like you liked her too. Why are you being like this? Do you know how long it's been since the last time someone was genuinely interested in me? She wasn't scared off, man, or even disgusted. I swear she was actually into it!"

"Maybe, but is she really going to be serious about an eight-legged freak." His words fucking hurt. That's the thing about Dylan—he's so fucking thoughtless with his words. He knows how fucking sensitive I am about being rejected by women. Sometimes I wonder if he does it just to keep me to himself, but then I don't know why he would. He knows that I won't commit to him even if he wanted it.

There's a loud knock on the door, distracting me from our conversation, thank god. I call out for whoever it is to come in before finishing applying my makeup.

When it opens, Magenta walks in. "Hey, guys. How's it going? You ready yet?"

The pretty Skarrian drops down on the couch next to Dylan, already dressed in her costume even though her face isn't made up yet.

"Hey, babe, how are you?" Dylan pats her on the leg and turns the charm back up, but she curls a lip up at him.

"Eww, don't touch me! I don't know where your hands have been," she jokes, pushing his hand off her knee, but I see Dylan's eyes flash reptilian. I don't know if it was her comment or pushing him off her leg, but something about that interaction genuinely bothered him."

"Yup." I stand up and grab a bottle of oil. "Just got to rub this in then I'm good to go."

She rubs her hands together. "Whoop, this is my favorite part!" She leans back to enjoy the show, and I roll my eyes. Magenta has never been disgusted by me, but we also friendzoned each other very quickly. She's like the sister I never had, which is actually nice.

Dylan rolls his eyes and stands up, coming over to me. "Here, let me do it." He grabs the bottle out of my hand and pours some into his before slapping it on my chest.

"Hey! You're blocking my view," Magenta complains, and he growls in response, a little bit of smoke leaving his nose. There's that unwarranted jealousy again.

He oils all the exposed skin for me, his hands gliding seductively across my chest, but after Lila and the feelings she inspired in my beast, Dylan does nothing for me. Thankfully, he doesn't notice. His torso is already gleaming in the light, so I take the bottle back from him and put it back on the table.

"Hey, Mags, have you met Lila yet?" I ask as Dylan washes his hand in a nearby sink. Oil on the hands is *not* a smart idea for jugglers.

"No, but I'm dying to meet her! I've been harassing the boss men daily. I'm sure they're close to caving. Don't you think it's weird they haven't been introducing her to us? I know they've been busy and she's met the crew, but you'd think they'd be excited for her to at least be around some of the other performers."

"Maybe she's too good to slum it with the freaks?" I glare at Dylan even though his words are an echo of what I just accused her of. People have already seen him getting friendly with her. What game is he playing now?

"No, I'm sure that's not the case. She seems…" I break off, not sure how to describe her. I can't very well say *fuckable*. "Cool."

Mags stands up, slapping her hands together. "That's it! If they don't introduce me tomorrow, then I'm going to find her myself. Do you know where her room is?"

She looks at Dylan. Circus gossip hasn't hidden the fact that he's been hanging out with her. He rolls his eyes and points to me. "Actually, she's next door to octoman."

Huh, I didn't know that. Well, that makes things interesting. I think now that I know she's not going to reject me, I'm going to do my best to convince her that spending time with me would be a good thing. My kraken opens one eye inside me and agrees, baring his teeth in Dylan's direction. Jesus, he really doesn't like that dragon.

A smile crosses my lips, and Mags raises her eyebrows. "Oh, I see how it is. Good for you, man. You go get yourself some."

Before anyone can reply to that, one of the stage-hands sticks his head in. "Five minutes, guys. Let's get moving."

So the three of us head toward the stage entrance, all talk of Lila done with for now as we get ready to wow an easily wowed audience.

"I wish all audiences were as easy to entertain as humans." Mags voices exactly what I had been think-ing. "Anyway, break a leg as the humans say, and I'll catch up with you later."

Dylan is strangely silent as we wait for our cue, but I don't have time to worry about him now. I have plans to make and a woman to woo. There's a huge smile on my face as I take the stage, happy with my decision and having something to look forward to.

CHAPTER TWELVE

Half an hour later, I find myself in the tiered seating, ringside seat. My mind is still occupied by what just happened despite the mystery of what I'll see tonight. How is it I haven't been able to manifest any cool powers but the whole mate thing is now an issue? At first, I felt like I'd gotten the short end of the stick.

But as my mind's been fixating on this for the last thirty minutes, I'm starting to think that something else is happening too. Since the event in the elevator, all my senses are on high alert. The noise of the crowd is like the sound of waves pounding on the ocean, thunderous and constant, and the smell of popcorn and cotton candy permeates the air… along with the regrettable undertone of excitement in the form of body odor. I lean over and whisper in John's ear.

"I think something's happening. Everything around

me is just… *more.*" John's eyebrows raise in surprise, excitement crossing his face as he leans in toward me.

"Tell me what you feel?"

"I can hear, smell, and see *so* much better. Like, I can see all the way across the other side of the arena. There's a little girl, and she wants a Galaxy Circus shirt, but her parents are telling her she has to wait until after the show." I point in her direction, and he turns to look before nodding.

"Yes, that's good, Lila. This might be the start of it all. Maybe you just needed to ease into it slowly." He rubs his hands together, and a rush of excitement flows through me followed by another bout of the stench of body odor and anticipation.

"Eww. Can't say the better senses are a side effect I'm thankful for." My nose wrinkles as I try to clear the smell. The scent of beer and peanuts gets stronger when William sits down on my other side.

"Here," he says, waving a beer under my nose before handing it to me. "This will make it easier. Big crowds like this always affect the senses, but you will get used to it the more you are exposed. Once you become ringmaster, you will be doing it all the time. Your senses will adjust."

"How did you know?" I ask him in surprise, and he taps his ears.

"We all have enhanced senses, so I heard you telling John. When you get more experienced, you will be able to pinpoint one conversation even in a crowd this big."

Grabbing the beer from him, I take a sip before

turning up my nose. It's definitely not as nice as the last alcoholic beverage I tried, but I guess they can't very well offer that to humans.

Looking around the area closest to us, I watch a small child a few seats away, bouncing up and down in her seat. The pure happiness on her face as she waits for the show to start is infectious, and I grin and wiggle in my seat as well. After a quick conversation with the adults sitting with her, she starts furiously waving her arms up and down to get the attention of the man selling balloons a few rows away. He starts moving toward them, slowly going to get through the rows.

"I don't recognize that man selling the balloons." I gesture to the guy when he gets to the little girl, an indulgent smile on his face. I might not know all the names yet or have the ability to pronounce their species correctly, but I'm good with faces. Call it one of the few perks of being a bartender.

"No, you wouldn't," John says, taking a sip of the beer that William handed him. "We hire locals to sell the concession stuff." The man hands over a balloon and a glow stick that looks like a multicolored firework. "Most of them have full-time jobs, but it's a little extra they can earn, as we are after-hours. They help with ushering, concession stands, and merchandise. The humans come in around showtime and leave straight after. It's a way for us to establish good will with the locals," he says, shrugging like it's no big deal.

William interrupts John, adding his own two cents. I'm starting to think the grandpas can't have any conversation that's not a team effort. "That will be one of your jobs. After tonight, we're going to throw you in the deep end. We will be getting you to work with the show both behind the scenes and with the performers."

"Yes," agrees John, "in Nevada, we'll let you handle the screening and employment of the locals, *and* you will start working with one of the acts." He mulls this over. "Not the first act, I don't think. Not much you can do to help with that one unless you have some kind of juggling, fire breathing, or knife throwing skills you haven't told us about?" He raises an eyebrow at me, but I shake my head.

"Not to mention the tension between you and Caspian," William mutters beside me. I throw a dirty look his way, knowing he totally deserves it, what with the *enhanced senses* and all. Gramps definitely knew I would hear that comment.

"We're not even going to continue that discussion at the moment. I don't have time for men, nor do I even want a man, considering all that's going on. Plus, if I'm in as much danger as you say, how can I ever learn to trust that they want me and not the circus?" I finish off in a soft voice. William glances away, but not before I catch the hint of sympathy in his eyes.

"The mark will fade if it is not a true romantic attachment. If they are faking it for personal gain, it will disappear. And then I will kill them," he says matter-of-factly.

"And I will bury them," says John. "Actually, I may feed them to the Magila worm on Stol." I'm not actually sure how to respond to that sweet sentiment, so I let it go.

The lights start to dim before I can even respond. A noisy wave of anticipation spreads through the crowd and then drops to nothing but the occasional cough or throat clearing. A spotlight shines down, illuminating a figure standing in the middle of the circus ring. It looks like he appeared out of nowhere. Eric strikes a pose like he's Madonna circa the nineties, and his clothes definitely fit the bill too. He has sequins all over his jacket, looking like a glitter ball on steroids, but the overall effect is amazing. Top hat, cane, and long black boots over his jodhpur-style black pants. Slightly different to the outfit in my closet. The man is truly a show pony. If he hadn't been married to my grandma, I would think we batted for the same team. He has the crowd on the edge of their seats and in the palm of his hand.

"Welcome to the Galaxy Circus." He spreads his arms wide, cane in one hand, as his voice projects around the dome, the microphone in his lapel amplifying his voice. He turns in a circle as he continues to speak.

"Welcome to an evening of excitement, enjoyment, and eye-opening extravagance." Smoke drifts across the floor, surrounding him and drawing the eye of the audience to ensure they are focused on him. "We have performers that will blow your mind. Your eyes will not believe what is happening before you, yet it is truly real. After tonight, you will walk away questioning everything you have ever believed." He starts to strut his way through the drifting smoke, heading to one end of the arena and drawing the audience's eyes with him, away from where the first act will appear.

I can see hints of movement in the dark as the performers and crew move all their props into place, some of it done by hand and some with some "special" assistance.

"First up to tantalize your senses, we have a troupe of performers whose skills are out of this world. You will see jugglers with amazing hand-eye coordination. You will see knife throwers with deadly accuracy and fire breathers with flaming talents. You will see things that you will not believe. Sit back and hold on tight to your seats, ladies and gentlemen. Here is State of Fluxx!" He disappears in what looks like a flash of smoke right before a blaze of light appears down the other end. Dylan, Caspian, and troupe are all there, the men wearing tight pants but nothing on their torsos. The women are wearing one-piece bodysuits with sequins scattered artfully over them. There are plates, batons, balls, and rings flying every which way. One group is surrounding a man riding a unicycle while holding balancing poles, the others throwing plates on them. The plates are stacking up, but he continues to balance them with ease.

There's another group, three men and a woman, juggling glowing rings between them. They throw the rings back and forth, up and down, everything happening so fast it's hard to focus. I can see Dylan juggling those batons that light on fire, unlit as of yet. Off to the side, there's a man with a woman against a board, throwing ninja stars at her, and in the middle of all these people is Caspian. He's just standing, watching everything going on.

The audience is transfixed. Every now and again, there is a gasp or a round of quick applause as the performers flourish and bow. One by one, the performers finish and leave the ring in a rush of feet and props until only Dylan and Caspian are left.

The two men start to throw the batons back and forth. Once Caspian has all three, he starts to juggle them in his hands while Dylan spreads his arms wide to show everyone he has nothing in them. When he turns to watch his partner, Caspian throws the batons higher. All of a sudden, as one of them reaches the zenith of its flight, Dylan blows out a deep breath. Flames shoot out of his mouth, setting the baton alight, and the audience gasps in unison. All around me, the whispers start.

"How did he do that?"

"Wow, did you see that?"

By now all three are flaming, and Caspian begins sending them back to Dylan. He catches them and whips them around his body—up and down, through his legs, under and over. All of a sudden, he starts catching them all in one hand. While the crowd is waiting on the edge of their seats, eager to see what's coming next, he holds one of the batons high for show-manship then puts the flame into his mouth and closes his lips around it, putting it out.

"How does he do that?"

"Doesn't it burn his mouth?"

"Maybe he really is a dragon."

One by one, he puts out the batons, smoke swirling around his head and billowing out of his mouth every time he opens it to put out another flame. More artificial smoke drifts across the arena and up into the stands, joining the haze left over from the batons. It's very cleverly done. The artificial smoke also has a distinct smell to it, which must be what the grandpas were telling me about on the first day. Makes people suspend their disbelief while fogging their senses ever so slightly.

He puts out all the flames then takes a flourishing bow. The audience erupts into applause while Dylan puts the batons down and steps to the side, giving Caspian the centerstage spot. He's holding eight balls in his hands, all glowing brightly. He hands five to Dylan then starts juggling the other three, and after a while, Dylan starts throwing extra balls into the mix. By the end, Caspian is juggling all eight. As this happens, Eric reappears on the stage in a flash of smoke. "Audience of all ages, are these men not amazing?"

"It's good but nothing I've never seen before."

"The guy before was better. This dude's only juggling balls."

"What's that, I hear?" he questions dramatically, holding a hand up to his ear. "Not so impressed? Well, what if we doubled the amount? Watch very closely as I wave my cane and say the magic word. Abracadabra!"

In a burst of light and sparkles, with some special effects smoke thrown in, two-legged Caspian disappears. Eight-legged OctoCaspian reappears, juggling all eight balls with his six legs... um... tentacles and his two human arms while two more tentacles hold him up. There's stunned silence throughout the dome, the audience so quiet you could probably hear a pin drop. More whispers.

"Holy shit."

"No fucking way."

"Wait, is that a costume?"

"How did they do that?"

"It's got to be animatronics."

"Oh, did you think I meant we were going to double the amount of balls? I obviously meant legs, though it's more like quadruple." Eric laughs, gesturing to Caspian, and then he and Dylan start throwing more balls until even I lose count.

The audience erupts into thunderous applause, and Eric gestures with his cane again, cueing another flash, sparkle, and some smoke. All the balls drop to the floor and bounce away before Caspian appears again in human form. The applause continues while Dylan and Caspian take a bow.

"Wow," I whisper to William and John. "That was just... *wow.*" I lean back in my seat and release a heavy breath. The performance has been going for about thirty minutes, but it's so fast paced I didn't even notice the time. "Just wait," William says smugly.

John interjects next, basically as expected. "That was only the warm-up. Pay close attention to the next act. As the future ringmaster, you'll be heavily involved in it as you become the 'lion tamer.'"

I turn to him, mouth open in shock. "I'm sorry,

what did you say? Because I *thought* you said I would become the lion tamer, but that's just not possible. I know nothing about lions. I thought you were just joking when you told me that the first day!"

"Oh hush." That's William this time. I must have gotten a bit loud in my confusion because I've attracted the eyes and much too interested ears of a few audience members sitting near us. He whispers in my ear, "They're not real big cats. Well, they are, but they're the shifters you met the other day. If you have their respect, you have nothing to worry about. They will follow your lead."

John grunts, and I turn to look at him. "Have you got something to add?"

"Yeah, after what you did to Natalia, that may be a bit tricky. She thinks that all the other male cats belong to her. Having another female come in, especially one above her in the pecking order, is going to be a big problem." I bite my lip in worry, sneaking a glance at William.

"No, it won't," he says, sitting back and crossing his arms. "I've sorted it. They don't play nice, then we get new cats. Maybe a new species, who knows, but I'm pretty sure between Maxsim and Echo, they will fix it. Now, shush and watch."

While we were talking, the crew collected the balls and cleared the arena for the next act. Eric is now talking again, his voice booming out.

"What an act! Weren't they amazing? Well, we warmed you up with that one, and now we are going to cool you down... way down. If you need to, feel free to reach under your seats. We have provided blankets for people to wrap around themselves as the temperature is about to drop."

"Cold?"

"Why is it going to get cold?"

"They can't make it that cold, can they?"

I can see people following Eric's directions, their brows furrowed in disbelief.

Meanwhile, Eric continues, gesturing to people in the first tier of seats. "People in the bottom row, can you make sure you have nothing sitting on the banister in front of you? If you have handbags, food, or drinks, please move them now. Very shortly, a barrier will be appearing out of there." People hurry to do as Eric asked as more smoke fills the arena and the lights start to dim. Suddenly, just as he said, a clear glass-like barrier rises out of the banister in front of the bottom row. People's eyes are drawn to it, the distraction delaying their notice that the inside of the circus ring is changing as well. It now looks like a frozen tundra with mounds and dips throughout the space. A small section rises out of the middle with Eric perched on it.

"Alright, I think we're just about ready for our next act," he announces, drawing everyone's attention back to the center ring and earning more gasps and exclamations of surprise.

"You've all seen big cat acts in circuses before, but our big cats are just a little different. All the way to us from the planet Iceeen." He gives a huge exaggerated wink, and they titter and chuckle like the good audience they are, playing to his cues. "I'd like you to welcome our Lightning Cats!"

A thunderous roar, followed by some spine-tingling screeching, sounds through the arena, but the oohs and ahhs from the audience drown it out as the next act stalks into the center of the ring. Holy crap, Dylan wasn't wrong when he said they looked like saber-toothed tigers. Larger than any Earth cat I've seen, their fur is varying colors on the blue spectrum, though one is pure white.

"That's Echo," William says, gesturing to the pure white one. "Natalia is the light blue one that's slightly smaller, and Maxsim is the really big one with all the black markings." The magnificent blue ombre cat stalks his way around the arena. Muscles rippling, claws flexing, teeth baring, he is definitely king of the jungle. He growls and roars, playing up to the audience, pacing back and forth in front of the glass screens.

The white one walks close to him and nuzzles his head against him, but Natalia chases him away from Maxsim, swiping a paw with huge claws in his direction and baring her teeth.

There are three more cats involved in the act, wrestling and rolling around on the snow-covered ground, bringing smiles to the children around the arena. Suddenly, Natalia roars loudly. Her tail points straight up, lightning arcs shooting from it and bouncing around the arena before striking the three who are playing. They all jump when it hits them, then rush behind Maxsim, almost like they're using him as some kind of shield.

"I thought you said they were a matriarchal society?" I ask Willam.

He nods his head ruefully. "They are, but between you and me, Natalia is a raving bitch, and although their council was hoping this group would become a streak, I'm pretty sure that's not going to happen. The others all look to Maxsim for protection when she's in a shitty mood because he will and does stand up to her."

John practically giggles on my other side. "And I can guarantee she is still in a shitty mood from when you zapped her in the dining room. She knows how to hold a grudge."

"Great," I grumble, slumping down in my chair. "Do you think I'll survive to actually do a show with them?" John pats me reassuringly on the shoulder while William chuckles.

"Don't drop your guard around them, and you should be fine. Remember, if she comes at you, you can levitate her around the dome if need be once your powers kick in. You may have to once or twice to put her in her place until she understands that you're not a pushover either. It's also forbidden for her to use her lightning against you, so that's a little safety net to keep in mind. Although they can absorb it, it's lethal to just about anyone else." Oh yeah, I had forgotten I'm not a vanilla human anymore. Not that I've ever been very vanilla.

Eric waves his cane, and with a flick of his wrist, it unravels into a whip. Immediately, he cracks it, the sound like a shot across the dome. The big cats' eyes are now all on him. The surrounding terrain has shifted, and he has them jump from space to space, over each other, and then commands them to roll over and play dead, causing the audience to laugh.

"Isn't this a bit demeaning for them?" I ask. "I mean, they're huge animals and prideful when in their humanoid shape. How can you get them to do this without complaint?"

"With great difficulty," mutters John next to me.

William shoots him a scowl before answering, "When they shift, their personality recedes. They become more animal than intelligent being, so it really is like training a wild animal, and we treat them as such. They don't have a problem with it. Without the strong handling, they would tear Eric apart and feast on his entrails." My heart thuds to the bottom of my stomach, and a wave of nausea crosses my body.

"And you want me to train them? What the fuck!!"

CHAPTER THIRTEEN

After more spectacular leaps, thunderous roars, and air-splitting flashes of lightning, the show finishes with the cats jumping through a flaming hoop before leaving the arena with Eric riding on Maksim's back, the others following in a V formation.

The arena of ice slowly starts to disappear in a cloud of mist and smoke, and all eyes are drawn to a spotlighted single figure hanging from the roof. Lanky pale limbs, a stark contrast wrapped around shiny black silk, her long bright pink hair adding a splash of color to the monochromatic sight. The white leotard she wears sparkles in the spotlight, the flash of diamantes and sequins adding some pizzazz to the elegance.

A hauntingly beautiful melody fills the arena like a siren song, captivating the audience as she twirls and twists herself through mesmerizing movements.

"That's Magenta, a Skarrian. I keep meaning to

introduce you to her, but you've been so busy this week," John explains.

William leans closer to my side and adds, "She's definitely a good one to be friends with. She's smart and feisty and will be a loyal friend as long as you don't cross her."

"What happens if I cross her?" I ask curiously.

"She'd probably shank you." Given the seriousness of the statement and my very strong impression that he's *not* joking, I really don't see how William is laughing as he says that. "Her act is modified for our Earth performances. On the other planets, she slowly moves from two silks to one to none."

"No silks? How does that work?" Disbelief must be obvious in both my question and my tone because I can feel the grandpas stiffen.

"You're still thinking like a human," William snaps. "You need to remember we have talents that Earth people only dream of possessing. She can levitate. We put objects up in the air, and she floats through. We even give the audience a chance to play dodgeball with her! If they hit her, they get to take her on a date. No one has yet, but it's always fun to watch them try."

Her act keeps the crowd focused as the rest of the icy landscape disappears. Frequent gasps of amazement fill the arena as she wraps herself then completes death-defying drops supported only by the flowing black silk. At one stage, she binds herself completely, looking like a sexy offering to a bondage god, before unraveling all the way to the floor, stopping inches from the crowd.

The haunting melody comes to a close, and she strikes a final pose as the crowd bursts into applause. With her waving to the crowd and blowing kisses, the silks rise upward and the spotlight shines back down onto the floor.

In rolls a little yellow car with Eric riding on top. He's had a costume change. Same style of outfit, just different colors. The little car jauntily makes its way around the arena with Eric waving and smiling. Suddenly, it comes to an abrupt stop and he flies forward. With great skill, he somersaults in the air and lands on two feet with a flourish. I turn to William to say something, but he rolls his eyes and waves at the action. "Just keep watching."

"Ladies and gentlemen, please welcome to the floor... our clowns!" He runs out of the ring, but the soft mutters of the crowd begin to pile on top of one another when nothing happens. The little car just sits innocuously, its windows blacked out so nothing can be seen inside. The muttering increases in volume, and from the corner of my eye, I catch people wiggling in their seats, children standing up as though just getting a different vantage point will magically give them something to see. I open my mouth again to say something, but before I can, the little car begins to shake. The muttering stops abruptly as the audience's eyes are drawn back to the car. The motion continues, this time more violently, and with a sudden drum roll that comes from nowhere and everywhere all at once, the doors to the car fly open and out of it pour the clowns. There are so many of them, my mouth drops open in surprise. Looking around the arena, I can see I'm not the only one in shock.

First, five dwarf-sized clowns exit. Next, an extremely long leg pokes out one of the doors, followed by the second leg, two extremely long arms, and an equally large torso, and last to emerge is the head. Once this clown stands up, he's close to nine feet tall. He waves to the crowd and moves out of the way. Next, an extremely wide clown eases himself out, followed by three more dwarfs. Just after that, some normal-sized clowns get out. In the end, once they have all exited, there are almost twenty clowns standing around the arena. One of them tries to close the car doors, but another runs over, shaking his hands and gesturing no to the others. He reopens the door, only for two little dogs that look like Jack Russells and then three brightly-colored poodles to jump out.

Finally, the car doors close and it rolls back out of the arena. Stagehands roll a whole heap of props into the center of the arena, and the clowns and the dogs spend the next fifteen minutes entertaining the crowd with a kind of slapstick performance mixed with magic tricks, mostly sawing bodies and parts in half. The children are giggling, and the parents are smiling indulgently at their offspring.

William leans closer again, though I can forgive him invading my space all night since it's usually accompanied with some kind of explanation. "These guys are called Nenghe, from a planet with the same name. Have you ever seen that 80's movie about the girl who goes into a maze and all the wonderful creatures she comes across before meeting the king?" I know the movie he's talking about, so I nod my head. "Do you remember the creatures that could remove their body parts and throw them around?" I grimace because that bit kind of grossed me out. "Well, these guys can do that, and instead of juggling balls and things, when we're off world, they juggle each other. They also have the ability to change shape. All the ones that are tall, short, or wide are actually the same size as the normal-sized ones; they've just changed their shape for the act."

Turning back to the action, I look closely but I can't see any signs. "Mamu, the one who is really wide today," he says, pointing at the performer, "actually gets into the car in his normal size. He wouldn't be able to fit in the car otherwise. As he climbs out of it, he shifts the dimensions of his body with each movement."

Out of the corner of my eye, I can see John holding a hand up to the earpiece he has in. He'd been quiet while William explained things to me, but now I can see him replying to whoever is talking in his ear.

He stands up and holds out his hand as the clowns race off , allowing Eric to re-enter the arena. "Come on, Lila, you'll have to catch the rest of the show at the next stop. We've got some pre-flight checks that need to be done before we are ready to leave this evening, and we want to get a start on showing you those."

Taking his hand, I allow him to pull me up, and the three of us leave before the next act can begin. We make our way to the control deck of the ship where we are greeted by Captain Lester. He and Captain Potter, who is back on the command ship, take turns with each vehicle. Both are Skarrians who have been with the circus for a long time.

"Good, just in time." His voice is rough, like he smokes a pack of cigarettes a day. "We need someone to put out the hologram emitters, and I thought that Lila should learn to do it as well."

"Hologram emitters?" I ask. "Nobody has mentioned them over the last few days."

"Yes, it's how we trick the humans into believing that the tent takes a day or two to dismantle. We place them on the ground, and they show a pre-recorded simulation of a large group of people packing up the circus into trucks. Meanwhile, the ship has actually returned to the main one and we're halfway across the world, hovering over our next destination."

"That's awesome, but what happens if someone sees what's really happening?"

"They don't. The emitters have their own cloaking abilities, and when the program finishes running, they are pre-scheduled to be beamed back to the ship."

My mind has been a nonstop tornado for the last week while I try to assimilate all this new information and technology. Is it any wonder I've been crashing every night, asleep before my head even hits the pillow?

"Ok, cool. If you show me where they are and how to use them, I'll get started on that. How hard can it be?"

"I can't spare any of the crew at the moment.

They're all busy with the show," the captain says gruffly. I kind of get the feeling he doesn't like me all that much, but John has insisted that's just his way.

"That's okay. I've arranged for someone to show Lila what to do," John assures us all.

"Who?" demands the captain. "There is no one else."

"Captain Lester, I'm quite disappointed to find out that I'm so easily forgettable." The melodically accented voice has us all spinning around. Standing at the entrance to the control deck is some kind of humanoid shape that's shrouded in darkness. Like a shadow, you can't quite make out who it is. The captain blanches at the sight of the newcomer.

"Prince Xavier, I assure you, you are anything but forgettable." The shadow steps forward, practically pulsing with power. Being near him is like standing next to a power grid, and it makes my jaw hurt from clenching. Holy shit, this is the warlock. My gaze darts to William and John who look completely unaffected by this man … creature... alien? I really have to figure out the polite thing to call someone. This is starting to get ridiculous.

"Xavier, thank you for doing this." The shadow shrugs what I think are his shoulders.

"Anything for you guys, you know that." William and John exchange a look, but they both nod.

"This is Lila, our granddaughter. She needs to learn how to put up the holo-emitters. Lila, this is Prince Xavier Colest, heir to the warlock throne and our man in charge of anything mystical."

William gestures to the blur, and I wave. Yeah, it's super awkward, but what else am I supposed to do? It's kind of hard to greet someone when there's no hand to shake or eyes to meet. Considering I really only have a vague idea how tall this dude is, I could be making eye contact with his nipples right now for all I know. In fact, I'm not sure how he's even going to show me how to operate the holo-emitters either.

The captain holds out four palm-sized devices, and the blur reaches out and picks them up. Well, okay then, I guess he's solid, not a mist or shadow, though maybe that's some kind of illusion. My eyes scan his form, looking for some hint of solid shape or mass, and it's not until I get to his head that I see a flash of something. Deep within the mist, a light shines, and the closer I try to look, the brighter it becomes. It's a pale, pale green, and I feel myself sinking deeper into its magnetism, my mind growing light and my body becoming insignificant. I want to touch the light, to be one with it, to let it *consume* me. It's calling me; I can feel how much it wants me, needs me. Suddenly, the feeling starts to change, and that warmth becomes desire. Our energies touch, making my nipples pebble and my breath become harsher, almost a pant. Oh my god, I'm going to orgasm in front of everyone. What the hell is going on? I grit my teeth so I won't moan, but then it suddenly feels like it's starting to drain from me. With nothing to tip me over the edge, the orgasm I thought was coming is just out of reach. That desire and teasing pleasure is slowly draining down and out through my limbs, moving toward the shadow.

"Goddamn it, Xavier!" William's shout knocks me back into reality, and I stumble as the trance leaves me. "What the fuck were you doing to Lila?"

"Shit, I'm sorry." The melodic voice sounds shaken and disgruntled, but there's no doubting the sincerity in the rushed apology. "I'm not sure what happened. It's like she locked on to me and dragged me under."

"Me? Uh, nope. That was all you. I'm human, remember? No freaking crazy mind powers here."

"*Not* human," William grumbles. "And that better not have been you doing what I think you were."

"Defective Skarrian then," I offer in an attempt to lighten the frigid tension in the room.

"Did you seriously not do that?" John asks Xavier, a curious lilt to his voice.

I watch as the blur shudders violently. "No, I'm not sure exactly what happened. It's like our consciousnesses merged until we became one. I've never heard of something like that happening to a warlock. We are taught how to do that from a very young age, so our minds are like steel cages. I'm going to have to consult with my parents about it."

I wish I could see his face and get a read on him, see if the surprise in his voice is mirrored by the rest of him. That's if he has a face... maybe this is his permanent state? Damn it, I wish I could ask about it, but that would just be fucking rude. Even I know that. *You can't just ask people if they have faces, Lila.* Those kinds of questions probably end with dueling at sunset or something else to make amends. I'll have to ask one of the grandpas next time I get a chance.

"Alright, come on, we need to get on with it. It's almost intermission, and people will be going out to smoke. We don't want them seeing the two of you out there setting up," Captain Lester grumbles.

I start to head toward the exit, hoping that Xavier will follow me, but John puts his hand out to stop me. "No time for that now. Xavier will have to teleport you down there; it will be quicker."

A nervous squeak escapes my mouth, but I slap my hand over it, hoping no one heard. But from the amused smiles on the men's faces, I'm almost certain they did.

"Teleport? Can he really do that? Is he allowed to take people?" I'm pretty sure Dylan told me all about warlocks that second day, but I've learned so much in such a short period of time, things were bound to be forgotten.

The blur rumbles, giving a sound of amusement. "Am I *allowed*? You are funny, young Lila. Nobody tells me what I can and can't do. Teleporting is child's play for a warlock. We have to put bands on our children to stop them from using these powers when they are small. Teleporting babies is stressful for parents."

Well, okay then. "Excuse me, Obi Wan Kenobi?" The sarcasm is strong with me. "I hadn't got to that part of my warlock knowledge yet." How old is this dude? His voice sounds young, but he called me 'young Lila' like I was a freaking kid.

"So how do we do this?" I ask, the butterflies in my stomach now a full-on kaleidoscope. Yeah, that's a group of butterflies. I'm good for more than just impressively weird dildos and erotica recommendations... though my erotica recs are on point, I have to say.

The blur moves toward me. It kind of looks like he's floating, but it also looks like he's taking steps on smoky legs. It's a little freaky that he's a perfect blend of shadow with just the barest hint of solid substance. As he comes nearer, the temperature around my body drops and goosebumps break out across my skin. He's close enough for the two of us to be standing chest to chest, if he had one anyway. The misty fog surrounding him starts to expand, and the squeak that escapes my mouth this time is more like a roar. I'm too distracted by the mist moving closer to worry about our audience's laughter this time. The shadow starts to engulf me, but instead of the frozen prickle I'd expected, it's a cool, sensuous slide across my skin. It's like it's reaching out and embracing me. Finally, it reaches my head and covers my face until I'm fully surrounded by the same shadow. I expected to feel claustrophobic, but it feels good, like I'm safe in a cocoon, cherished and comfortable. It's like being wrapped in a hug.

"Ready?" The grumbly voice is close now, just by my ear, and I have the phantom feeling of two arms wrapped around me. Swallowing nervously, I nod.

I can't explain the sensation of teleportation because not much really happens, but I guess it's kind of like a roller coaster ride. That feeling where your stomach starts in your throat and plummets very fast until it sits right in the bottom of your belly. It's happening before you know it, and it's over just as quickly.

"Are you all right?" Xavier's voice tickles my ear, and that roller coaster feeling prickles into another kind.

"Yup, I'm good." The words are breathy, but I can't move away from him... it... whatever. I'm still surrounded by the mist.

Slowly, that comforting hug starts to recede, the feeling of being wrapped in arms disappears, and the mist drains away from my body. First, my head, and when I can look around, I discover we're outside the dome, the giant black spaceship looming above us and making me feel incredibly insignificant.

When the mist recedes, I discover that England's weather is at its finest, and the magical shadow that just surrounded me was pleasant compared to the natural mist of the countryside. A cold wet fog surrounds the dome, giving it an eerie mystical feel. I know that the humans can't actually see it, which is a good thing because it would definitely start a panic.

A clearing throat makes me startle, and I realize that Xavier's stuff—cue the mental sniggering that I just manage to keep inside my head—has left my body.

"Are you okay?" he asks, sounding concerned, which is sweet of him.

"Yup, I'm all good." I'm excellent at putting up a front, good at deflecting too.

"So do you want to show me what to do?" Not that I'm sure I'm going to be able to see it. The things disappeared into his hand when the captain gave them to him.

"Yes, this might be easier if you could see what I was doing though, right?" He sounds amused this time, but it's a little too coincidental for me.

"Can you read my mind?" I demand, a little (read a lot) upset, crossing my arms in a defensive position.

"No, Phoeall, you have a very expressive face." And with those words, something begins to happen. The mist sort of absorbs inward, flowing backward to expose long limbs covered in clothing unlike anything I've ever seen before. A moment later, standing before me is a somewhat normal, albeit fucking hot, male indivdual.

CHAPTER FOURTEEN

Standing before me is an alien lover's wet dream. The man is all long, lean lines, and you can see muscle definition under the black skintight... armor, I guess, because it certainly doesn't look like any jumpsuit I've seen. The black material shimmers like lycra but has the solid look of leather. The skin on his hands is a lavender color, with swirls of silver decorating his neck. The swirl stops at his chin, though there's a more complex marking under his right eye. It's a set of swirls, lines, and dots. He also has what looks like kohl around his eyes, but I'm not sure if it's makeup or natural.

His cheekbones are sharper than an average human, and his ears have a noticeable sharpness to them as well, the end result looking elf-like. The pointed arches of his ears are pierced with many silver and turquoise rings, as are his nose and eyebrow. Indigo-colored hair is tied back in a high ponytail, and those eyes which appeared to be green through the mist are actually a purplish blue. Holy shit, no wonder he blurs himself. This man would have to fight off suitors constantly.

I'm sure I've been gaping at the man/alien in front of me for far too long because he cocks one eyebrow and folds his arms, classic 'yeah, take a picture' posture. *Whoops, shit. Lila, get it together. Let's not insult the man.*

"Sorry, I'm just surprised to see a solid form. I thought you were all mystical mist or something."

An amused snort escapes his mouth before he can contain it. "It's a defense mechanism. If a warlock's eyes can't be seen, their mind can't be invaded, which really hasn't been a problem for years. But once upon a time, our planet was rife with turmoil and intrigue, and you never knew who you could trust. You would only expose your real form to those whom you knew for sure wouldn't betray you. I'm afraid I still default to that time, particularly when meeting new people."

Curiosity getting the better of me yet again, I just blurt out my first reaction. Because that's served me *sooooo* well this far in life. "Does this mean you trust me?"

"No, Phoeall, but what could you do to me? I hear that your powers haven't been activated. You are no match for me and mine, and I need to show you what to do."

"Who told you that? No one knows except for my grandpas. And what is that word you keep calling me? Fo-ell? Why doesn't my translator translate it?" It's my turn to cross my arms, though I know it won't do a damn thing to protect me from him. Growing up in the system has done nothing to improve my self-esteem, and while I can keep going even when the odds are stacked against me, I've developed a real sensitivity to feeling embarrassed or vulnerable in front of other people. Lucky me, he's just hit on both of those nerves at the same time.

He shrugs casually like it's no big deal. "William might have mentioned something. Asked me if I could get a read on you to see if I can work out why your powers haven't manifested. But we don't have time for that now."

I also notice that he didn't bother telling me what the word means. For all I know, he's calling me an idiot and having his own internal laugh about it. *Damn arrogant alien.* That pisses me off, and I grit my teeth in anger. But for my grandpa's sake I let it go for now.

He holds out one of the holo-emitters, clearing his throat when I don't immediately glance down at it. "These need to be placed in four equal positions around the dome. They are pre-programed, so when you reach the right spot, this red light will turn blue." He points out the red light in the middle of the emitter then starts walking. Within a few steps, the light changes and the device starts humming at a low frequency. "Once it's on the ground in a stable position, press down on the top. It will go into standby mode, and once all four are in place and you press the last one down, they will all activate simultaneously. It's easy, really."

Knowing how curious and nosy humans are, I definitely have one concern to chew my lip over. "What happens if they're seen by someone and picked up?"

"The minute you push the button down, it will cloak, and the frequency it emits has a repellent in it. Humans will feel uncomfortable and move away."

"And Captain Lester said it returns to the ship automatically after a certain period of time?"

"Yes, the hologram is programmed to show a circus tent being dismantled, packed up, and loaded into big black trucks. Your primitive Earth minds wouldn't be able to cope if they saw an alien ship lifting off the ground and taking off into the sky. Once they've run the entirety of their programming, they send a signal to the ship. It will beam them aboard, no matter where we are surrounding the Earth." *Hey, buddy, who the fuck are you calling primitive?* I guess to him we probably do seem primitive, but he doesn't have to be so rude about it. Knowing the future leader of the circus can't just bite people's heads off, I push down my offense for my fellow man and focus on the important things.

"Wow, that technology is light-years ahead of anything the human race has. Honestly, I'm a little shocked that the powers that be—you know, the government or whoever—haven't tried to weasel more information out of you… or taken it by force." Let's face it, humans are better known for trying to take what they want rather than having the patience to develop it themselves.

"They are not completely stupid. They know that the big ship sits in the upper atmosphere, fully equipped for battle when necessary. It was made extremely clear to the human governments from the very first landing that they would get more than they bargained for if they tried to take anything by force. The Adams made sure they knew they'd live long enough to regret a foolish decision like that."

He holds out his hand with the emitters, shaking them just enough so that I know he wants me to take them. "Let's do this. People will be exiting the dome soon, and we don't want to be caught." I take it from his hand and follow the instructions he gave me. After placing it on the ground and pushing down on the top, it makes a clicking sound and fades from view.

"Perfect, it's all set now." There's a prickly feeling running down the back of my spine, causing me to step back and rub my arms, like that almost primitive fight or flight response. But this one is leaning heavily on flight. Xavier watches me with curiosity in his eyes as I start to back away.

"Well, that's very interesting. It shouldn't be affecting you if your Skarrian heritage has come to the forefront, though you're the first Skarrian I've heard of who has grown up without constant direct contact with the waters of Skar. Even those that migrate to other planets have bottles of it shipped to them for daily consumption. This latent development of your Skarrian aspects has to be connected to the lack of water in your system." He's eyeing me like I'm a science experiment, one he would really like to take apart and put back together, which makes me back away quicker.

"Whoa, it's okay. I'm not going to hurt you." He

holds his hands up in that universal way of trying to make someone feel better, but who knows what can come out of his hands!

"Can we just finish this?" The human repellant is working overtime on me, and I already want to run screaming from the area.

Xavier nods before his body explodes into mist, and it's just one sudden move too many while I'm feeling so anxious. Basically, I very smoothly and maturely scream and turn, running like the hounds of hell are on my tail.

"Lila, wait!" At least he makes the effort, but I don't stop. I want to get out of here. It's working just fine until misty Xavier appears in front of me, causing me to skid to a stop. I mean, it would be kind of rude to run *through* the guy. I don't know what that feels like for him. Maybe it's like the warlock equivalent of someone grabbing your dick without permission if someone wanders through you when your body is all one with the fog. That definitely wasn't covered by the info on the tablet.

My ragged breathing is loud in the quiet that surrounds us. "We don't have time to walk the whole distance, so I'm going to jump us to each position." I think he's trying to sound reassuring, but without the visual cues, it's hard to tell. "But from the way you're reacting to the repellent, I think I'll keep a hand on you. That way I won't have to waste time chasing you down after you activate one."

I'm breathing too hard to respond, so I just nod my head. Almost immediately, his mist reaches out, enveloping me again, and we repeat the process until all four holo-emitters have been put in the right place. Neither of us says much more to the other, and that's fine with me.

Finally finished, Xavier jumps us back inside the dome, our bodies teleporting into the corridor just outside the control room.

"There you go. How do you feel now?" he asks as the mist recedes from my body, and with it my breathing calms. With my eyes having adjusted to the darkness outside the dome and the shadow of Xavier's mist, the lights of the corridors are causing me to squint against the brightness.

A big sigh of relief escapes my mouth. "Better, thank you." His misty arm reaches up and tucks a strand of hair behind my ear. The sweet gesture is surprising from someone who routinely feels like they have to be on guard.

"I don't think I've ever seen a human run so fast." I think he means it as a joke, but my stomach sinks at his reminder that I'm human. Before I can respond, I hear someone call my name sharply.

Turning, I find Dylan in half-form, staring at us, with a thin trail of smoke coming from each flared nostril. "What are you doing?"

Smiling at my friend, I wave him over. "Hey, Dylan. Xavier here was just showing me how to set up the holo-emitters outside." He walks over, the frown on his face and quick steps telegraphing some kind of discomfort.

"Hey, Dylan," Xavier adds, and it sounds friendly,

but Dylan just returns his greeting with a short nod. Shit, I hope he's not jealous. Maybe Xavier is the guy he's got a thing with. I step back, putting some room between me and the shadow-shrouded warlock.

"Xavier showed you how to do that?" He sounds skeptical, and his brow ridges rise in surprise.

"Yes, Lila's grandpas entrusted me with the pleasure of showing her how to do it." If I didn't know better, I would say Xavier sounds slightly smug about it. There was almost a little emphasis on the word 'me' like he was trying to make a point. What point, I have no idea.

"Apparently everyone else was busy with the show. Isn't that where you're supposed to be?" I ask him, curious at why he's questioning things.

Dylan shakes his head. "No, I'm done for the night."

"Tut, tut, tut, Dylan, skipping out on the final parade through the arena. How rebellious," Xavier mocks with a slight edge to it. Hmm, maybe they're not as friendly as I first thought.

"I won't be missed for one night," he argues. "And I was worried when I noticed Lila had disappeared from the audience." Well, considering he hasn't been to visit me for a few days, I'm surprised at his reaction. "I was worried because all the animals are still in the dome for the final parade. I didn't want her to wander into the wrong area, especially because I think this is the first time I've seen her out and about during the show."

"Like her grandfathers are going to let her wander

off without them," Xavier argues back. "And why is it your business? Who went and made you her guardian?"

"Well, thanks for your help, but I've got her for now," he assures Xavier, ignoring his questions, almost brushing him off like he's unimportant. Once again, I watch as his misty outline shrugs, not rising to the edge of hostility that Dylan's pushing at him.

"Okay. It's been a pleasure, Lila. I'm sure I'll see you again soon." And with those parting words, Xavier disappears.

A hissing sound escapes Dylan's mouth followed by a little puff of flame which has me yelping and scooting backward. "What were you doing so close to him? Do you know what he is?" Holy shit, what the fuck? His voice has devolved, transforming his words into what could only be considered a growl, and his tight grip on my arm is definitely not what I would have expected from him.

I snatch my arm out of his grasp. "Dude, chill. You heard what he said; my grandpas asked him to help me. And yes, I know what he is. What is your damn problem?"

Another growl escapes his mouth, and I watch as his teeth lengthen and sharpen before he shakes his head and they shrink back to normal. "He's a warlock and not just any warlock. He's the crown prince."

"Yeah, and?"

"Warlocks are psychic feeders. They feed off of strong emotion. It's how they power themselves up. Warlocks as strong as Xavier have harems of feeders who they siphon emotions off of, usually through sex. I was worried he was doing that to you." *So he's a magical emotion-eating vampire? Also something to probably keep in my head. They should just let me define what all these species are. It'd be so much less complicated. Maybe that's why William was upset when he thought Xavier was doing something to me. Okay, Lila, stop talking to yourself and listen to what he's saying.*

"Feeders can become addicted to the feel of it. It can feel fucking amazing, but they can also inspire terror in their feeders too. Different emotions taste differently, and you don't know what his favorite *flavor* is." He's looking away by the time he explains that part, not meeting my eyes. Right, so it *was* jealousy. He's obviously fed Xavier in the past and didn't want me replacing him.

I wonder if Xavier has a harem? He must if he's as powerful as they say he is. Does he keep them on board the ship here or back up at the mothership? So many questions I want to ask, but I'm thinking Dylan might not be the best person for that right now. Maybe I'll ask Eric later. He seems like he would be pretty cool with any questions I have.

"Well, okay. No, I'm pretty sure that's not what was happening. He didn't show any interest in me other than curiosity in the fact that I seem to be more human than Skarrian."

"Make sure you stay away from him. You don't need to form any more ridiculous attachments," he snaps at me before turning to walk away.

"Excuse me, what the fuck do you mean by *that*?" It's my turn to grab him and demand an answer, though I don't have the intimidating eyebrows or smoke to go with how grumpy I'm now feeling.

"Your attraction to Caspian, of course. I saw a mark on his shoulder during the act, and when I grilled him about it after the show, he admitted it appeared after he had tried to scare you off. Why him? Lila, that is going to end in nothing but heartbreak. Caspian would never be interested in someone like you. He couldn't be." *And that's my last nerve for the night.*

Hurt like nothing I've ever felt slams into my chest, and I flinch involuntarily. Shit, I thought this guy was my friend. A tear escapes despite me not wanting to expose myself right now. "Fuck you, Dylan."

Dylan's features soften, and he grabs hold of me again, pulling me closer and wiping away the hot trail from my cheek. "Lila, he's an alien with very specific breeding needs. Yes, he has a human form, and yes, you can have sex with him in that form, but if he wants kids, he needs someone who can take the eggs he lays. I know that you've been trying so hard to be open-minded about everything, but you were raised human. There are some things that might just push you over the edge. Are you really saying you're willing to accept his ovipositor?"

Oh... well, wow! That escalated quickly. "His what?' I ask tentatively, but I'm pretty sure I know what it is. I've watched hentai.

"The ovipositor is another tentacle-like appendage that comes into play during breeding time. It's a thick tube which enters the woman and then forces eggs into her womb to be incubated until they're ready to be born."

Huh, I wonder if they're baby krakens or born in humanoid form. But I don't think Dylan would be receptive to that question either. Another for Eric then. Hah, can't wait to ask him that one.

"I mean, I hadn't been planning to start a family with him the minute we had sex. Eric told me Skarrians had five chances before any kind of bond would be sealed. I'm sure all of those things would have come up in conversation eventually."

Dylan's mouth drops open in surprise. "You're not freaked out? Most women avoid him because they know what he needs, and nobody is willing to risk accidentally sealing the bond." I guess even alien women can be super shallow even though they have their own weird "extras." Maybe that's why Caspian comes off as such a dick. I'd probably be pretty cranky too if I thought every woman I talked to was just biding her time until she rejected me.

"It's not like you can accidentally seal it. What, were they worried they were going to slip and fall on his alien dick the last time?"

Dylan sighs, relaxing a little bit now that I'm not freaking out and in need of some kind of therapy. "No, but his breed of alien has a rut. When they find a mate they're compatible with, sometimes something takes over and they are unable to control the frenzy. Even though the bond takes five times for Skarrians, it can be overridden with strong enough feelings. Really, his rut can override any species' breeding 'rules,' which makes a lot of women see him as a risky option. It's like fate steps in, making a decision when it decides it knows best. But you don't have to worry. Caspian's mark would have to show up on you too, or you wouldn't be able to even trigger his beast's rut." He chuckles like it's hard to believe it would.

Damn, another hit to my self-esteem. Before I can say anything, the control room opens and William pops his head out. "Oh good! Lila, I was just coming to look for you. The ship scan said you weren't outside anymore. I'm going to run through the shutdown procedure with you." He catches sight of Dylan, his head tilting as his brow rises.

"What are you doing here? Get back to the final parade." He shoos him away, and before I turn to enter the control room, I stop and lift my shirt up around my neck. William's eyes bulge out of his head, and I snort.

"Just because you're not attracted to me, Dylan, doesn't mean other people aren't." Glancing at the reflective wall behind me, I can see Caspian and Link's marks, and next to it is the new one I'd felt form earlier when Xavier's mist enveloped me the first time. I was so distracted by the coldness of the mist that I hadn't recognized the burning for what it was. He must have liked what he'd seen and felt.

Dylan's face just about matches William's when he catches sight of the three marks. Quickly dropping my shirt, I escape into the control room before he can say anything else. I guess I misjudged him. Not the kind of friend I thought he'd be. Oh well, I'll have to call Susie and tell her about the three hot guys who are interested in me. Leaving out all the alien deets, of course. Imagine telling her about Caspian and his ovipositor... She'd absolutely lose her shit. Susie isn't the most vanilla person on the planet, but there's a big difference between how adventurous the two of us are.

Me, I've got to admit I'm super fucking curious. I've watched anime tentacle porn before, and it definitely lit some kind of fire in me. Freaked out is the exact opposite of how I feel right now; honestly, Caspian's personality is much more of a deterrent than his egg-laying tentacle.

Wonder how krakens feel about ball gags?

# CHAPTER FIFTEEN

William and John take me down to the area behind the arena where they hold the animals while waiting for the final parade. It's apparently also where they store those creepy animatronics that they keep on hand to stave off any rabid PETA investigators. As we exit the elevator, a deafening roar thunders around the space, shaking some nearby equipment. I feel the sound deep in my stomach, and that primal part of me that knows I'm prey to whatever that was shivers in its shoes.

"Holy fuck! What was that?" But I don't need John and William to answer me because once we step out of the elevator the answer becomes very clear. A giant cage in front of me contains something out of a movie. Something that I never thought I would come face to face with, not even in my wildest dreams. A real life flesh and blood Tyrannosaurus Rex. Exactly like something out of *Jurassic Park* except for the color. Unlike the movie, this T-Rex is blood red, with black dorsal stripes. It looks like a preschooler was being rebellious during coloring time.

John and William step up to the cage, gesturing for me to follow. I warily eye the thickness of the cage bars as I follow them, albeit much slower, and my mind is even more blown when we get to the cage. The T-Rex turns, spying us, but instead of lunging with an aggressive show of teeth, he starts to thump his tail up and down and make little snuffling sounds as his big ass fucking head comes down to our level.

"Hey, Viggy, have you been a good boy today?" My eyes practically bug out of my head when John reaches in and strokes the giant beast's head, cooing at him like a baby.

"Of course he has been. We trained him perfectly." The haughty voice comes from behind the dinosaur right before Fiona steps up next to him, one hand on his leg and what looks like a cattle prod in her other hand. "And how many times do I have to tell you not to call him that ridiculous nickname? His name is Vigolash."

When she says that name, it's almost like Viggy flinches away from her, the ferocious beast shrinking in on itself. "Oh, does that mean something?" I ask her, trying to draw her attention away from the animal.

"Yes, it means 'obedient one' in old Aaz'axian." My interest picks up at that familiar word, and Viggy takes Fiona's distraction as a chance to move away from us all. He lumbers away, no more interested in us than any other kind of domestic animal now that our attention is elsewhere.

"Weren't the Aaz'axians hellbent on galaxy domination?" Fiona's gaze turns shrewd, her disgruntled eyes boring into me.

"Yes, they were a great warrior race, and they were misunderstood." William snorts behind me, and I catch John nudging him out of the corner of my eye. "How do you know about them?" she questions.

"Oh, well..." Shit! They told me about them when I got the lecture on the orb, but I probably shouldn't share that bit of information. "My tablet had information on so many different races, and I found it fascinating! I've learned so much over the last few days; it's why I've been so busy."

She seems to accept my answer, but I don't want her to ask any more questions, so I bound away from the cage to another nearby structure.

This one, unlike the giant tank that I saw that day with Dylan, is more of a portable one on wheels. It's probably the size of a caravan, and through glass side walls I can see movement in the water but can't make out what it is. Stepping up, I press my hands and my head against the glass, trying to get a better look at what's moving inside. Suddenly, before me is a dolphin. I startle slightly, stumbling backward, and John chuckles, catching me then pushing me back toward the glass.

Once I get my bearings, I study the creature before me. It's almost exactly like Earth's bottlenose dolphin, but I can see that unlike ours who have smooth skin, this one is scaled like a fish. Big dollar-sized scales that shimmer, the lights playing off their beautiful green and gold pastel tones.

I put my hand back up to the glass, and it presses its nose against the clear surface, rubbing its head back and forth so its nose makes a squeaky sound. A smile crosses my mouth as a chuckle escapes. Along with the simple happiness of this moment comes a hint of surprise. This is one of the first times I've just had an easy laugh since I got here. There are no strings attached, just a lighthearted moment with an alien dolphin. *And we're back to the weird again.*

"That's Nikos," John tells me as the dolphin starts flipping in circles before waving its flipper at me. I wave back, and it suddenly shoots upward. With an impressive burst of speed, he breaches the surface of the water, does a perfect flip, then crashes back down with a giant splash that sends water over the edge to soak John and me.

John shouts with dismay, but I just keep giggling. The water isn't freezing cold like I had expected; it's almost bordering on warm. While I'm shaking off the water, I notice more movement, and my head goes back to the tank in the hope of seeing the dolphin again, but this one is more humanoid. She's the very picture of a mermaid, except unlike human fairytales she doesn't have seashells over her breasts, only scales that match the pretty pastel blue and gold of her tail.

As my eyes rise to her face, I notice the gills in her neck pulsing in and out as she breathes in the seawater. When I get to her face, her lips are pretty pink and her eyes and hair match the gold of her tail. She's studying me just like I'm studying her. There's no annoyance or malice, just curiosity, so I lift a hand and wave, giving her a smile.

"Hi," I mouth, and her lips turn up into a smile before she opens them to reveal sharp shark-like teeth. Thankfully, she throws her head back with laughter when I flinch, bubbles exploding from her gills, and when she turns back to me, she's grinning and the sharp teeth are nowhere to be seen. She was messing with me.

She manages a wink at me before a rumbling sound signals the movement of the vehicle carrying the tank. She waves goodbye, and with a sad smile, I wave back.

"Well, I think it's safe to say that Nixie likes you." William has joined us, his eyes on the tank rumbling away to join the parade.

"That wasn't the same person as the dolphin?" I ask, remembering that they had said its name was Nikos.

"No, that was his sister." Before they can say anything else, the floor starts to shake. Whirling on the spot, I turn and find Viggy directly behind me, Fiona on his back. He's wearing a saddle and has a weird harness around his forearms. It looks so uncomfortable. Another dinosaur comes lunging forward a moment later. This one I recognize as a velociraptor despite its orange and yellow markings. Phillip is riding on its back but looks like he's struggling to keep it contained.

"I thought Htaed hadn't been cleared for a parade yet?" John sounds and looks worried as he slowly moves us back and away from the practically vibrating dinosaur.

"He's fine," Phillip scoffs, and before either of the grandpas can say any more, they barge past us and join the tail end of the parade. Everything else already entered the dome. Wow, that was brave to defy the guys in charge. I'm kind of stunned, really. Everyone else seems to respect them so much. You'd think that if Fiona and Phillip were hoping to eventually lead the circus, they wouldn't blow off the grandpas. At this rate, they'll never be the heirs even if I stay a boring human.

William brings his watch communicator up to his mouth. "Xavier, I need you in the arena to watch the dinosaurs. Those foolish children decided that Htaed was ready for the parade. Ready the tranqs. Lester, ready the beam to send him back to his enclosure on the big ship if needed."

I hear both men respond with affirmatives as the loading dock doors close behind them.

"Okay, Xavier and Lester are on top of that. Let's make our final checks of everything, and once the parade is finished, it will all be beamed back to the ship and we'll be good for relocation." William leads me further into the loading dock and the storage area, him and John pointing out everything that needs to be completed before we can leave the Earth's atmosphere. Even though the ship is powerful, Earth's gravity takes its toll on the thrusters, causing things to shudder and shake while we clear the atmosphere, so everything needs to be secured properly.

"This really won't be your job, but I want you to know the procedure. If anything ever goes wrong, they will eventually come to you, and you can't be floundering." William leads us back through the corridors to the main lobby as he talks. Once we get there, I can hear the cheers and applause of the crowd again, then the arena doors open, allowing people to flood out. Movement out of the corner of my eye shows two security guards standing at the elevator, not allowing anyone to enter even though a few enterprising people try.

"Everyone is encouraged to leave the premises, though the merchandise stand will be busy for the next hour or so. We will have you man that one too, so you get a feel for what we sell on Earth, which is different to the merch in the rest of the galaxy."

"What happens next?" I ask, watching the chaos of excited families making their way home with tired but happy children.

"Well, because it was the final show for this stop, there'll be a party tonight, but that won't happen until we dock back with the ship. Everyone has the next hour to shower and wind down from the show before we have to prepare for immediate departure."

Excitement flows through my body at the thought of what's to come. Fuck me, I'm going to space! "Is there anything specific we need to do for that?" I ask as we move through the crowd toward the merch stand. It's surrounded by people, their happiness and energy so palpable it gives me second-hand shivers of excitement.

"Yes, it's roughly four hours to make it back to the other ship. We need to pass a few of Earth's sensors and our cloaking technology on the arena can only handle slower speeds, so we can't go any faster."

I'm trying my best to focus on what he's saying, but there's a little commotion at the merch stand that's grabbing my attention. A young couple is arguing over the merchandise. The woman wants a poster with Caspian and Dylan on it, but the guy she's with is refusing to buy it for her. Poor girl looks like she's just about in tears. Before I can step in, John pushes past me to the booth, grabs a poster, rolls it up, and puts a band around it before returning to us. While he's in the process of doing that, the jackass boyfriend storms off, leaving the girl looking around like she has no clue what to do now.

My marshmallow grandpa walks up to the girl and hands her the poster, whispering in her ear when she continues to sob. Before I know it, he's escorting her outside. "It's not quite our responsibility to make sure the humans all get along, but it does benefit us to limit the drama that happens on the circus grounds," William explains. "John's likely calling the girl a taxi so she can get home safely. No one in the crew would ever take advantage of her, but it's good to care for others if you have the means to do so."

My white knight grandpa rejoins us, and as we walk back toward the elevators and the two men guarding it, William continues to tell me about the trip.

"It's too short a journey for lightspeed, not to mention the arena isn't lightspeed capable on its own. You need to be strapped in for the first part of the journey, and it takes roughly ten minutes to leave the Earth's atmosphere. Most people choose to nap for the journey since the bed converts into a secure capsule which you can be strapped into for safety purposes. There's no real point being up and about. We don't serve a meal, and apart from the control deck, there are no windows. Best that you wait until we dock with the main ship."

"Once we get there, I can show you to your permanent quarters and all the other cool things on board. Because the ship travels most of the time, it's virtually a little city." John butts in as the guards step away to allow us entrance.

"We will have a few days of rest and relaxation, then we will take the arena to the US and do the show all over again. After that, we hit Asia and Australia, and then this rotation on Earth will be done." William presses the button for the employee floor, and the elevator moves smoothly upward. "Oh, and when we are in the US, we also take on anyone who wants or has been asked to leave Earth. We have holding cells on both this pod and the main ship so that visitors can travel with us without being a potential threat to any of our regulars."

My mind spins with all the information. Just when I thought I had a handle on it all, it seems I haven't.

"Come on, Lila. Let's take tea in our quarters. Eric will be cleaning up after the show, and we usually do a debrief before take-off." The guys lead the way off the elevator, past my room, and all the way down the corridor to a set of double doors.

John opens them with a flourish and marches in, with William gesturing for me to go first. As I enter their private space, a whistle escapes my mouth.

"It is good to be the kings."

"Well, there are three of us," William grumbles from behind me as I take in the huge luxuriously appointed space.

"And there used to be four," John adds in quietly.

I take a seat on one of the plush sofas and decide to address the elephant in the room.

"What happened to Grandma? I don't think anybody has said," I ask gently, and they both join me on the large sectional sofa, each giving the other space.

William rubs a hand across his suddenly tired face. "We're not sure. She disappeared, and her body never surfaced. We're not even sure *where* she disappeared. We were performing on Earth, but she hadn't made the journey from the bigger ship with us. Said she had some things to do. She'd been very secretive, and her sister was also coming to visit from Skar on a transport. They'd been estranged for a while, but with the birth of their grandchildren, they'd decided to try and mend fences. When her sister arrived, your grandmother was nowhere to be found. We used every single resource at our fingertips to try to find her, and believe me, they are extensive, but it was like she vanished into thin air." William breaks off, the toll of telling me about it showing on his face.

"Then your parents were killed, and we decided it would probably be best for you to be hidden and not come to live with us for your own safety," John adds, and I feel so much sympathy for these men. We haven't known each other very long, but they are worming their way into my heart. I reach over and squeeze John's hand before doing the same for William.

"Thank you for telling me that. I know how hard it must have been for you both."

An internal door opens before anyone can say anything else, and Eric steps out in sweats, rubbing a towel through his wet hair.

"There you all are. I wondered where you had disappeared to during the Nenghe." He throws the towel over one of the chairs surrounding the huge dining table then joins us on the couch. He squeezes in between me and John even though there's plenty of room further down. Our bodies bang together, but he just chuckles and throws an arm around me.

"So, our little princess, what did you think of the show, especially your most amazing grandpa?" With his words, the tension in the room relaxes. I'm not sure if he'd been listening, but he's successful in lifting the mood.

"I'd have to say the overacting ringmaster was a bit much, but the rest of it was spectacular," I reply tongue in cheek.

He squeezes my shoulder and growls, "Cheeky." Once I burst into a set of giggles that I hadn't anticipated, he removes his arm and gets up, stretching. "God, I'm looking forward to a week off. This week seemed to be more work than normal," he complains before heading to a hutch in the wall and typing something in.

"You want a beer?" he asks the rest of us, and both William and John say yes.

"Can I have one of those pink things? Rilaxious, I think they were called." With how good they tasted, I'm going to grab one whenever I can. He brings us over our requested drinks and takes a seat again, this time not practically on my lap.

"Is it always a week off in between each place you play?" I ask, curious to know more.

"Yes, usually, but it depends how far we have to travel. A week is typically long enough to get us where we need to be," William explains after taking a sip of beer.

"We also take a month off each year and return to Skar. The performers all take vacation, unless their contract is up. We also audition any new acts during this time. It's the equivalent to Christmas and New Years on Earth," John adds in.

"Yes, and this year we actually have someone to celebrate it with us." The excitement in Eric's voice adds to the happy relaxation I'm feeling right now. Poor guys have been alone for the last twenty years since my parents and Grandma disappeared. I want to know why they haven't rebonded or whatever, but we've moved past the sad part of the evening, and I don't want to bring it up again.

"When you bond with someone, it's unbreakable

except through death," William says quietly, and I swing to look at him.

"How did you know that I was wondering that?" I ask, worried about mind reading again.

"Princess, you have a very open and expressive face," Eric says gently. "The thought of moving on has never been easy. When a bondmate dies, there is usually a severing of the bond. The mate mark disappears, and the remaining bondmate usually falls into a coma. Most of the time, they don't survive. On the odd occasion they do, they will never form a bond again. When someone is bonded to multiple mates, the chances of survival when one of them dies is much higher. In that case, the Skarrian has other mates to sustain them. It doesn't lessen the emotional pain, but it helps to keep the body alive."

"That severing never happened to us, so we hold out hope that maybe she is out there somewhere. We have all stayed true to our vows. Not to mention it makes us nauseous to think about starting a relationship with someone else." John looks resigned to his fate, but not like he regrets it. Their loyalty is not what makes them sad. It's the unknown that has brought such exhaustion and defeat to their faces. Before we can talk anymore, a siren sounds through the room.

"Ah, the ten-minute warning bell. Come, Lila, I'll show you how to set your room up for transport." Eric jumps to his feet, draining his beer and putting the bottle on the coffee table.

I decide to bring mine with me instead of downing the potent concoction. Getting to my feet, I lean over and give John a kiss on the cheek before doing the same to William.

"Have a good nap, dear. I can't wait to show you around the ship when we arrive." John's face lights up with excitement, and the same feeling runs through my body.

I'm going into motherfucking space!

CHAPTER SXITEEN

Eric walks me back to my room through corridors that are busier than I have ever seen. People are loud and chatty, with no one paying too much attention to us. But as we get to my room, I can see Dylan standing outside of the one next to mine, arguing with someone beyond the doorway. The super nosy part of me, which is most of me, is dying to know who it is since I haven't met my neighbor yet. Eric and I pause while I pull my lanyard from around my neck, but before I get a chance to swipe it, Dylan notices us and clams up. The situation only becomes more awkward when all my wave gets in response is a nod. Okay then. That hurts a bit, especially after our most recent conversation, but as I turn to open my own door, the person he was arguing with steps out.

Caspian is in human form this evening and looks like he's freshly showered, wearing only a pair of sweatpants. His vivid purple hair and skin are glistening with water, and his skin is the same color as mine at the moment unlike when I first met him. I feel my mouth go dry at the sight of him.

Oh, will you look at that. Caspian's room is directly next door to mine. Nobody said anything about that. I scowl at Eric, but he just winks at me and steps toward the two guys. I feel the mark on my back pulse when Caspian catches sight of me.

"Are you guys all set for departure?" Eric asks them both. "Maybe you should make your way to your room now, Dylan, since it's down the other end of the ship." He slaps Dylan on the back a little harder than necessary then gives him a shove. Alright, that confirms it. Those shifty grandpas have some kind of telepathy because there's no way he heard what Dylan said to me earlier.

"But, but..." he tries to argue, but Eric's having none of it.

"No, go. I don't want to tell you again. And Dylan, you might want to think about the things you said to Lila and how they may have hurt her."

Yep! Let's add telepathy and really good hearing to the list of grandpa abilities. Super snoopers, for sure.

Dylan's eyes brighten with flames, but he turns and does as instructed. "I'll catch up with you when we're on the big ship, Lila," he shouts back over his shoulder before he disappears around the curving corridor.

"Please tell me his room is far away from mine on the big ship too?" I ask Eric. "His mood swings make me dizzy."

Caspian has been quiet through the whole

exchange, but I could feel his eyes on me the entire time. Another siren sounds out, this one slightly different from the first.

"Fuck. That's the five-minute warning," Eric curses. "Quick, I need to show you what to do and then hightail it back to our room."

"If you would like, I could show Lila what she needs to do so you could make it back before the ship departs," Caspian offers.

"Yes!" Eric practically shouts. "Thank you." He leans in and gives me a kiss on the cheek. "Enjoy your first *ride*, and I'll see you on the other end." He gives me another wink and disappears in a blur of speed. Damn creepy grandpa and his innuendos.

"Ah, do you want to come in then?" I'm left asking the hottie octoman now that it's just the two of us.

"I can't very well show you what to do out here, can I?" he says gruffly, and all awkwardness disappears. There he is, the grumpy man I've seen each time. There's something a little comforting about that. His attitude might not be as pleasant as Dylan can be, but at least he's not giving me emotional whiplash.

I swipe my card through the door, and it buzzes us in. Stepping into my little room, I make room for Caspian to join me, the two of us now alone once that door closes.

Looking around, I wince. Fuck my life. On my bedside table is my favorite bad dragon dildo and a book of alien erotica. I've been horny all damn week, and last night I finally did something about it.

I hurry toward them in the hope he doesn't notice,

shoving them into a drawer as nonchalantly as I can, which is probably a huge failure. When I turn back, his eyes are on the drawer I just closed. Yep, I'm still going to pretend he didn't see anything. Avoidance, thy name is Lila.

"So what do I need to do?" I ask, hoping to distract him. He scans my room then picks up the control tablet.

"See this icon here?" He points to a rocket ship taking off. "This is the icon that sets you up for space re-entry." With a tap of a button, things start to whirl around.

The chair tucks under the desk before both of them retreat into the wall. I can hear things going on in the bathroom and closet, so I stick my head in to check it out. All the drawers have done the same as the desk, and the hanging space now has a wall in front of it.

"It gets a bit shaky on take-off, and things can bounce around if they're loose." Caspian is so close to me now, I can feel his breath on my neck. Whirling, I find him chest to chest with me, and my heart skips a beat. With his stormy blue eyes and those nipple rings practically at mouth height, he's just daring me at this point.

I place my hand on him and gently push him away as something starts to happen to the bed. With a chuckle, he moves over, letting me watch the bed transform from something you'd find in any bedroom to something that is definitely futuristic. It shrinks a bit, turning from a king-sized bed to something probably closer to a double. Once the shrinking settles down, a lid, I guess, is lowered from the ceiling and clicked into place. A section of the lid slides back, allowing me access.

"Climb in," he says, once again super close to me. Is he trying to make me uncomfortable, or does he just find it hard to stay away? If he feels the same kind of pull that I do, it must be messing with his mind since he was so anti-me to begin with.

The warning siren sounds once more, and a panicked look crosses Caspian's face. "Shit! Hurry, I still have to get back to mine, and that's the one-minute countdown."

I kick off my shoes, hoping that they survive the trip, and awkwardly climb into the pod as the ship starts to shake. The inside of the pod is different too. The texture of the mattress has changed to a thick almost jelly-like consistency, and I sink down. The ship starts to shake even more.

"No time. Move over," he demands and crawls in behind me. Once in, he pushes another icon on the tablet that has the pod closing then being covered in a thick gel. I guess it's the same as what we're laying in. Once Caspian takes his place next to me, he presses one more button then pushes the tablet into the thick gel matrix where it rests. Straps come up and over the both of us, holding us in place.

"I'm sorry to barge in, but the take-off from Earth is too dangerous for anyone not to be strapped in. The g-forces and turbulence will kill someone." He does sound apologetic, but I can't turn my head to look at him thanks to the strap.

Suddenly, the lights in the room turn off until only the pod is lit up with a strange bioluminescence.

"Here we go." Surprisingly, I feel his hand in mine as the ship starts to move. "Breathe, Lila, everything will be okay. I've got you." Huh, Caspian actually said something that was… *nice*. Well, that's not good. It was easy enough to ignore our attraction when he was being a douche, but this could change things.

I gasp as I realize I'd been holding my breath, and without any other signs of warning, the ship starts to move. Nothing changes in the pod, thankfully, and although the ship is bucking like a bronco, the two of us are stable.

The ship lurches to one side, and I scream, unable to stop it before it leaves my mouth.

"Shh, it's okay. That's perfectly normal," Caspian croons to me, and I manage to move my head so that I'm facing him. Who the fuck knew Caspian could *croon*? He's watching me with soft eyes and a gentle smile. It's the most open I've seen him so far.

A tear trickles from one of my eyes as my terror gets the better of me when the ship lurches from side to side. My heart is racing, and I fist my other hand in the substance below me. It shudders even more, so I squeeze my eyes closed, expecting a free fall back to Earth at any second.

"Hey, Lila, look at me," Caspian orders, but I keep my eyes closed. "Lila." He growls my name this time, but I still refuse to open them.

Suddenly, movement on my leg has my eyes popping wide open. There's a gentle caress around my naked calf followed by the suckling motion of what feels like hundreds of little mouths giving me kisses.

My now wide open eyes meet Caspian's, and he smirks. "Lila, a mark showed up on my shoulder this evening after I accosted you in the elevator. Do you want to talk about that?"

"Shall we talk about what is currently wrapped around my leg?" I deflect, wondering if he'll admit to his own attraction.

"I can partially shift, and I thought you needed the distraction. You didn't seem to mind it in the elevator, and by what I saw on your nightstand, I think you're probably just a little curious. Are you curious about me, Lila? I'm not like your human men." Caspian's words are a little mocking, like he's worried I'm going to say no and he doesn't want to get hurt.

"I am *very* curious, Caspian, but you haven't really gone out of your way to make me feel welcome. So either you're playing games with me, or you're afraid to admit how you feel." If he can call me out, I'm going to do the same thing to him, especially since he can't run away from me at the moment. I'm not opposed to the idea of speaking my own truth, but he and I didn't get off on the best foot. Tentacle? Whatever. So if I'm going to put myself out there, I think I'd like to get some honesty from him too.

"But the mark that appeared on my own shoulder tells me something different. Are we going to both keep pretending, or do you think we might fuck and see where this attraction takes us?" I guess going into space is making me bold, but from the look in his eyes, I don't think he minds super bold Lila.

"You know what I am, but are you really ready for all of me?" he challenges as his tentacle creeps further up my leg and under my skirt. Just as it reaches the seam of my panties, its little suckers still caressing my skin, the ship makes another lurch and shudders violently.

Another scream escapes my mouth, but the sound turns into a moan when his tentacle slides under and slithers its way across my mound until some suckers hover over my clit. The feeling of a thousand kisses caresses my clit while his tentacle secretes some kind of lubrication I definitely wasn't expecting. Instantly, I'm on the edge of an orgasm, squirming against the sensation like multiple tongues licking and sucking.

"Oh my god," I pant out at the incredible sensation. Another tentacle creeps under my skirt and pulls my panties off, allowing him free access to *everything*. Once they're removed, the tentacle returns, its tapered end teasing my lips to send ripples of pleasure across my body. I'm wound up as tightly as I can bear, panting and sobbing with need. It's barely been two minutes, and he's already got me ready to beg. What the fuck is this alien magic?

"Open your legs and let me give you a taste of what being with me is like," Caspian croons, licking his lips. "You taste incredible." He must be able to taste through his suckers, which could be weird, but I'm too turned on to give a fuck right now.

"Please," I plead, " I want it all."

"Good girl." He groans as he pushes his tentacle into my pussy until I'm full, the pulsing on my g-spot sending me over the edge. Another scream bursts from my lips, this one undeniably full of pleasure, and I'm seeing stars as I explode, coming the hardest I ever have. The tentacle rocks back and forth through my orgasm, giving me maximum sensation, and all I can do is vocalize my pleasure, trapped and unable to move. Caspian's grunting and groaning like it's his dick in me, and all of sudden, the tentacle stops, swells, then floods my pussy with fluid as he moans long and loud.

Whoa, did he just cum through his tentacle? Fuck me. Literally. If that's the case, it's like he has eight extra dicks.

Once he's finished and the aftershocks of my own climax have ceased, he gently removes them both from my body, but one of them comes up and caresses me on my cheek before sliding across my lips as if asking for access. Opening my mouth, it slides in, and I suck the fluid from it. Sweet and sticky, I clean it up, the suckers tickling my tongue as I do. There's zero question about it. I'm straight up ready for round two after the dirty act.

It's only as the tentacle pulls away that I realize the shuddering of the ship has finished and the straps restraining me have retreated. Not wanting to wait anymore, I throw myself toward Caspian. He grunts as he catches me, wrapping his arms around me, our bodies pressed together as my lips come down on his. I kiss him like my life depends on it, running my hands across his naked chest.

I think I surprised him because he hesitates for just a moment before he's kissing me back with equal enthusiasm. His hands quickly remove my top, bra, and skirt as I push his sweatpants down his legs. I have no idea where his tentacles came from or how, but they seem to have disappeared now. His cock jumps up as soon as it is no longer confined by the pants. Pulling my mouth away from his, I look down at what he has to offer. Much like his tentacles, it's long and thick. He has no hair around the base, and it's covered with suckers. I take a deep breath in excitement, but he must mistake it for something else because he pulls away from me and growls.

"I warned you I wasn't like human men." Even though he growled the words, trying to use that grumpy attitude of his, I hear something else beneath it. What Dylan told me pushes to the forefront of my mind, and I think something just clicks into place about Caspian. I'm not ready to just totally excuse his attitude, and I'll totally snap right back at him when he deserves it, but this moment right here is not about me.

I grab a handful of hair to hold him in place. "Caspian, don't mistake me for other women either. I can tell that you have been hurt in the past, but do not put me in the same category as anyone else. Humans can be open-minded and accepting too, all women can, regardless of species, and you're just going to have to learn that I'm not at all what you expect."

Using his hair, I pull him closer to nip at his lip, his

eyes flicking in between humanoid and cephalopod as I make my way down his body, placing tiny little kisses. I wish that I had tentacles to repay the favor for him, but I'll make do with what I've got. Licking, nipping, and sucking, I pause for just a second when I get down to his cock. He tries to squirm away, but I have his legs trapped under my body, so he is going nowhere. His breathing gets faster, and when I look up, his eyes are hooded with desire as he watches me.

Taking his cock, I run my hand up and down it a couple of times. Lubrication weeps out of the suckers as they ripple with my stroking motion, making a smooth glide for the both of us. Despite the lube, there's still the slightest bit of pressure, no disguising the texture of those little suckers. *Fuck, I can't wait to feel that inside me.* But before I do, I want to taste him. Using my tongue, I run it along the underside, the suckers pulsing with the motion and tickling my tongue as I lick my way up the length of him. Like his tentacle, the secretion is sweet and sticky, a little like passionfruit, and I can't get enough of it. *How the fuck are these alien women not lining up?* Taking his whole cock, I pull it deep into my throat, hollowing out my cheeks and swallowing so I can get most of it down. A shout leaves his mouth as he realizes I have no gag reflex. That's my superpower.

I feel him in the back of my throat as my nose meets the suckers around the base of his cock. They flutter gently over it before I pull back. I do this only a couple of times before Caspian is tugging me off and flipping me over.

"You really aren't like other women." He looks at me with reverence as his mouth takes mine. He pushes my legs wider with one hand as his cock nudges up against my pussy lips. Then, as he kisses me like he's starving, he thrusts in, and I groan with appreciation.

"I'm sorry, but this is going to be fast and furious," he apologizes with a slight blush, not quite able to meet my eyes.

I put my finger under his chin so that he looks at me. "Fuck me hard, Caspian. Give me everything you need."

And with that permission, he starts pounding into me, and it's an entirely new and entirely hot mix of sensations. His cock pulses inside me at the same time the suckers surrounding the base lick and suck on my clit every time he thrusts inward. Within only a few thrusts, I'm back at the precipice of an orgasm, and as he leans in and takes a nipple into his mouth, I discover something I hadn't noticed when he was kissing me. He has suckers in there too. Holy fuck, that's enough to send me over the edge. I throw my head back and scream as I tightly clamp my legs around him, my hands gripping his ass.

He continues thrusting as I ride out the bliss, so many sensations sending my nerves haywire, and my mind blanks out for a moment. When I come to, he's crooning to me in another language, petting and caressing me as he holds still while his cock pumps me full of cum. This sets off another orgasm, deep inside me, and I feel my pussy ripple as it takes everything he has.

CHAPTER SEVENTEEN

Lying there, my head against his chest, his arms wrapped around me as he strokes my back, I feel more cherished and loved than I ever had before. I'm also feeling a little sticky since cum is dripping out of me, but it's not like I can get up and move. We're stuck here for the next couple of hours while our ship makes its way toward the large one.

Rolling onto my back, I properly take in the capsule for the first time since I was too distracted by panic when we first took off. It's cozy and secure, but we are obviously going nowhere because it looks completely sealed. I guess it's still not super safe to wander around even though the initial turbulence is over.

Caspian removes his arm from me, and it's like I can feel him retreat into himself. Someone has really done a number on this guy. All the emotions from before are gone, and the atmosphere turns awkward.

Now, we can't have that. I refuse to let him do that. I roll onto my side to watch him, and he stiffens at my perusal.

"Is this the form you're the most comfortable in?" I ask him directly, but he refuses to look at me or answer. So I grab him by the chin and make him look at me. *Obviously.*

New rule of thumb: Boundaries belong to people whose cum isn't currently dripping out of my body.

"Fuck, you are a moody bastard. I'm not grossed out or disgusted, just genuinely curious. You saw Dylan before. He wasn't hiding himself from me because I asked him not to, and I don't want you to feel you have to do the same. Especially because you and I just became very intimate with one another's bodies. I would think that very situation shows that I'm not going to run away screaming if you let your body be its most comfortable."

He still has a stubborn set to his jaw and doesn't answer. "Would it help for you to know that when I saw you on that first night, I thought you were one of the sexiest things I had seen? Sure, I was a little surprised since I'd only just found out aliens exist, but once I got over that, I could see how fucking sexy you were. Who do you think I was using as spank bank material with that toy you saw before?"

His eyes widen with surprise like he doesn't believe me. "You say that now, but the novelty will wear off. All women say that until the reality of getting up close and personal with it happens," he snaps at me, his defensiveness on high alert.

"If you weren't in this pod with me, but in your own, would you be in this form?" I ask him, and he shakes his head. "Then please change. I want to see and feel and get to know you, the real you. The marks on our shoulders tell each other we're attracted, so let's explore that further."

He looks at me a little longer like he's trying to see if I'm telling the truth before he breathes out a big sigh. "Fine, but we're trapped in here for another three and a half hours, so don't freak out on me." His skin changes color, becoming mottled blue and purple, his eyes transform, and his body ripples. In a flash of magic, his bottom half is now all tentacles. Tentacles that instantly wrap around my body and pull me closer, causing me to giggle.

"Oh my god, it tickles," I choke out through the laughter as I'm pressed against his chest once more. His arms wrap around me, and I look up at his face. His eyes are wide with wonder and reverence as he strokes my hair.

"Lila, you are one very special woman. I can't believe you aren't running."

"Well, it's not like I could go anywhere," I tell him, gesturing to the pod. "And why would I? Seriously, being hugged by so many limbs is amazing." And it really is. I feel like I'm being wrapped in love. I'd expected the tentacles to be cold and slippery on my naked body, and they were cold to start with, but it's like they warmed to make me more comfortable.

"Is the secretion a sexual thing? Can you come out of every tentacle?" I ask him, my need for knowledge getting the better of me. Right now, the tentacles feel cozy, but they're also dry, like his body knows that we're not getting down and dirty right now. I run my hands up and down his delicious chest, plucking at one of his nipple rings as I wait for his response, and he nips at my shoulder in return before nodding his head.

"Yes, I can cum out of every tentacle. Unlike the Earth breed of octopus that uses one tentacle for mating, I can use all eight. And I also have another appendage which is used for breeding." Again, I wait. Dylan already broke this news to me, but I try to keep my face blank so I won't need to tell Caspian that his friend was sharing his secrets with me.

He sighs, some of his tentacles exerting just a bit more pressure as if they're seeking some kind of extra comfort from me. "I guess we should discuss this, so all cards are on the table before we go any further. My species has *very* specific breeding needs. The male lays the eggs, and the female incubates them. The secretion is a sexual thing. It has a muscle relaxant which helps the female partner's womb relax so that the male can implant his eggs into it for incubation. The female then carries the eggs until they are ready for birth. "

"Eggs as in plural?" I squeak, a little surprised.

"Yes, usually somewhere between three and five. Incubation time is completely up to the mother, and the babies can sit inside her for up to a year. Once she's ready, she will drink a cup of the male's cum to activate the enzyme inside of her womb. When that time comes, the enzyme will melt the eggs' coating, allowing the babies to be born. It's why it doesn't taste offensive.

If the female isn't of the same species, mating with the kraken changes them biologically to make them a compatible breeding pair. The babies are born in their animal form, but they usually shift to their human form within two weeks of birth."

"Oh wow, okay." That's a lot to take in, and I guess he must take my silence for rejection because his arms and tentacles move from my body, leaving me shivering. The temperature in the pod is much colder than before.

"Too much, wasn't it?" he grunts out, despair deep in his tone. I huff in annoyance and gesture for him to roll over. He moves away from me, and I stab a finger at his shoulder.

"No, Caspian, it wasn't too much, just a lot to take in at once. If the attraction had faded, that damn mark on your shoulder would have faded too. Instead, it seems to have gotten even darker." I haven't seen my marks up close, but I can now see both our marks clearly. His is clearly a sideways eight, almost like an infinity symbol, and mine is a pair of wings with long trailing feathers. One of the grandpas had said it was a Viking symbol for protection. Both of them are a deep black against the purple and blue mottling of his skin.

I let him roll back over then snuggle into his body, not wanting to look at his face when I ask the next question.

"But what about you? Yes, we're attracted to one another, but wouldn't finding a female of your own species be a better idea?" I feel his whole body shudder at the suggestion, and when I look up at him, it's fear I see in his eyes, not desire or longing.

"Fuck no. Kraken females are rare, and they also like to eat the males after the eggs have been laid. It's why I'm so thankful we can breed true with other species. Otherwise, I'm pretty sure we would be extinct by now. No, I'm ecstatic to have found you and that I haven't frightened you away with any of the information. My inner beast is riding me hard to not let you get away."

"What's it like having an inner beast? Are you of the same mind, or is there another entity in you so to speak." His tentacles creep across my body again, almost restlessly, like they're going to take any chance they can to explore me. There are a lot of them, and they caress the skin they touch, giving me a soothing full body massage. I pick one up and slide my hand back and forth across it, waiting for Caspian to answer. When he doesn't, I look up into his eyes again. The heat and desire have returned, and I realize I'm basically stroking one of eight cocks.

"Whoops, sorry," I apologize, starting to remove my hand, but he stops me.

"No, don't stop. It feels good. When in this form, he takes a backseat, but it's like he whispers to me constantly. In full animal form, my mind takes the backseat while he has control, but I'm still observing everything. It's hard to explain unless you have your own beast."

We're both quiet for a moment before he sighs again. "I noticed you had two more marks on your shoulder next to mine. I know Skarrians are a mostly polyamorous race, and as much as I and my beast want to keep you all to myself, I'm aware that isn't what you need."

It's my turn to sigh. "This is all so new to me. Up until a week ago, I thought I was human and living a normal life. Now, here I am, having my world rocked by an octoman with another two potential suitors out there somewhere on this ship. Yes, I know who they are, but at the moment, I'm happy getting to know you."

"Don't ignore what your body is telling you. Sometimes it will take matters into its own hands and force you to face its wants. Don't get caught unaware." His warning must cause my hand to tighten on his tentacle because he moans again, and the little suckers start to suck harder against all the skin they're touching.

"Oh my god," I groan again. "That feels amazing."

Caspian leans in and kisses me aggressively, but I want to tease him as much as his body is teasing mine, so I pull away from him and lift the tentacle in my hand up to my mouth. My eyes not leaving his, I suck and lick it, bringing it in and out of my mouth like I did his cock. He throws his head back in pleasure as two tentacles cup my breasts, plucking at my nipples with their suckers. Two more part my legs and creep up toward my dripping pussy. As they start to play with my folds and clit, the tentacle in my mouth thickens.

"Lila, I'm going to cum," Caspian warns me between clenched teeth, but I ignore him and keep going. With a moan, he floods my mouth with a rush of cum, so much I can't swallow it all before it leaks out a little. Swallowing as much of it as I can, I lick and suck his leaking tip, but it starts to vibrate. In fact, all the limbs on my body start to vibrate.

My eyes swing to Caspian's, but they're squeezed shut, the rest of his body vibrating the same way as his tentacles.

"No, not like this," he grits out. "Don't you dare!"

"Caspian, are you okay?" I ask tentatively, letting go of his tentacle and stroking his face. "I'm sorry. Did I do something wrong?"

His eyes flick open, and gone are the colored eyes; now, they're pitch black. "Oh no, you did everything right." His voice is all gravelly and thick, the new tone simultaneously worrying and intriguing me.

I swallow nervously as I realize Caspian's beast is now in the driving seat, but I don't struggle away or anything. If Caspian and I are going to attempt to get to know one another, then this is a part of him. He has a different presence than Caspian, somehow taking up more of the space around us, but I don't get the feeling that he would hurt me. His beast feels curious, but he also feels like he wants to care for me.

Before I can say anything, his limbs contract against me and he pulls me closer. Slowly, he lowers his mouth to mine, his eyes on me the whole time like he's waiting for me to flinch away, but I just melt into him. This is Caspian, and I'm not afraid. Whether it's his beast puppeting the body or him, they're still one and the same. This is just a more primal part of him. When his lips touch mine, I kiss him back with as much enthusiasm as I had before, and when his tentacle breaches my entrance and thrusts deep inside me, I throw my head back and moan. Much thicker than his cock, there's a slight bite of pain before a flowing wave of pleasure. An immense feeling of fullness has my pussy spasming with joy.

"More," I beg him.

"Yes, good girl, ride it," the beast mutters as his mouth bites, licks, and sucks much the same way his tentacles are across my body.

They start to lift me up until I'm suspended above him, splayed out like an offering. The whole time, his tentacle continues to thrust in and out. I'm a panting, writhing mess, the suspension adding a whole new dynamic to the sensation. A little bit of fear is creeping in because I'm floating in the air. It's not too high, we are in the pod after all, but I'm hovering over him with no support except his tentacle, and that's a mind fuck within itself.

He lifts his body up and sucks on my nipples, my breasts being supported by a tentacle each. They all start to secrete a fluid from them that makes my body tingle, and even though the liquid runs all over my body, making me a slippery mess, he still holds me tight.

The combination of the fluid against my clit and the suction is an added sensation that has me tipping over the edge, and I scream out my orgasm as my pussy clenches tightly around the tentacle. His beast's black eyes watch me with approval, the tentacle inside me picking up its pace until he's grunting, with more liquid flooding my pussy than I ever thought possible.

He slowly lowers me back down onto the bed, his tentacle deep within me, as he coos encouraging words to me. "Such a good mate, such a good mate taking all my fluid." I'm a shuddering ball of over sensitized nerves now, and his words become nonsense when his tentacle starts to move again, those suckers doing their job once more. His tentacles caress across my belly, massaging and rippling.

"God yes, again… more, give me more, please," I beg him.

He leans closer and kisses me. "Shh, it's okay. I'm giving you just what you need. I'm going to make you ours," he promises me, and all I can do is beg. A small part of me latches onto his beast's words, finding comfort in what he's saying to me. *Ours* sounds kind of nice.

"Yes, make me yours. Give me those big thick tentacles, please." My pussy is pulsing around his tentacle, the limb not feeling as thick as it had before. I need something more to fill me up.

"Are you ready for something bigger now?"

"Please, oh please, fill me up." The tentacle in me leaves. "No, please don't take it away!" I sob as a tear trickles down my cheek. There's a part of me, a tiny awareness in the back of my mind, that is amazed at how much of a mess I am right now, but I can't find it within me to stop. I don't want to stop what's happening between us even though I have the tiniest prickly feeling that there might be something bigger happening here.

He sticks out his tongue and catches the tear before licking its track. "Oh, you are *so* perfect for us. I'm going to give you what we both need."

This time, the tentacle that pushes against me is blunt and even thicker than the one before. I try to look down, but he catches my chin and kisses me at the same time a tentacle atop my clit starts to pulse. Bit by bit, it pushes its way into me, and I start to force myself down onto it, needing him to ease the empty feeling inside.

Sobbing and panting, it finally gets to where I need it, and I moan with the feeling of complete fullness. I have never felt this way, but there's something about it that's just right. My body is thrashing, trying to move up and down on the huge appendage, but Caspian's beast clamps me tightly against him.

He starts to growl and grunt, then the thing inside me moves. He's muttering, but my mind is so gone with desire that I don't really hear what he has to say.

"Breed, carry, perfect mate."

Suddenly, I feel something start to happen. Around the entrance to my pussy, it feels like another tentacle is trying to push itself in next to the other. But the tentacle across my clit ups the vibrations, and another orgasm pounds its way into my body. By now, I'm incapable of any movement so I just ride the waves of ecstasy.

"Yes. More. I need more," I sob as sensations rip through my body. Over and over, my body orgasms, and all I can do is beg. It's a rolling feeling, like something is pushing its way down the tentacle inside of me, but it hits my g-spot every time, so I don't care. He nuzzles at my shoulder, and I feel a sharp pain in the location of the bondmark, but the sensation turns to pleasure as I feel him lick across the mark.

Eventually, my voice and energy give out, leaving me a quivering, slippery mess. The motion in my pussy stops, but the thing in their stays lodged deep inside, giving an occasional vibration that keeps me on that edge of orgasm. Once the sensation ebbs again, it vibrates once more, stopping just before release. With the onslaught of pleasure, tears are leaking out of my eyes, and another tentacle slips inside my mouth. As my lips close around it, he cums, forcing me to swallow the liquid once more. I eagerly take the fluid, thirsty like I've never been before.

"Good, drink," the beast commands, and the cum keeps going until it overflows from my mouth and dribbles down my chin.

Suddenly, everything stops. The tentacle in my mouth retreats, but the others maintain their contact with me, one caressing my belly with massaging motions while others stroke and pet me.

The beast plasters kisses all over my face, praising me, telling me what a good girl I am, but as I drift off to sleep, the beast's eyes change and Caspian takes control once more. He scans my body, and a look of sheer panic crosses his face. I just barely catch a whisper of words.

"Fuck, Lila, I'm so sorry, baby."

CHAPTER EIGHTEEN

CASPIAN

As I gaze down at the woman my beast just mated, a stranglehold of terror grips my heart. I'm scared that when she wakes up she's going to reject me before we can even get started. This was only supposed to be a bit of fun to distract her from take-off, but when she insisted I change form, my beast took over. I fought him the whole time, *begging* him not to do this, not to take away her choice, but he pushed me too far back, telling me this woman was perfect for us and he wasn't going to let her get away. He was taking the matter out of our hands by doing the thing I couldn't make myself do—take away her choice.

But the asshole didn't just give her the mating bite; he also implanted her with our eggs. Lila is going to wake up mated and pregnant, and she's going to hate me.

I feel a tear slide down my cheek as I push her sweat-drenched hair back from her face. Her body is completely wrung out by what we did to it, but she just kept begging for more. He's not wrong about her being perfect for us, but women don't like it when the choice is taken out of their hands. That's a universal fact no matter what their species, and all I can feel right now is shame. I don't get to feel the satisfaction that my beast says I should, nor do I get to be excited about the eggs she's holding. What should be one of the best moments of my life is so far from that, I don't know what to do.

I had been an asshole to her from the start, afraid of getting looks of horror from the practically human woman the bosses had brought aboard—their heir. But she had taken everything I threw at her and given it back without flinching. Despite that, I was stunned when I felt her mark appear on my shoulder. She was as attracted to me as I was to her, and I wasn't going to allow that to go by unexplored. I couldn't. It's been so long since I was more than a novelty. Fuck, since I had even the chance to become more than that to someone. How could I walk away from the chance for someone to truly want me?

When Dylan cornered me before take-off and warned me away from her, I argued with my best friend for the first time in a long time. He tried to tell me she was fragile and over her head and that she didn't know what she was doing. Didn't realize the consequences of her actions. I told him to fuck off, like the asshole I am. Finally, I'd found a woman who was interested in me, and she was hot and feisty, and I was going to get to know her better.

He's going to cook me when he finds out I mated and impregnated her all without her agreement. That hot and cold act of his as far as Lila is concerned might very well spell out danger for her too. I have fucked up on so many levels.

Oh god, not to mention her grandpas are going to kill me. If she doesn't first.

Reaching into the impaction gel, I take out the tablet and hit the clean cycle on the pod. Warm gel flushes over our bodies and the surfaces around us, leaving us clean and refreshed. Maybe she'll be in a better mood when she doesn't wake up looking like a crime scene under a blacklight. Changing into my other form in the hope that it won't be as triggering when she discovers what my beast has done, I gather my mate into my arms and cradle her carefully against my chest, placing kisses all over her still-flushed cheeks. She doesn't stir, snuggling into my body instead.

Using the tablet, I press another button. The gel seeps up and over us, leaving only our heads exposed, and then it warms to a comfortable temperature. I close my eyes, feeling content for the first time in a long time, with my mate wrapped in my arms. I only hope it won't be the last time it happens.

Looking down, I can see our mating mark on her shoulder now. Both our marks have combined and are settled into her skin, not like the other two marks next to it which still have the flatness of a painted tattoo. It's a pentagram with an eye in the middle, and the other one is a series of cogs sitting on top of a staff with two snakes twined around it. Dylan had thrown in my face that she had not one, but *three* marks, but it hadn't bothered me. I knew it was a possibility, and from what I know of Lila, she seems to have a big heart. I'm sure she's capable of equally loving as many of us as she takes.

I breathe in her scent, which is now a mix of both of ours, and pray to the universe that this woman forgives my beast and is willing to make a go of this. If she doesn't, I will have to leave the circus. There's no way I could be around her every day, knowing she's mine but not being able to touch her. My beast nearly forces himself forward again at the notion that I might be willing to keep him away from our babies, but I manage to win this time, tugging Lila closer and letting myself focus on nothing but the warmth of her in my arms.

Closing my eyes, I allow myself to drift off to sleep, taking this stolen moment in time to enjoy this feeling because it could shatter at any moment.

LILA

As I wake from the deepest sleep I've had in weeks, I notice my body aches all over. A bone-deep ache that I know has come from really, *really* good sex. The warm arms around me make me feel cherished, and I smile to myself as I snuggle deeper into them. It's nice to feel wanted, even if only on a superficial level.

Damn, that was some sex session. Not only did he completely distract me from what was happening, Caspian rocked my fucking world, and I'm not sure I could go back to normal vanilla sex after that. I mean, seriously, he made my books come to life. The first round was better than any I'd had before, but when he got all freaky? Fucking sign me up for more of that.

He shifts in his sleep, and I notice that his legs are now back to normal, all tangled up with mine. There isn't a part of our bodies that isn't touching, and I can feel his thick cock hard against me. I should give him a treat to wake him to say thanks for working me over so well. Realizing I'm too tightly clenched against him to move, I start to place kisses against his chest until a glint of silver catches my eye, and my mouth zeros in on one of his sexy as fuck nipple rings. Licking the hard bud, I take the ring into my mouth and worry it gently with my tongue, using my teeth to scrape at the skin around it. Caspian shifts in his sleep, thrusting his cock into my hip as a small moan escapes his mouth.

When his arms loosen, I smile to myself and wiggle my way down his body, licking and sucking and placing love bites all over his body. With that gorgeously alien skin of his, the marks show up as bright purple rather than red. They look so pretty that when I get to his hip bone, I get the urge to really mark him. *Not really sure what that's all about, but let's go for it.*

He grunts when my teeth clamp down, and a hand brushes through my hair, grabbing hold of some strands.

Running my tongue across the imprint I've left, I drop lower until I'm face to face with his sucker-covered cock. The suckers ripple with movement. Again, I take it into my mouth, loving how the suckers tickle my tongue and cheeks as they pulse in and out. I suck and lick and moan my enjoyment, feeling entirely unashamed. Fuck me, it's like his cock is laced with ecstasy. My pussy instantly starts to drip, and I'm panting to be filled. Caspian must be exhausted because when I climb back up his body and line myself up with his cock, he only moans.

This is like the third time we've had sex, but I still can't get enough. Thank goodness for his natural lubrication, otherwise I would have to be investing in a jumbo-sized container of it, though maybe a carton of cranberry juice might not be a bad idea. *Enough, Lila. Dick first, UTI prevention later.*

Feeling naughty, I lower myself down his thick dick, gasping as I watch it disappear into my pussy. Fuck me, that's hot. When I'm flush with his pelvis, I lean forward, bracing my palms on either side of his head so the suckers surrounding the base can work my clit while I gently ride him. Still watching it all, I frown when I notice my belly. My normally flat stomach looks like I've just eaten a huge meal. I must be getting my period soon because it's slightly bloated. But the suckers soon distract me, and I throw my head back as I rock myself up and down on my lover's cock.

"Fuck me, princess, you look like a goddess. You're beautiful and amazing." Caspian's voice is filled with reverence as I work myself over. "Please don't hate me," he whispers as he sits up and takes one of my nipples into his mouth, thrusting upward at the same time.

"Fuck me hard," I shout, ready to lose myself in him again now that he's awake.

I'm a sweaty panting mess by the time we both orgasm in sync, but when I lean down to take his mouth with mine, he pulls out of me and rolls away.

Hurt lashes at my heart, and I'm making no effort to hide it. It might end up being awkward as fuck, but the kraken just came inside me for the third time. He can explain himself no matter how damn uncomfortable it is. "Oh, baby, please don't look like that. I want nothing more than to kiss and hold you tight now and forever. I know it's soon and we barely know each other, but I'm hoping that you will grow to love me like I think I could love you."

Whoa, did he just throw out the love word? I mean, yeah, I love his cock and his mad sex skills, but full-on emotional love? I'm *so* not there yet. Seeing the incredulous panic that's probably just flooded my eyes, he sighs.

"I need to talk to you about a few things, and I'm worried you're going to hate me afterwards, but it would be wrong for me not to tell you what my beast did. Once I've told you, I don't think you're going to want anything to do with me. You may even feel the need to demand retribution, maybe even my death, and that would be within your right. I won't fight whatever course of action you believe is best. My beast might have made the mistake, but I will respect your wishes on behalf of both of us."

"What are you talking about, Caspian? You're scaring me." I'm tense with worry at this point, and it feels much too vulnerable to be hearing this news while naked. The level of exposure that I'm dealing with right now is comfortable for sex or some other kind of playtime, but no one wants to hear bad news with their vagina exposed to the world. Somehow, that just makes the tension so much worse.

Caspian must understand what I need because he pulls the tablet out of the gel stuff and presses a button. A hatch pops open, revealing a large Galaxy Circus t-shirt. He grabs it and helps me pull it over my head before grabbing out the pair of sweatpants that he pulls over his body, covering his distracting dick.

He sits cross legged. There's just enough room in the pod for him to do it without ducking his head, and he pulls me closer to him so that I mirror his position.

"You met my beast, right? He overwhelmed me and pushed his way to the front."

A shy smile crosses my lips as I remember what happened. "Yeah, he was intense, but fuck he blew my mind. I liked playing with him."

Caspian grimaces slightly before sighing and running a hand through his own hair. The bright purple locks are in disarray after our fuckfest, but it's a good look for him.

"Well, he took matters into his own hands last night. He mated you without asking permission." He blurts it all out, and my heart skips a beat.

"What do you mean... *mated* me?" I ask cautiously, not sure what he's saying.

"Normally, Skarrians have to have sex more than fives times with one person to seal the bond, but he overode that by giving you a mating bite. I'm so sorry, Lila. I couldn't stop him. I tried as hard as I could, but he decided that you were perfect for us and didn't want to chance you getting away. "

I feel my body freeze, trying to take all of this in. A mate... Someone who is now irrevocably all mine. Someone who will be there at the end of the day to give me foot rubs or just cuddle on the couch as we talk about our day. Someone who won't find their person then leave me behind in the pursuit of their own happiness. Instead, my mate and I can each be part of the other's happiness. We'd be on this journey together, neither of us leaving the other in the dust.

A pulse of something surprisingly positive rushes through me. Fuck me, this sexy as fuck octoman is all mine. Despite what's whirling around inside of me, this weird blend of excitement and happiness and this sense of almost peace, I try to keep my face blank. I don't want to let him off the hook just yet, even if I am thrilled and it wasn't completely his fault.

The grimace on his face makes it clear that he's feeling something that might be close to nausea. Taking a deep breath, he rushes out, "Does it make it any better if I tell you the matebond wouldn't have worked if a part of you wasn't open to the idea? It takes more than just physical attraction. There had to be a part of you that wanted something concrete between us, some type of bond to connect us."

"Okay, but I have two questions." He nods slowly, looking wary.

"Will you be mating any more women, or am I it for you?"

He shakes his head quickly, almost violently, and a hint of black starts to overwhelm his eyes like his beast is ready to get involved. "Absolutely not. You are it for me."

"Ok, good. Because I would kill anyone else if your beast decides to mark them."

"Mine," his beast growls, those eyes fully flashing black this time.

A sly smile crosses my lips. "Yes, yours," I confirm for him.

Caspian's eyes return to normal with a shake of his head. "And the second question?" he asks cautiously, still not sure of my reaction.

"Will you promise to dick me like that every single fucking time?" I launch myself at him and fuse my mouth to his, kissing him with everything I've got. He catches me and hesitantly returns the kiss before pushing me away with a sigh. My stomach jumps to my throat at the look on his face.

"Oh, baby, I will give you whatever you want, whenever you want it, if you will only forgive me for the next thing I have to tell you."

I cup his cheek with my hand, not liking to see my new mate so sad. "Tell me what's wrong. I'm sure we can work it out together."

His eyes drop to my belly, and he runs his hand over the little paunch that's there.

"Hey," I complain, "I must be getting my period because I'm a little bloated. Not nice to point that out on the first day of matehood." I slap his hand away, but he returns his hand to my stomach, caressing it with a sad look in his eyes.

"No, baby, this is not bloating. When my beast mated you, he also... bred you. He implanted his eggs into your womb to ensure you couldn't get away from us. To him, the matebond still left too much room for you to reject us, and he's adamant that there is no one else who will ever fit us like you could."

My mouth drops open, and goosebumps erupt across my skin. "I'm sorry, but I don't think I heard you right."

"Baby, you're carrying our eggs. You're pregnant."

"What the fuck!"

CHAPTER NINETEEN

"I'm sorry. I must be mistaken because I thought I just heard you say that your fucking beast *knocked me up*." I'm shouting by the end of my sentence, unable to wrap my head around his announcement. "Becoming mates is one thing. I mean, I can work with that, but me? A mom? I don't know how to watch a fish, let alone a baby! I killed a goddamn succulent, Caspian. Do you know what that is? Do you know how hard it is to kill a *succulent*? And you said fucking eggs, *plural*. What the actual fuck? Eggs, like more than just one. A litter of baby octopus. What do you call a group of octopuses?" I'm babbling now, panic having taken over my mouth.

"Not octopus, kraken," he replies much too patiently, though he does begin to shrink away when I growl in response and bare my teeth at him. "A family group is called a Kake."

"I was being sarcastic, you tentacled idiot!" I scream at him, tugging at my own hair in frustration. "I don't really fucking care at this moment. Except for the fact that you've just told me we're about to become a ready-made one."

"No, baby, not yet. The when is all up to you," he coos, trying to make me feel better, but I'm just confused.

"What do you mean 'not yet'?" I take a shuddering breath in and release it slowly, calming down just enough to hear what he has to say. Don't get me wrong, I'm still on the edge. On the edge of what, I'm not sure. Hysteria? Fear? Anxiety? An overwhelming sense of doom like I'm standing on the edge of a cliff, blindfolded, while wearing impossible to walk in heels after doing one too many shots? Okay, the last one might be a bit dramatic. With one more breath, I try to let the more rational side of me take the lead even though it's barely rational at all right now.

"Remember, I said the birth process is completely controlled by the mother. You incubate them as long as you need to. They won't be born until you are ready for them." Oh. That. I do remember that, though only a man of any species would think that's a bonus in this situation.

"And walk around like a whale?" I screech at him. "That's if I can even walk with however many babies you implanted into my stomach."

"Only three this time... He didn't want to overtax

you for your first breed." Another screech leaves my mouth as I pummel his chest.

"Let me at that over-tentacled idiot. I'll show him *over fucking taxed*. Maybe when he feels my foot up his ovi-whatsit, he'll think twice about knocking me up."

Caspian grabs my flailing arms and pins them to my side, the contact feeling more comforting than I would ever admit unless under penalty of death. Right now is the time to be angry, not sink into a cuddle. "Baby, the eggs go into hibernation. They won't grow or get any bigger or do really anything until you say so. When you're ready, we will give you what you need to start the process. For a month, or however long you choose, you will carry them as they grow in your belly, then you will secrete the hormone to break the eggs down. The babies will just slide out! Much easier than a humanoid birth because they have no skeletal form."

I blink at him, stunned and possibly horrified. Tentacles going *into* my vagina, well, that's one thing. A very hot thing that got me into this very situation right now. Tentacles coming *out* of my vagina? What the fuck? "Easier... much easier? I'm going to give birth to octopus?"

"Kraken," he corrects me, and I growl again. "Yes, it is much easier and safer for your body. In either form."

Trying to hang on to the last shreds of my sanity, I stop my ranting and blink once more. "What do you mean by *either form*?"

A pleased smile covers his face. "Now that we're

mated, you should be able to shift just like I do. My beast is very excited to meet yours."

That's it. I'm done. I can't take any more today. I flop backward into the gel matrix, staring up at the lid of the pod.

"Lila?" Caspian's voice is small, with one emotion coming through too clearly for me to ignore it. He's scared shitless right now, and doesn't that make me feel like a dramatic bitch? Sure, yes, I am 100% entitled to my anger right now, but if what he said is true, his beast totally threw him for a loop as well. He wasn't ready to put himself out there, as both a mate and a future octo-daddy, but now he's in this situation too. Sighing, I flop my hand out, offering it to him to hold. A deep breath of relief escapes him before he grabs hold and snuggles into my side. If I'm being honest, it actually makes me feel a bit better too.

"I really am sorry. I know none of this was what you thought would happen when I hopped into your capsule tonight."

I turn my head to look at him. "No, Caspian, I really didn't, but you're a fucking sex god and I'm a horny bitch, so I guess we're a match made in heaven. But you will have to excuse me if I ignore the pregnancy thing for a moment. I need to wrap my head around it all, so let's just start with the mate angle and then jump back to the whole egg, vagina, tentacles situation. Please don't push me," I practically beg him, and he nods immediately.

"I promise. I'm just glad you're not outright

rejecting me. I wouldn't know what to do if I had to leave you now."

Somewhere out in my room, a siren sounds. Oh god, what now? Caspian's hand comes up to cup my cheek as panic fills me. "That's the docking siren, meaning in about five minutes, the pod's going to open up and let us out."

"Okay, so what happens now?" I ask him, suddenly a little shy. It was all well and good while we were locked away in our little bubble, but now we're back to reality. Are we telling people, keeping it to ourselves, what? How are the grandpas going to react? I doubt aliens have a version of Dr. Phil or Jerry Springer, but if they did, we'd be a perfect feature for the next episode. I can see it now, an entire special with extended footage, called, "Is that your ovipositor, or are you just happy to see me?"

"Well..." He places a gentle kiss on my lips. "We find your grandpas and ask to be assigned mated quarters." A wave of relief flows over me as I realize he's ready to start making this work immediately. It would be easy for him to use my panic as a way to get himself some time to deal with all of this, but he's not hanging me out to dry. I mean, I know his beast has no second thoughts, but I needed some outward proof that he wasn't changing his mind now that the real world is closing in on us. "Because I don't want to be away from my mate for one single second if I can help it. Then we can work on your shifts, if you want, or I can show you around the ship. Anything you want."

"And the babies?" There's a thud in my chest at

saying those words, and my hands come up to cup my little bump. Holy crap, babies. A family of my own.

"Whatever you want to do. We can tell your grandpas, or not. I'll let you lead. Especially because they're probably going to kill me anyway." He moves down and peppers kisses all over my belly, whispering to it, and my heart bursts. Oh my god. I hate insta-love in my stories, but I get it now. Boom! Heart gone. Just like that.

"Is there anything else I need to know?" I ask, almost ready to start holding my breath, and he looks up at me from my belly and winces again.

Rolling my eyes, I give him the get on with it signal. "You might as well tell me."

"You're going to be extra… horny, between now and whenever you give birth. It's the hormones the eggs give off. It's a survival thing. Lots more can fit in there, so they give it off in the hope that you will want to carry more."

A lot more can fit in there? Absolutely fucking not. I grab Caspian by his beautiful blue hair and yank him forward. "Let me speak to the beast," I growl, and Caspian's eyes instantly blacken as his beast pushes forward. He nuzzles into me, but I yank him back by the hair.

"Listen here, buddy! You may have gotten away with the first implantation." He chuffs joyfully, and a weird grin crosses Caspian's face. It's all teeth, which isn't exactly the most sane look, but I think his beast is trying his hardest not to look intimidating. "But there will be *no more* eggs implanted into my belly." His grin turns down, and he whines mournfully. "There are things you don't know yet, and to be honest, I want to be involved in these kinds of decisions. You and I will not be vibing if you take the decision from me again. I am not saying a permanent no to the idea of growing a family in the future, but I will have an active say in that future. Do you understand?" He nods once, and the blackness recedes from Caspian's eyes.

"Wow, baby, he's sulking in the corner. Don't be surprised if he's not going to encourage more of those fuck me vibes just to mess with you. He can vibrate at a certain frequency which encourages the eggs to do the same. If you thought the tentacles were an experience, well, just be ready in case he gets a little vindictive."

I shrug. "Meh, there are worse things to be than horny, and at least I have a sexy mate to take care of all of that." His eyes heat as he crawls back up my body, but he shakes his head to clear away the fog of lust. Damn him.

"Yes, but not just with me. You will also emit… *fuck me pheromones*, to put it bluntly. It's those same hormones hoping to influence your mate into giving you more eggs. Unfortunately, it's not just exclusive to my species. Yes, I'd be the only one to implant more eggs, but the effect can also influence others around you."

I bite my lip as I think about what he just said. "Okay, is there anything I can do to stop that?"

He shakes his head. "I'm not sure. Maybe the owners of the two other marks can help you with that."

"Shit!" I sit up straight, remembering said marks

for the first time. I turn to look at my shoulder, and Caspian reaches over to help me push my hair out of the way. "Are they still there?"

"The warlock's mark?" he asks, and I look at him sharply.

"How did you know?"

"It was one of the things that Dylan threw in my face when we were arguing earlier. Though he didn't know who the other one belonged to."

"I think it's Link's, but I'm not completely sure. I haven't seen him again since I discovered it."

"The doctor's?" His eyebrows rise in surprise. "Well, that's interesting. He usually keeps to himself. Women chase him because of where he's from and because he's the heir to Pleasure Bot Industries, but I've never seen him accept any of the offers. I just assumed he had his own pleasure bot for any sexual needs he has. The cyborg race is somewhat of a mystery; they keep their secrets close to their chests." As he speaks, he gently strokes my back, and some of that heat from earlier is giving way to feeling comfortable, almost cozy. It's just nice, and I could easily sink into the contentment of this moment.

"Do I need to know what your argument with Dylan was about?" I ask him warily, and he shakes his head and gathers me fully in his arms.

"No, let's not worry about it now. And don't worry about me. If the warlock ends up in our family, then we have powerful protection. If he loses interest now that you're mated to me, well, he wasn't worth it to start with. Stop stressing and let me hold my mate for five more minutes of peace before the world butts in once more."

Once the pod opens, we're both reluctant to leave our safe space, but I know my grandpas will come looking for me if we don't. I'd rather be the one to tell them about us, as opposed to them accidentally discovering it. Caspian uses the tablet to return the room and bed to normal while I take a minute to make sure that I don't look like I've just been ravaged, mated, and impregnated by an alien octopus sex god. Need to hold on to a little of my dignity while I can.

The corridors are busy when we leave my room, and Caspian takes me by the hand, leading me toward the elevator. "This pod docks with the main ship, slotting into a space underneath it. It's not used at all when we're docked with the main ship, and the elevators are locked down to stop people from coming down here. For the next week, we will relax and wind down until we make our way back to the pod and take it to the United States. While we are there, anyone who wants to return home will be transported back, as will any aliens who were caught messing up and are being deported. I'm sure your grandpas will want you to help with that process, but for now, let's enjoy our time off."

We get to the elevator, and there's a crowd of people already waiting to board it. Amongst them are Phillip and Fiona. Both give me identical sneers, and

Fiona's eyes just about bug out of her hair when she notices my hand in Caspian's.

"Oh my god. You know he has tentacles, right?" she gasps, sounding disgusted. There's something so loud and exaggerated about her tone that I just know she's saying this to hurt him. Or me. Well, probably both of us. Everyone in the elevator is watching the drama unfold in front of them, not even pretending not to.

Caspian stiffens and tries to pull his hand away from me, but I won't have any of it.

"Oh, honey, I definitely know what he can do with his tentacles." I fan my face and wink at her, and her mouth drops open in shock.

"Are you serious?" she screeches, looking a little pale, and I step forward.

"One hundred fucking percent. Krakens certainly aren't lacking in the mad sex skills department. I've never been so well satisfied in my life."

The elevator comes to a stop, and as we step out, apart from Fiona, all the other women are eyeing Caspian with renewed interest.

"And let me warn you all now. Caspian is *mine*. I licked him first, so he is mine. That means I will cut any one of you that thinks they can try *my* kraken out."

With that announcement, the doors close, forcing the rest of them to ride it back down again. I have to nudge Caspian to get his attention, and when he finally looks at me, his eyes are filled with wonder.

"You just told everyone in the elevator that we were having sex. That I was *yours*. You claimed me in front of them all, including your cousins." He sounds awed by this, but I honestly just don't understand why it's a big deal. I mean, I get why it is to him since he told me a bit about his history. But we're on a spaceship surrounded by aliens, for fuck's sake. How are tentacles the weirdest equipment someone's packing around here?

"Ah yeah, of course I did. I'm fucking proud to have such a sexy mate. And don't think I didn't notice that you were on your human legs. You don't have to do this for me. We already covered that."

He shakes his head and shrugs. "No, I do it because… Actually, the only reason I do it is because Fiona freaked out the first time she saw me and said some horrible things. It's easier than having to listen to the nasty words that come out of her mouth."

Oh wow. "My grandpas allow this?" I really am surprised to hear this considering how much they warned me about offending the performers.

"God no. She's never done it around them. You remember your first night, where she didn't say a thing. They wouldn't stand for it if she did, but she knows that and likes her job too much. It's just become a habit, and now I don't really care either way. It's nice to be in my half-form, but I'm just as happy in this one."

I stop our movement, pushing him up against the corridor wall. "Well, as long as you know I think you're sexy either way." I brush my mouth across his, nipping his lip to ask for entry, and when they part, I slip my tongue in. For a quiet moment, we enjoy each other.

He pulls away first with a sigh. "You still have to see my beast form. You might not think that when you do."

"Hmm, he might not be excited to meet *me*. I still owe him a kick in the ovi-whatsit," I grumble back to him as he once again takes the lead. "When will I meet him?" I can't deny that I'm curious. How he pushed his way to the front was sexy in a primal sort of way.

"There's a big pool on one of the levels for the Aquilians. It takes up the whole floor, and it's where their quarters are. I use it to set my beast free because let's just say he's a little bigger than an octopus." He smiles as if he thinks of something. "Yours probably will be too. In fact, you may be bigger since female kraken often are. My mother is bigger than my father."

Before I can jump on the subject of his parents, he continues to tell me about the pool.

"Their homes are really cool. They're split-levels with the bottom located in the pool and a dry area floating on top for when they want to take human form. It doesn't happen very often. They prefer to be in the water, but they need one day a week on dry land, or they will become permanently shifted, only able to switch between mer form and dolphin. Some choose to do that, but most like to still have the option for legs if needed."

The corridor opens out onto a huge viewing platform, and before me is a sight that leaves me speechless. A huge viewing window is located in the very center of the area, with plush seating scattered around it. But it's the view beyond the window that has me mesmerized. Like something out of a sci-fi movie, stretched out before me is infinite space, an unfettered view of the cosmos, and it has me gaping with amazement. I slowly walk all the way across the large area until I can put my hand up against the window.

"Oh my god." Up until now, reality really hadn't hit me. Even with the mad crazy tentacle sex and now being mated to a kraken, I could still pretend nothing had changed, but now *this* *is* just undeniable. I'm in space, and not only that, but I'm mated to an alien and pregnant with his eggs... offspring... young?

I think everything has finally caught up to me because I feel my mind short circuit, and with a muttered, "Fuck me," it's lights out.

CHAPTER TWENTY

When I crawl my way out of the darkness, I realize I'm settled on a soft surface. Sitting next to me on the bed, with my hand in his, is Link. He notices I'm awake and smiles at me but doesn't drop my hand. Those eyes of his are doing that weird body scan thing again, so I know I'm not going anywhere until he's ready.

Link's eyes widen when they get to my stomach, and he looks up at me, his eyes switching back to normal as his eyebrow rises.

"I've got to say, Lila, I'm a little disappointed that you found someone else to take care of that other problem," he says with a cheeky wink. After that, he's all business again, his eyes changing and resuming the scan. His hand in mine is cool and comforting, and I kind of wish it was on my face. I'm feeling slightly warm, but I don't know if that's from me passing out or my proximity to Dr. Hottie and the memory of his offer.

Finally, he finishes his scan and drops my hand before getting up off the bed, my thighs mourning the loss of his weight against them. *Down, you thirsty bitch, your mate is waiting patiently in the background while you lust over another. He's going to regret it all if you keep this up.*

Once he opens the door to the room, in walk three very concerned grandpas but no mate in sight. Panic fills my veins. Does he not want me anymore? Has he decided I'm just too much trouble like so many other people have in the past?

"Caspian?" I croak out, and they part, showing me my sexy mate behind them for barely a breath before they block him from my sight again.

"Lila honey, you had us worried," John says quietly, sounding concerned. "How is she, Link? What's wrong with her?"

He looks to me, and I shake my head slightly. I don't want him to tell them about the eggs yet, not like this. With the barest tilt of his head in return, he turns back to the four worried men.

"Lila is fine, though she's once again dehydrated and exhausted." He starts as I struggle to sit up, but he quickly helps me, his touch firm and steady as he places a pillow behind me. "She also needs to eat. None of these things helped, and I guess seeing the view of space for the first time was the icing on the cake. Overwhelmed, her body did what it's designed to do, so it shut down. Forcing her to take what she needs —rest."

John and William look worried, but Eric is downright pissed, from his crossed arms to his tapping foot.

William pats me on the hand. "Why don't you take the rest of the night to get some rest? We can give you the tour tomorrow."

"I'm actually a little hungry now." The second I get those words out, my stomach rumbles rather loudly.

"There's a replicator out in the main room of your suite," William assures me. "We can get you something to eat."

"I'm sure you are freaking hungry and exhausted. After all, you spent the flight mating our fucking kraken," Eric all but spits out, unable to hide his annoyance.

"Oh! So you know about that..."

"Yes. *Oh*." Eric throws up his hands and starts pacing. "What did I tell you, Lila? Try *before* you buy. You get five times to ride the pony before you have to either get off or commit. How is it you end up with a mate on the first go round?" He sounds exasperated, like a parent telling off a wayward child. But when he looks at me, his eyes are soft again.

I shrug. "I don't know. It just kind of happened." Yep, that's me. I have officially turned into the teen cliche from every Lifetime movie ever. Now I'm just waiting to see if one of them asks if I slipped and somehow fell onto his tentacle dick.

"No, it didn't," Caspian says from behind them, sounding guilt ridden. "My beast took over and forced it."

The grandpas let him through, and even Link

moves out of the way, allowing him to sit on the bed next to me. He grabs my hand and leans in, pressing his forehead to mine, eyes closed, and whispers, "Thank god you're okay. I was so worried when you went down." I rub my nose against his before giving him a kiss.

He pulls away and turns to them. "Not only did we mate, but my beast also impregnated her. She's going to have my babies."

Well, shit. Of course Caspian has blown *that* out of the water too. We really need to have another talk about establishing some ground rules here. Along with no more "accidental" egg drops, let's add "leave the life-changing news for the grandpas to Lila" there as well.

The grandpas are all silent. The only indicator that they've just had any kind of bomb dropped on them are the slack-jawed expressions that say they've been hit in the face by a two-by-four.

"Pregnant!" Unsurprisingly, Eric is the first to recover, screeching it to the room. "You can't be pregnant! We've got a circus to run, and you've got so much to learn, not to mention the inherent danger." He throws his hands up in the air and storms out.

Caspian frowns at his words, confused, but I know what Eric is talking about.

"Are you sure?" John asks quietly. "Did you see this?" he asks Link, looking between him and us.

"Yes, I did, but it wasn't my place to say anything. It doesn't read like a normal pregnancy. I don't know much about krakens' breeding habits, but I would love a chance to update my files on them. What can you tell me about it?"

"The eggs are in a sort of stasis, and Lila will carry them until she's ready to give birth. It's a kraken thing. A throwback to the need for the babies to be born when it is safe and away from predators. Really, life will go on the same until she's ready. She can still do anything she needs to. The babies are well protected, so basically nothing will harm them. Nor is her body going to change until she decides she's ready." Link looks fascinated, pushing back his shirt sleeve to make notes on his built-in technology.

"Okay, I'll update my files. When you feel up to it, you should come to my lab so we can make sure everything is okay." Link takes his leave after I assure him I will see him soon.

John and William both let out relieved sighs, then a bright smile crosses John's face and he slaps Caspian on the shoulder, maybe a little too hard. "I guess a welcome to the family and a congratulations are in order."

William looks at me, frowning again. "Are you sure this is what you wanted?"

"I can't deny I probably would have liked to have had the five tries as Eric keeps calling it, but I'm not upset about it either. In fact, I'm a little thrilled to know someone wants me." Both John and William look a little guilty when I say this.

"Oh, I didn't mean it like that, but I've never had someone who wanted me so badly that they lost control. It just... feels nice. Caspian says it couldn't be forced, that I needed to be receptive for the bond to take, and I believe that." Without getting into details that I'm totally not ready to say in front of my grandpas, I feel confident in the fact that my non sex-fogged mind knows I definitely wanted him in more than one way while we were… stuck in the capsule. "I'm looking forward to getting to know him." I reach out and take his hand, squeezing it reassuringly.

"Well, okay then." William leans down and gives me a kiss. "We'll leave you two be. Caspian, make sure she eats something and gets some rest. We will be by in the morning to give you the tour."

"Don't worry about Eric. He's all bluster and drama," John reassures me, then he too gives me a kiss on the cheek and squeezes Caspian's shoulder before they leave the room. "Great grandbabies, William, how exciting!" I hear John whispering to his brother, and it brings a smile to my lips.

"Come on, let's get you something to eat. I'll run you a bath after." Caspian helps me get up and leads me out into the living area.

"Wow," I say as I gaze around the room. "Where are we?"

We're in a huge space with a kitchen area which has a sink and a breakfast bar with a replicator built into the room as well as plenty of cupboards. The rest of the space is filled with sumptuous couches overlooking a large picture window that shows me the same view I had seen before, the vast expanse of space.

"On this floor is the command deck for the whole ship as well as suites for the ship's owners and the two captains. This was your mom and dad's suite when they were with the circus," he explains gently before taking my hand and leading me over to the breakfast bar. With a thoughtful nudge, he pushes me to sit down before he goes to the replicator.

A touch of sadness hits me at the thought that this was my mom and dad's, that I will never get to experience it with them. I could have grown up here if it wasn't for the person who took their lives. Right then and there, the sadness starts to burn with an edge of anger, and I vow to find the asshole who did it and get my revenge for them.

"Lila." When I face Caspian again, he has a strange look on his face, a worried scrunch of his nose that tells me what he's going to ask. "Are you okay? You kind of zoned out. I had to call you a couple of times; you really must be tired."

I conjure up a smile and shake my head. "No, I'm okay, just lost in my thoughts. What did you say?"

"What would you like to eat, baby?"

I screw up my nose this time. "Do I need to be on some special diet now that I'm carrying the babies? Like... I don't have to eat seaweed and raw fish, do I?"

He bursts out laughing and shakes his head. "No, baby, nothing like that. Though when you decide it's time, you may get weird cravings." It's nice to see the carefree look on his face. I guess it's all been a bit much for him too. Now I feel like I failed at this mate thing already. He's been worrying about me, but I haven't returned the favor very well.

Getting up and walking over to him, I wrap my

arms around my sexy blue and purple mate's waist and rest my head on his shoulder. His arms wrap around mine and hold me tight, a ragged burst of air escaping his lips before he leans down and presses a kiss against my forehead. "Thanks, I needed this." His breath brushes across my ear with his words.

We stay locked in place for a moment, just breathing each other in, before he pulls away and gestures to the machine. "Come on, food and then a bath and bed."

"I'd like tomato soup and grilled cheese, please." He pushes a button or two, and within moments, my food is sitting in the hatch, hot and steaming. I groan when the scent hits my nose.

"Gah, that smells amazing." He carries it over to the breakfast bar, and I take my seat again, practically inhaling my food while he goes back and returns with the same thing for himself. There's a comfortable silence between us as we quickly eat our food then load the dishes into the dishwasher. It's a nice little snapshot of what normal life could be like between us, being able to sit and do simple things with each other.

Caspian brings me back to the bedroom, pointing out a few things on the way. "There are six more bedrooms in the suite as well as a theatre. The bathroom is communal, and all bedrooms lead onto it. Anything else you could need you will find in the ship proper. There's a library, game rooms, a number of restaurants and shops... Basically, anything you would find on an Earth cruise ship, that's the kind of thing you will find here."

This time, I take a moment to actually investigate the bedroom space. The room is just as lavishly decorated as the rest of the suite, and the bed is fucking huge. Way bigger than anything Earth has to offer, but I guess that's needed in a polyamarous society. He pushes a button on a blank wall, and it slides away, revealing a Roman bath-style bathroom. In the middle of the room is a large sunken tub, and to one side there are some sinks lining the wall. Beyond the tub, there's a walled-off area which I'm going to assume has a shower and toilet.

Stripping off my clothes, I don't wait for Caspian before I step down into the steaming tub, groaning when the hot water hits all of my sore muscles. But then I have a thought and stand up quickly. "The hot water isn't going to cook the eggs, is it?" I ask him, cradling my tiny bump. I may not want them yet, but I don't want anything to happen to them either.

He snorts with amusement before realizing that I'm serious. "No, Lila, it won't cook the eggs, just like it doesn't cook your own eggs inside you." He strips off his shirt, exposing all his blue and purple skin, and I lose all interest in the conversation. I drop down into the water, leaving only my head above it, and continue to watch as this beautiful male strips off the rest of his clothing. He slides his jeans off, revealing his tentacled cock, already erect, and my exhaustion suddenly disappears beneath a wave of raging need. Still in his human form, he steps down into the water and makes his way across the small pool to stand just in front of me. There's a cocky smirk on his lips, and his eyes sparkle with mischievousness. Licking my lips, my eyes trace the nautical tattoos on his well-defined arms. There's an anchor, ships, and sea creatures, including a topless mermaid.

"That doesn't look like the mermaid in the tank; she had scales covering her breasts."

He grins, the smile lighting up his face. "Yes, but that was because we were on Earth where they are very puritanical in their views. On the other planets, naked breasts are very much accepted and wanted. You'll see."

"So is that modeled after anyone in particular?" I ask, jealousy making me take a small step back from him. "Please tell me that I won't actually come face to face with the woman on your arm with those amazing tits."

He chuckles and lunges for me. I squeal and try to get away, but he's just too quick. He pulls me in, and I automatically wrap my legs around his waist, his thick cock sliding through my lips, and I moan. He nibbles at my neck. "No, baby, it's just a tattoo, not modeled after anyone. Mermaids are incredibly snobbish creatures, so they tend to stick to their own species. They wouldn't be caught dead with a Fluxxian kraken shifter."

I rub myself up and down his thick length, and a moan escapes my mouth. "Really? The one I saw in the tank seemed friendly enough."

"Was that Nixie?" he asks as he palms my breast and leans in to nibble on the nipple.

"Yes," I groan out as the nip of his teeth sends shocks of pleasure straight to my core.

"You'll probably find she's the nicest of the lot, though her brother is a fucking asshole. But enough about them. I want to make my mate scream." And with those words, he thrusts himself deep into my channel, both of us grunting as he seats himself fully.

"Mermaids? What mermaids?" I pant out as Caspian proceeds to do what he said he would. My screams echo through the bathroom as he makes sure I am well and truly sated before bed.

The following morning, Caspian and I are up early, following another blistering round of sex. We can't seem to keep our hands, mouths, or tentacles off of each other, which is fine by me, but it means we haven't really gotten to know one another on more than a physical level. So I'm not surprised that when I suggest another round of bath sex, he counters that we should bathe separately then enjoy breakfast together, learning more about each other.

I agree, albeit with a pout, and hurry through a quick shower, not wanting to miss out on one-on-one time with him before my grandpas come and pick me up.

"Are you going to do the tour with us?" I ask him while eating my bowl of fruit salad.

"No, I thought I would give you some time with your grandpas. I have to go back to my quarters to grab a change of clothes and catch up on my mail and stuff. It tends to build up while we're on Earth."

His quarters? "But I thought you would be moving in here?" I reply, suddenly afraid that maybe he doesn't want this as much as I thought he did.

His eyes light up at my question, and he sits up straighter. "Really? That wouldn't be going too fast?"

I snort, almost blowing my coffee out through my nose. That was bad timing. "Too fast? That horse has already left the stable, buddy. Fast was your beast deciding to implant his eggs into my womb without checking if it was okay first," I tell him dryly, and he has the grace to look embarrassed. "No, I want you here. While the grandpas are showing me around, why don't you move all your stuff in? Take whichever bedroom you want for your things, so you have a space if you ever need a break from me." He looks thrilled at my suggestion, already hurrying to finish his breakfast so he can get started.

"Why don't we meet at the Aquilian pool a little later? You can show me your beast." God, you would have thought I told him he'd won the lottery with how he whoops and nearly smashes a kiss on my cheek before putting his plate in the sink and hurrying out. Well, that's something to look forward to anyway.

It's about half an hour later when I pull the door to my suite closed and follow my grandpas to the bridge of this ship. I missed most of it last night, having been unconscious when they brought me to my room, but the ship is apparently so big they use sideways elevators to get around. They slide around on a track that circles each level. When we step out of the one we're in, I'm greeted by another huge picture window with a similar-looking setup to the circus pod but on a larger scale. There are quite a few crew members here that I don't recognize, so I whisper that to John, sure he'll drop some info on me.

"All of our crew are Skarrian, and most of them stay aboard this ship while the circus pod is on Earth. This ship requires a lot more people to keep it running efficiently," he whispers back before introducing me to Captain Broderick Potter. He's a tall rugged redheaded gentleman with a bushy moustache and beard, but unlike Captain Lester, this man has a twinkle in his blue eyes.

"Well, who do we have here?" he asks, looking me up and down.

"Rick, this is our Lila," William says, sounding proud, which warms me inside. "Lila, this rogue here was your father's best friend."

He sticks out a large hand, but when I reach out to shake it, he pulls me into a huge hug. "Of course she is! Spitting image of her gorgeous mother." He pulls back, and I can see the sorrow in his eyes despite his grin. "Thank the universe she doesn't look like her ugly father."

Everyone chuckles, while I frown in confusion.

"Your father was a very handsome man. How could he not be with us as parents?" Eric is still chuckling as he gestures to the three of them. I roll my eyes, but then I realize I can't remember what my parents looked like. Any photos I might have had got lost in the system, and that's something that just makes me sad. Sure, I'm reclaiming a part of my heritage now, but that doesn't help bring me closer to them if I can't even picture them in my mind.

"It's nice to meet you, sir," I tell him quietly, immediately receiving a shake of his head in response.

"Oh no, none of that. You will call me Bubby, like your mother did. You and I are going to be firm friends. Now, let me show you the bridge of this hunk of junk." He offers me his arm, and for the next hour, 'Bubby' gives me a rundown of the technical aspects of the main ship. He introduces me to the staff, and by the end, my head is brimming with so much information that it starts to throb a bit. It's John who notices me rubbing my temples even though he and the other two grandpas have sat out of the way and let Bubby run the show.

"Right, I think that's enough. We've still got a lot to get through, and Lila probably needs to drink more water." Ugh, even the mention of the water has me grimacing. With no signs of Skarrian power, this seems like an exercise in futility. I guess I'll at least be an octopus now, though I'm not sure if that will be as important to the grandpas.

"Maybe we need to get the doctor to have another look at her." Eric sounds concerned, his ranting about the mating and pregnancy having fallen into the past.

"He said she was fine, Eric," William reassures him. "Come on, let's show her some of the fun stuff. All this information overload is too much for even me. And let's face it, with Rick and Captain Lester around, she doesn't really need to know all this. I can't remember the last time any of us needed to fly this beast."

"Okay fine," John concedes. "But water first."

And with that, I receive another hug from Bubby before we say goodbye and the grandpas whisk me off in search of water and fun.

XAVIER

Even on a ship as big as this one, gossip spreads like Laomanian flu, and even though most people go out of their way to avoid me, I have ways of knowing everything that's going on around me. When you can travel with your body shrouded in mist, it's easy to ferret out secrets from oblivious shipmates. So it is of no surprise when whispers of Lila are a hot topic, but the rumors themselves, much like the woman herself, are surprising in nature.

Lila has mated with Caspian, the Fluxxian kraken shifter. Isn't that an interesting piece of gossip? In fact, I find myself floating around the ship more than normal, seeing if I can pick up any other juicy details. I've made it my mission to be unapproachable and aloof in my relationships, apart from a few select people, so my circle of trusted companions is really quite small. It's been a while since I've been even remotely tempted to add to it in any way. But Lila wasn't thrown off by my misted form, and her curiosity and simple naivete was just alluring. Everyone usually knows better than to look a warlock in the eyes, and I couldn't help myself when our gazes met. It was like my soul leapt out of my body and latched on. Taking the decision out of my hand, it wanted to consume hers, to meld us, mate us in the warlock way. When was the last time I was so intrigued by someone that my instincts nearly took over?

It was all I could do to stop it from happening, but I fed deeply on her. That one woman, practically a human, was such a smorgasbord that I haven't needed to use any of the feeders since, much to their disappointment. I hear my harem's whispers, their speculations and bets on who I must be feeding on if not them, but I simply roll my eyes at their audacity. Though it's an inevitable risk that they form attachments, they have no real claim to any territorial feelings. Unfortunately, that desperation for more, which I will never give them, starts to taint what I draw from them in my feedings. Think about it like tasting something that's just about spoiled. Your stomach may fill, but the satisfaction is no longer there, and the aftertaste is far from desirable.

Sure, in the past, I've used them to assuage both my sexual hunger and my biological needs, but recently they haven't been fulfilling me. Their emotions are bland and unsatisfying and certainly don't feed me like I need. I find myself using more at once to get full than I have in the past, which can be dangerous for them. Same goes for sexual satisfaction, I find that I don't get the same kind of rush from fucking any of my harem members like I used to. No, something is definitely not right anymore. It seems it might be time for me to refresh the members of my harem. Send them back to the warlock home planet and find myself some new ones.

Saxon would gladly supplement me as long as I would be willing to return the favor. For whatever reason, I've been able to stomach him, even crave him, in ways that no one else appeals to me lately. Though I certainly wouldn't mind adding Lila into that mix. The thought of that has my cock hardening in my concealed form, but my arousal is tempered by the thought that her mate may have something to say about her getting involved with me. That could be tricky business, getting in between a matebond, though the Skarrian attraction mark hasn't disappeared. So there may still be hope for me and my little feast.

I had felt the mark form on my shoulder, but hadn't wanted to push the issue, especially when the dick dragon was trying his best to get between us, not to mention among the rest of the circus. Most of the rumors surrounding her are stemming from him, including the one about her having no powers. What kind of friend would open her up to that kind of vulnerability?

My personal outrage aside, his meddling has at least opened up the perfect opportunity for me. With the bosses asking me to look into this power situation, I have a convenient excuse to get closer to Lila. This is my chance to get to know her a little better. Discover if the attraction is still there and whether or not she is a good candidate for feeding.

Even now, I can feel where she is on the ship; it's like my soul has become attuned to hers, and now it must constantly remind me of her existence. I've never heard of that happening with a non warlock. In fact, I don't know of any warlocks who have mated outside of our race. Warlocks are all about purity, so for this to be happening with Lila is an anomaly. It would be frowned upon back home, but I've never been very content to just do what was expected of me.

For now, I head back to my quarters with the plan to have one last taste of my harem, but with every step closer I get, the queasier I start to become. More strangeness to puzzle over. Change of plan, I'll go find Saxon, he did nothing but bitch and complain about the lack of variety of blood available to him. I'm sure he will enjoy the treat almost as much as I would. All that delicious anger and aggression has always proven to be incredibly tasty in the past. Combine that with his sexual tastes, and, well, I'm in for a very, very good night. For some reason, the idea of seeing Saxon doesn't inspire the same physiological illness as the thought of my harem, which only solidifies my decision.

I don't bother to knock on Saxon's quarters when I reach them, sliding through the gap in the door and floating through until I get to his bedroom. His bedroom is cloaked in darkness with only a slight luminescence emanating from somewhere, with seductive rock music playing in the background. Once there, I remain invisible, silently staring at the sight that greets me. Saxon's kneeling on his bed, naked, with his fist locked onto his cock. Those painful and pleasurable fangs are buried in the neck of a fully clothed female who's begging for a taste of what he's refusing to give her.

"Please, Saxon, why won't you touch us any more?" she sobs, and he yanks his fangs from her neck with a growl.

"Get out of my room. Your incessant whining is ruining my dinner." He shoves her away with his free hand. Without another word, she runs through the harem door, letting the door slam closed behind her. *So dramatic, all of them.*

"Stop hovering, Xavier. Get over here and take care of this," the moody bastard snarls, and I feel a shiver of want flow through me as I allow my shadows to recede.

"Having a problem there?" I ask, cocking an eyebrow and nodding toward his thick, albeit unusual length.

"Nothing I can't fix by pounding into your ass." The direct bastard's dirty talk is always on point. Normally the silent type, nobody would guess he becomes filthy as fuck in the bedroom. "Now get over here so I can choke you on it."

Submission in the bedroom is usually not my thing, but there's just something so delicious about giving in when it comes to Saxon. In more ways than one. Literally, the flavor of all that growling, snarling dominance is mouthwatering, at least usually. Tonight, there's a slightly bitter undercurrent, something that tastes of a faint resentment. But if I know Saxon, which I do, I won't get any information out of him until I get off on him.

With a shrug, I disrobe, moving over to the bed and engulfing his thick pulsating, ridged length with my mouth. His groan echoes through the room as he grabs hold of my hair and starts to fuck my face, all while I drink down the confusion, want, and need he emits.

CHAPTER TWENTY ONE

"So this is one of the rec rooms set up for sports and fitness as well as rehearsals for the trapeze act," William explains as we walk into a spacious open room with high ceilings that has trapeze rigging set up on it. There's a large catching net below it, but that's still double head height above us. The rest of the room is a multi-purpose ball court. Skarrians have their own kind of ball sports, but they also love Earth basketball. Who knew it was a galactically popular sport?

It smells like sweat and disinfectant in here, a not altogether pleasant smell, but it's not offensive either. The trapeze really interests me because of my gymnastic background, and there's no one using it currently. But on the far side of the room, I can see that someone is using the aerial silks that are hanging there. They're wrapped up enough so I can't make out who it is, but I'm curious. Leaving the grandpas squabbling about their last one-on-one game, don't ask me how that works with three of them, I walk over to where the crash mat is sitting underneath.

Stretching my neck back, I watch the woman with the long pink hair wrap the silks around herself in an intricate pattern until she looks like an offering to some primordial god. With a flick of her body, she's tumbling downward, but something goes wrong. One of the silks unravels and floats away from her body, leaving her hanging by the single silk wrapped around her ankle. A gasp escapes my mouth as I look around for something to help her.

"Fuck!" Before I can offer my assistance, the girl floats up into the air so that she's no longer hanging. She reaches down and unravels the silk from around her ankle before floating down to the ground, landing just in front of me. She's about the same height as me, with a slimmer frame and smaller breasts and ass.

The girl straightens her clothes and pushes her long pink hair back from her face before looking at me. She scans my figure; her eyes are a pretty light blue, almost gray color. When her gaze travels back up to my face, she holds out her hand in greeting. "Hi, I'm Magenta, but you can call me Mags. By the look on your face, I'm guessing you haven't seen someone fly before."

I close my mouth as my heart rate starts to slow once more, realizing I'm probably being a little rude. I grasp her offered hand, giving it a shake. "Fuck no, I thought you were a goner. I mean, I've seen the grandpas levitate things but never themselves."

She throws her head back and laughs, a musical sound that seems to echo through the room. "Oh, you are delightful! I can tell we're going to be great friends." She links our arms together and drags me back over to where my grandpas are still arguing about basketball.

"Hey, boss men," she shouts over the top of them, and they stop arguing and turn around. "I'm going to borrow Lila for a bit. We're going to get drinks, and I'm going to show her the places to shop."

William visibly shudders at the word *shop*, and you can practically see him tap out, but John and Eric look pleased.

"Thank you, Mags. That would be great. We've got some stuff we have to do for the deportation detainees. I guess you can learn how to do that tomorrow." John turns away, studying the court like he's already planning his redemption shot.

"And don't forget you promised to meet Caspian at the Aquilian pool later." Eric shoots me a suggestive wink, so I guess all is forgiven regarding the mating.

Earlier in the tour, we'd had a whispered conversation, smoothing out things between the two of us. He wasn't truly disappointed in me or Caspian for forming this bond or the prospect of our future kids. Octopuses. Krakens? That's something to iron out later; I don't know that I can say I'm giving birth to a kake. In any case, it was sort of an accidental trigger for him, I guess. With how hurt he and the other grandpas have been by my grandma's disappearance and my parents being gone, he just sort of got scared and flew off the handle. I'm still excited to explore my future with Caspian, but Eric did remind me of something important that I might have forgotten about. The bond ties our lives together, so Caspian is automatically at risk given our family's true job with the circus. That's something we'll have to figure out in time since Caspian can't be in the dark forever, especially if we're really going to make a life together.

Heavy stuff aside, it was a good talk. He apologized and told me how thrilled he was that Caspian was my choice. All three grandpas really like him and are happy to welcome him to the family.

"I won't forget, don't worry. I'm excited to see him shift." The grandpas now looking reassured, Magenta practically drags me away. When I turn back, it looks like the important detainee stuff is going to be forgotten if the basketball in William's hand has anything to say.

"I've been dying to talk to you, but your grandpas kept you so busy all week. Every time I tried, they shooed me away." She leads the way to another of the side slip transports, and with a press of a button and a woosh, the doors close and the pod starts to move. "Girl, that lightning that exploded out of you on the first night was freaking amazing! You must have some wicked cool powers," she gushes, and a wave of embarrassment flows over me. I stare down at my feet, avoiding looking at her.

"It was a fluke," I mutter quietly, hoping she doesn't hear me.

"What?"

I breathe out a defeated sigh and look up at the friendly girl. "It was a fluke, a one off. I have no powers except for heightened senses. I didn't even get speed like Eric."

Her mouth drops open in surprise, but she tries to hide it quickly. "Nothing?" she pushes.

"Not a scrap of power. Eric talked about getting Xavier to look at me, but I think I'm just broken. I've been on Earth too long, and the waters of Skar are rejecting me." This thought turns my embarrassment to sadness.

She stops suddenly. "The warlock? Holy shit, you called him *Xavier*." She looks around like he might suddenly appear. "He's scary as fuck. Have you seen him? It's freaky that you can't see what he looks like.

"He didn't seem to mind me calling him Xavier. Should I have called him something else? And I know what he looks like. He had to get rid of the fog when he was showing me how to work the hologram emitters."

She gapes at me like I told her aliens exist… well, you know what I mean. "Everyone calls him Warlock. I've only ever heard the boss men call him by his name. And I can't believe you saw him. Warlocks only ever show themselves to their family or their mates. Or maybe their harem? I've never had the pleasure of being in one."

A hint of jealousy spikes through me at the thought of Xavier using a harem to feed. Dylan had mentioned that before, but he had also just dumped a whole heap of information on me, so this is the first time I've really thought about it since. What does that bite of jealousy mean? How can I be wishing it was me being the one to feed him instead of his harem when I've just mated a wonderful man beast? Fuck, this Skarrian thing is tricky. I feel guilty for having all these thoughts, but I bet Eric would be crowing and encouraging me to tap that.

I shake off my thoughts and go back to the important issues. "But how do they have sex before they're mated if they don't take solid form?"

She shrugs and smirks. "Girl, you and I are going to get along just fine if your mind goes straight to the important questions."

I smirk back. "Well, those are the kind of things any red-blooded woman needs to know." The pod comes to a stop, and she drags me in the direction of what looks like a shopping mall, giving me no chance to even take my own step. There are shops on either side of the wide open space.

"This is the place to get everything you need, though we can order online from the GIN." I raise my eyebrows in question. "It's our version of the internet. It stands for Galaxy Information Network. We have the equivalent of an Earth postal box on all of the planets the circus visits, and if we receive any packages or mail after we've moved on, they have the schedule and will send those items to our next stop. The only one that doesn't is Earth. We get a post shuttle from Skar when we're here." She gestures to a shop with cute outfits in the window; there's everything from Earth-style clothes to really strange outfits unlike anything I've seen before. "This is Infinity Beyond. They have the best range of casual clothes and will have things that you'll need to fit in on different planets. Like when we visit Rilu, the surface is extremely hot and dry, so there's an appropriate outfit for there."

My eyes are stuck on one outfit in particular. It looks like it's fur, but it's shaggier than anything I've ever seen before. It's a full-length coat, and it's paired with equally shaggy knee-high boots and a hat that looks like a furry hunter's cap with ear flaps. A pair of aviator goggles finishes off the look. All of it is a pale blue, like the color of an iceberg.

"Cool, huh? That's for when we go to Iceeen. It's freezing there, like nipple freezing. I always find myself someone to snuggle up with when we're there too, if you know what I mean." She gives me a cheeky wink. I know exactly what she means. "The lightning cats we have with the show have their own big suite, and it's apparently kept at a lower temperature than everywhere else on the ship. I've never seen it because that Natalia is a raving bitch and won't let anyone near the rest of them, but rumor has it that their room is all frost and snow. Anyway, let's go and get an Achom! It's hot and yummy and will give you a burst of energy. It's made from the anal secretions of the Silax worm, but don't let that fool you!"

I must turn slightly green at the description because she just laughs again and drags me along to a café where we take a seat.

"Trust me. It tastes like a blend of Earth coffee and chocolate but has a kick to it like there's a dash of chili and vodka."

She orders two on a screen built into the table, and

within a minute or two, a hatch opens in the middle and they rise up out of it.

"What do we do for money? I didn't think to ask the grandpas about it because I haven't needed it up until now." I start to panic, the thought of how dependent I am hitting me for the first time. I hate not having a way to take care of myself, but I've been a bit distracted up until this point. "I haven't got any. How am I going to pay for this?"

Her hand on mine, she gives me a gentle squeeze and a smile. "Relax. Everything like food and drink is included. As for shopping, well, we all get paid a wage, and I can't imagine you would be any different. The boss men have probably added you to their account too. All the information should be available through that." She points to the watch on my wrist.

My panic ebbs, and I make a note to talk to the grandpas about it. "Okay, thanks. It's all just a lot, you know?" I take a cautious sip of my drink, and wow, it's amazing, like a mocha with a kick. "Finding out about all of this, and then learning I'm not even from Earth and now the mating on top of that." The words just slip out of my mouth, and it's only when I see her reaction that I stop and think about what I said.

"You're mated? Holy fuck! When did that happen? Who is it? Was it good?" She fires the questions at me without giving me a chance to answer. "Didn't you know about the five tries before you buy rule? How have you managed to have sex with someone five times while I haven't even been able to grab a meet with you?"

"Ah yeah, I did, but it sort of just happened. His beast kind of took over and forced the mating. I know how that sounds, trust me, but honestly, I'm not upset. I mean, I *was*, but when I thought about it, I realized I'm actually really excited. Let's face it, he's sexy as fuck, has mad dick skills, and he's sweet and kind and loving. I could end up with a lot worse." I'm rambling slightly, but it doesn't seem to matter to her. My brain and maybe even those first stirrings in my heart are almost desperate for her to not judge Caspian. The situation is complicated and doesn't look the best from the outside, but I've already seen such good signs of the man that he is. I want to know more, and all these little glimpses have just confirmed that he and I could be good together. I have a lot to learn, but he seems like he will be ready and willing to give me things that I need and haven't found yet in my other relationships.

"Oh my god, a beast means it's a shifter. Which shifter? I saw you with Dylan and Caspian the first night, and gossip around the ship says that you'd been hanging out until you had a falling out." Movement behind her catches my eye, and I look around the little café for the first time. It's set up mostly like an Earth business would be, minus the servers because everything happens automatically. But there's a cozy little fire toward the back of the shop, probably for ambience because the ship's not cold or anything. Surrounding the fire are heaps of cozy-looking double pods, like mostly enclosed booths. Sitting in one of these pods is Dylan and another guy, the two of them in some kind of intimate conversation. I'm happy for him; he looks like he's flirting with the guy, so he must like him. He glances up, catching my eye, but he only returns my wave with one of those impersonal bro nods.

Ouch, that hurts. Seeing my face drop, Mags turns around. "Oh, look at that. Dylan the manwhore is on the prowl." She turns back to me, rolling her eyes. "Don't get me wrong, he's a great guy, but wow, he knows how to love them and leave them. He changes his partners like he changes his moods."

Huh, maybe I misjudged him altogether. He was the first friendly face I saw, and I latched on to him like the new girl at school. I guess that friendship wasn't as genuine as I thought, but I can't imagine what I did to piss him off.

I decide to let it go. Although I thought we'd be good friends, he has no reason to be pissed at me about anything. I'm sad, but not heartbroken about it. I just hope he doesn't cause problems for Caspian. Caspian's family now, and nobody fucks with my family. According to the grandpas, anyone who messes with my mate can easily find themselves replaced.

My watch beeps, and I look at the message flashing across the screen. I've got twenty minutes until I'm supposed to meet Caspian at the Aquilian pool.

"Hey, Mags, this has been fun and I definitely want to do it again, but I need to meet Caspian. Can you show me the way to the Aquilian pool?"

She jumps up. "Of course, let's go to the elevators. It's up a floor." She takes off, and I hurry after her, not wanting to get lost. "Is it Caspian who's your mate?"

she asks in an excited voice once I catch up and the two of us are heading up in the elevator.

"Ah, yeah."

She grabs hold of my hand and squeals in excitement. "Wow, that's awesome. You'll have to tell me all about it. What was the mating like? Do you remember every blissful second of it?"

I blush a little at the memory. "No, not really, my mind was pretty much mush."

"Oh! Do tell?" she asks, curiosity in her eyes.

"The man has mad fucking sex skills. I swear I've never been dicked so well in my life. I didn't know those kinds of orgasms were possible. Seriously, it's no hardship to have those for the rest of my life."

Her mouth drops open in shock before we both dissolve into peals of laughter just as the doors open, showing a room filled with water.

"Holy shit." The giggles disappear as I take in the sight in front of me. There is a section just in front of the elevator to step out onto, and from what I can see, it runs the rims of the walls. Apart from that, the whole room is like an ocean with a few houses floating as their own islands. "How does this work? How does the water not go everywhere if there's space turbulence or whatever?"

"There's a special gravity field that holds all the water down while allowing bodies to pass through it." She looks around the pool. "I thought that maybe Nixie would be here. Unlike most mermaids, she's friendly with other races. She regularly takes her human form and comes hang out, but I can't see her."

Right now, the water is still, not a ripple to be seen. "It looks like they're all gone. I'm going to leave you here since Caspian should be here any minute. I'll catch up with you at dinner. I want to hear all about what it was like to meet his beast." She leans in and gives me a kiss on the cheek before stepping back into the elevator.

Once she's gone and I'm all alone, I realize how quiet the room is too. No lapping sounds because the water is so still. There's no wind or anything because of the artificial environment.

Stepping up to the edge of the pool, I toe off one of my shoes and dip my foot into the water. It's warm and balmy, like a tropical beach, and I pull off the rest of my clothes, so I can go for a swim. I told Caspian I didn't have a swimsuit with me, and he suggested I swim naked. I wasn't keen on that, knowing that other creatures live in this area, so we compromised. Underwear, it is.

Sitting down on the edge, I swing my legs into the pool, but before I can do anything else, there's a frenzy of motion and something launches itself out of the water. I have just enough time to suck in a lungful of air before I'm dragged under.

Fuck my life.

CHAPTER TWENTY TWO

Whatever it is drags me through the water so fast there's nothing I can do but close my eyes, hold my breath, and hang on. The noise of the water rushing by my ears is thunderous and shocking after the calm quiet of the topside.

My lungs start to burn as the urge to expel the breath I was holding increases. I start to pound against the scaly creature's body, desperate to get away, my self-preservation having kicked in. Suddenly, we stop, and before I can open my eyes and continue my fight, something closes over my mouth, drawing the trapped air from my lungs before forcing in fresh air. When my eyes pop open, I find myself wrapped in the arms of a merman.

My hair swirls around my face, making it difficult for me to see him in the dim light of the depths, so I try to push it out of the way. His body is glowing, that slight light illuminating the area, and as my eyes reach his face, I recoil in fright. His pale golden eyes are narrowed, his razor-sharp teeth bared in aggression, and his gills are rapidly opening and closing like he's breathing harder than normal.

His own long hair floats around his face, metallic gold like Nixie's was. Is this her brother? Looking down, I can see his long, thick muscular tail beating back and forth to keep us afloat. It's covered in pastel green and shimmering gold scales that stop just above his pelvis, giving way to pastel green skin. Or I thought that it was skin, but it seems like it might be another layer of scales, these ones so itty bitty that it almost looks like they'd lay flat to the touch. Maybe protection against predators?

As we stare at one another, my lungs start to hurt enough that I beat against his chest once more. With a lazy flip of his tail, we head upward, the pressure on my ears easing as we get higher. Fuck, I hope I don't get decompression sickness. Our ascent is much slower than our descent, with him stopping more than once to fuse his mouth to mine, forcing in a new burst of oxygen. The last time, however, he lingers, locking those cold, aloof eyes to mine. Honestly, I have no idea what he wants from me. I guess he doesn't want to drown me, thank god for that, but I'm otherwise clueless.

Pulling away, he continues toward the surface, not paying any attention to me. I look around, not really able to see now that we're moving again, but I recognize that we're swimming into a tunnel that leads out into some kind of room. It's hard to make out what

I'm seeing, but I think it's furnished, or as furnished as it can be for a merperson. Not soon enough, we get to a ramp and swim up it until we break the surface. He pushes me up onto a small platform before he joins me, his body towering over mine while his large fin sits half in the water and half out.

"Who are you, and what are you doing in my pool?" he growls, his teeth still sharp and aggressive.

"Fuck you!" I slap at him before trying to scoot backward, but he holds me in place.

"You were with the boss men the other day before the parade. Who are you, and why are you in my pool?" he repeats, shaking me.

"She's Lila, you asshole, and the boss men are her grandpas. So kindly take your fucking hands off my mate, Nikos." Caspian's voice comes from off to the side, and when I turn, I find him in front of the platform but still in the water. His tentacles shoot out of the water, wrapping around Nikos and dragging him backward. Unfortunately, with Nikos still having a hold on me, I get pulled along with him.

"Caspian, stop, please!" The scream escapes my mouth, and Caspian immediately stops what he's doing just before we go tumbling into the water. Nikos loosens his grip and moves back, holding up his hands in surrender while looking contrite.

"Caspian, my apologies. I had no idea that you had taken a mate." I slap at his hands, noticing that they're a little too close to my breasts. "I just saw a stranger in my pool, and I reacted."

"You didn't even stop to ask!" I growl at the

merman as he flops his way back into the pool, leaving me on the ramp.

"Why did you bring her to your home?" Caspian growls as he swims closer to the ramp, one of his tentacles shooting up to wrap around my ankle, caressing it.

Nikos' eyes widen in surprise as I giggle when the tentacle strokes my skin. "Well, I figured anyone who was stupid enough to swim in my pool was offering themselves to me. It's been a long time since I had a chance to be with a woman of another race. Could you blame me for making the assumption?" He looks embarrassed now, and I feel a little bad for the guy.

Caspian grows in size, just enough to give him a more looming presence, and wraps a tentacle around Nikos' waist before picking him up and throwing him across the room. "You idiot! You must invite women to have sex with you these days. Kidnapping and ravishing is no longer appropriate," he shouts as the merman splashes down into the water.

Kidnapping and ravishing. Damn, doesn't sound too bad to me. I squirm slightly with the thought. Caspian's eyes shoot to me, and they widen in surprise as he breathes deeply, a small grin crossing his face. His tentacle around my ankle drags me toward him, but this time I allow myself to go. I drop down into the water, and he drags me close to his body, wrapping his arms around me. "You are a curious, lusty wench, aren't you?" he whispers to me as he nuzzles into my neck. "Well, your merman curiosity is going to have to wait until another day. We have to introduce you to my beast. It's all I can do to hold him back at the moment, and we also need to see if you can shift."

Nikos is silently brooding from where Caspian threw him, but there's curiosity on his face as he watches my and Caspian's easy affection.

"I'm going to have to take you back through the tunnel to give ourselves more room. Close your eyes underwater since I'll be going fast." He shifts me onto his back, placing my arms around his neck. One of his tentacles wraps around my waist, anchoring me to him, and with a wave to the silent sulky merman, I take a deep breath before my mate plunges under the water.

He shoots through the water at a rapid pace. When we get to the end of the tunnel, he moves toward the surface so I don't have to worry about breathing. Very quickly, we breach the surface, and I gulp in another breath of air as he swims us to an open platform with large sun lamps sitting over it. He helps me onto it, his tentacles caressing my ass as I climb, and a snort escapes. Playful, flirty Caspian might be my favorite Caspian so far.

"The mermaids need sun to keep their scales in pristine condition in both their mer form and their animal form. They use this platform for sunbathing."

The lamps aren't on at the moment, but he sees me looking at them. "They come on at a certain time, but you wouldn't be able to sit under them anyway. The sun from their planet is a lot hotter than the one from Earth. It's why the water in the pool is warmer too."

His tentacles slip away, but he stays half out of the water. "Okay, the shifting process is very easy. Or it should be. When we mated, it should have added the shift gene to your DNA. Once you see my beast, all you have to do is picture yourself doing the same thing and will it to happen."

I can't help but roll my eyes. It feels a little like when someone who can actually draw tries to explain something to the artistically challenged. Yeah, it's simple if you've actually got the talent. Otherwise, you wind up with a stick figure who looks vaguely suicidal. "Sure, sounds easy," I say back, but his narrowed eyes tell me the sarcasm is coming through loud and clear.

"Careful, baby. Naughty girls get spanked if they push their boundaries." I squirm at the thought of Caspian spanking me. *Yes, please! Sign me up.*

He chuckles, but there's heat in his eyes too. He *did* say something about fuck me pheromones, so it's not like this is my fault. "Concentrate, Lila, I can't hold my beast back any longer, sorry." And with that, his eyes change, and in the same flash of magic that I saw when he transitioned into half-form, his whole body follows suit.

When the flash of magic clears, my mouth drops open. Caspian has tripled in size, and although he's similar to an octopus, he's got a large mouth full of razor-sharp teeth. How do I know, you might ask? Well, his beast is apparently so excited to see me that he lets out a platform-shaking roar, showing off those deadly beauties.

When he finishes roaring, his tentacles shoot out and wrap around me, dragging me into the water. My heart races as he lifts me up, pulling me close until he's nuzzling my whole body. Little purring sounds start to vibrate from him when he gets to my belly, and all I can do is stroke his big head as he coos and chirps and strokes me. It's actually kind of relaxing, and I find myself beginning to doze off until he decides to put me back on the platform

He waves his tentacle at me as if to say "your turn." Oh crap, he wants me to try and shift. The big lug is just so excited that I know I can't disappoint him by refusing to try. Okay, I gather an image of what he looks like in my mind, making sure I have the right amount of tentacles, then I will it to happen. I swear I must look like I'm constipated or something because the beast starts to make a funny sound, kind of chuffing like he's laughing at me. I flip him off but try not to push so hard, thinking that maybe it should be more natural. There's a tingling all over, and whoosh, that flash of magic happens to me.

I can feel my body rearranging itself; it's the weirdest sensation ever, but it doesn't hurt, and before I know it, I unbalance and tip over, slamming to the ground. Looking down, I have managed a half shift. My clothes are gone, and I'm naked from the waist up, my skin a lighter version of Caspian's mottled blue and purple. From the waist down, I'm a mess of writhing tentacles. Holy crap. Why didn't I shift all the way? I swear I had a picture of the beast in my mind. Damn it!

Using my tentacles, I lift myself upright. They kind of work like legs in the sense that you don't even have to think about making them move, they just do. I shift myself toward the edge of the platform but hesitate before I drop off. How am I going to breathe underwater? Does it just happen?

Even Caspian's beast must understand the indecision I'm feeling because he shifts back to half-form and swims over to me. "Look at my pretty mate, all those beautiful tentacles," he crows as he takes me in. "Come swim with me, baby." He holds out a hand, but I still hesitate.

"Why didn't I shift into a beast? That's what I was aiming for." He shrugs, that same pleased expression still on his face. I guess he and his beast don't mind which form I can take so long as I can come swimming with them.

"I'm not sure, but maybe it's for the best. Quite often, the female kraken likes to eat their mates, so I'm more than glad for you to not get that beastly instinct. We can try again another time."

"How do you breathe underwater?" I ask him, not seeing the gill slits until he turns and angles his neck for me.

"They only appear once you get in the water. Come on, yours should do the same." I slide gracefully into the water, at least as gracefully as I can, and my tentacles instinctively propel me toward my mate. Once I get to him, they automatically tangle with his, wrapping us together. His arms do the same, and before I know it, his mouth is on mine and he's kissing me like I'm the very air he breathes.

Moaning, I pull back as the sweet taste of Caspian floods my mouth. "Oh my god! You really can taste through your tentacles." He chuckles. I try to fuse my mouth back to his, keen to continue what we're doing, but he pulls away and grabs my hand.

"Come on, let's swim."

He drags me under the water, giving me no choice but to go with it. He's stronger and bigger than me in this form. Closing my eyes, I let him pull me along, holding my breath for as long as I can until I eventually need to take in more oxygen. I start to panic and pull against him, but he must have known this would happen. Instead of feeding into my anxiety, he just wraps everything around me and we hold still.

"Breathe, baby." Caspian's voice is suddenly in my head, shocking me, and the air explodes out of me. I struggle to get away, but he holds me tight. Eventually, I stop struggling and accept my fate. The minute I take a breath in, water floods my lungs, but I don't drown. The tight feeling in my chest disappears, and oxygen inflates them. It becomes an automatic response, and my body relaxes in his arms.

"That's my good girl," he coos in my head, and my eyes shoot to his face. It's only then that I notice I can see everything clearly.

"I can see you!" I project back, hoping it works, and it must because a wide grin crosses his face.

"Yes, we have a special lens that flicks down over our eyes, protecting them and making it so you can see. Are you ready to swim now?" he asks gently, but I can tell he's eager to get moving.

"Lead the way," I tell him, and with a rush of water, he darts off toward the bottom of the tank. I can't

believe that it's this deep, and my eyes can't stop darting around as I follow him. This spaceship keeps surprising me. There's even a coral reef with fish swimming amongst it. No species that I recognize, so I stop and watch them. There's so much to see, and I don't know where to look.

In fact, I'm so distracted that I don't see the approaching monster until it's practically on top of me. Teeth like a shark, I can't make out anything else as it comes closer and closer. My fear response takes over, and my tentacles act on their own, squirting purple ink at the monster just as it's tackled from the side. It tumbles away into the murky ink, and I take my chance to escape, propelling myself to the surface as fast as I can. With a burst of speed that has to be thanks to this new form, I launch my body out of the water and onto the platform. My heart races and my chest heaves as I gasp for air.

What the fuck!

CHAPTER TWENTY THREE

I'm still trying to catch the breath in my lungs when a commotion breaks the surface. I can hear Caspian and Nikos arguing, but it's in another language that I don't understand. Shit, did my translator crap out because of the water pressure?

They both swim over to me, and Nikos has a contrite pout on his face until he looks up, his eyes glued to my chest. Yep, I'm definitely doing my best impression of one of those heaving bosom ladies from a tawdry romance book cover. Exposed nipples and all. I guess that's enough to draw anyone's attention. Noticing where he's looking, Caspian smacks him in the back of the head. "I know my mate's breasts are distracting, but don't you have something to say to her?"

A flow of words comes out of his mouth even though his eyes stay on my breasts, but I hold my hand up.

"Wait. I can't understand him. Something must be wrong with my translator."

"He said that he is sorry. He forgot to warn his pet about you, and she was just protecting the pool."

"His pet?" I know I sound skeptical, but sure enough a head pops up next to Nikos. The razor-sharp teeth are hidden behind a closed mouth. Its head looks similar to a turtle, but when it flips a tail, I know I've gotten it wrong. It thrusts its tail again and launches out of the water. The thing that lands on the platform next to me looks like a cross between a seal and a turtle. It has a small turtle-like head with a longish neck that sits on a wide seal-like body. Its skin looks like the shell of a turtle, but it's colored with camouflage-type blues and grays. Nikos' pet flops its way over to me and gently nuzzles his head against the hand I held up, my heart melting when it makes little grunting noises as I scratch its hard surface.

Another flow of words comes from Nikos, and I look to Caspian to translate. "Sweetpea says she's very sorry for scaring you and would like to be your friend. She says you're welcome to come and swim whenever you want." Caspian frowns and looks at Nikos as another torrent of words comes out.

"Of course my mate can come swim! You can just get over it. What? Since when did you want to find a non-Aquilian mate? I don't know if she will bring any friends. She's only just arrived; she hasn't met many people yet."

"Oh, I met Magenta today." Nikos shudders visibly,

as does Caspian. I gesture to them both. "What's all that about?'

"Mags is nice enough, but she really is a maneater. She chews them up and spits them out. Commitment is *not* in her wheelhouse."

Huh, guess it's kind of ironic that she called Dylan a manwhore then. Must take one to know one.

"That's the only other female that has been nice to me, apart from Nixie, kind of, but she's your sister, so that's out." I pause. "That *is* out, isn't it? Or do some aliens have different thoughts on sibling relationships?"

Again, they both shudder. "Fuck yes. Definitely out," Caspian confirms.

"Well then, I'm sorry I can't help him." Nikos' pout becomes more pronounced, but it has a twist of disappointment this time. He doesn't even say goodbye before he disappears below.

"Come on, don't worry about him. I'll show you how to shift back, then we can get Doc to have a look at your implant." My heart skips a beat at the mention of Link, and Caspian gives me a knowing wink. "Maybe we should invite him to dinner."

I feel a little guilty as I make my way back over to the edge and slide into the water. "You would be okay with that?" I swim up to my mate and wrap my arms around him, feeling like I need a little close contact right now.

He leans in and kisses me gently. "Of course, baby, anything you want."

We swim back to the elevator entrance holding

hands, and when we climb out, he shows me how to change back.

It's hard to ignore the fact that I'm completely naked when I shift back. Especially when Caspian sidles up to me, now back on two legs himself, his erect cock sliding between the gap in my legs to rub deliciously against my pussy lips. "It's the magic. Better to shift with no clothes on because they always disappear." His mouth meets mine, but just when I think it's about to get interesting, he pulls away. He moves to a nearby bag on the ground and pulls out two large towels, returning to me and wrapping it around me. "As much as I'd like to continue this, we should get that translator checked out, and I don't want everyone ogling my mate on the way."

I grab the ends and pull them closed around me as he wraps the other towel around his waist. My skin has returned to its normal peachy complexion, but Caspian has stayed mottled blue and purple. He shoves the rest of my clothes and my shoes into the bag and throws it over his shoulder. Grabbing my hand, we head to the elevator and get on the way to see Link.

"I'm never going to remember how to get anywhere," I complain to Caspian, lost as to how we're getting here.

"Your watch has a built-in GPS," he tells me, grabbing it out of the bag and helping me put it on my wrist. "You just have to type in where you want to go, and it will give you verbal directions. You can also pull up a map of the ship and zoom in and out to find things."

He pulls me into his arms and kisses me again. It's like we can't keep our hands off one another; I've never experienced something like this before, but I love it. "And if you ever truly get stuck, all you have to do is call me and I will come and find you." He's so freaking sweet. Who would have guessed that aggressive, angry man from the first week would be such a fucking sweetheart?

We're giggling as we make our way into Doc's waiting room. Stopping at the desk, we wait for the nurse to acknowledge us, Caspian kissing me in between giggles as he takes his sweet time.

He still hasn't acknowledged us even though there is no one else in the room when the dividing door swings open and Link pops his head out. "I thought I heard you, Lila." He smiles and gestures for us to come in. That's when Nurse Ratched decides to come to life. "But Dr. Tesla, you have an appointment in five minutes." Link looks around the room.

"Well, they're not here, and these two are. They can wait," he tells him, and he scowls.

He and Caspian are talking as they walk into the exam room, so both miss the evil glare he gives me. What the fuck is his problem? I flip him off, not willing to play nice if he doesn't want to, and let the door slam behind me.

"Caspian says your translator is malfunctioning after your swim. How about you hop up onto the bed so I can fix it for you." Link pats the examination bed again, so I climb up on it. Caspian comes over and gives me a kiss.

"I'm going to arrange some dinner in our room," he tells me before turning to Link. "Doc, why don't you join us?"

"That would be nice, thank you. I'd love to." Despite his initial surprise, he seems genuinely pleased by the offer.

Link goes over to a cupboard, and Caspian quickly whispers in my ear. "Have fun, baby. Maybe Link can take care of the frustration you're feeling now." He winks then quickly departs before I can react, leaving me with my mouth dropping open.

Did he just rev me up on the way here so that he could let another man take care of it for me? *Best mate ever.* I squeeze my legs tightly together under my towel, trying to relieve some of the pressure.

Link moves back over to me, placing that same tray down. Once again, he pushes my thighs apart and tries to slip between them, but my giant towel stops him. He looks down at it, a frown crossing his brow, before looking back at me. The shimmer on his skin seems to be brighter today, and there's a slight glow to his eyes. I can't say that I ever read many books about cyborgs before, but I'm itching to update my library now.

"Lila, I have updated my files with all the information regarding kraken breeding. I would like to make sure that everything is okay if that's alright with you."

"Yeah, that's fine. What do I need to do?"

"Well, I'd like to scan your body again with my new

program. It might be better if you remove the towel and lie down."

Lay down in front of the doctor naked? Yes, please. Dropping my towel, I shift my body to lay down on the table, but as I move my shoulders, Link's hand clamps down on one. "That mark… *Your* mark is on my shoulder." He turns around and looks at my other shoulder, adding, "And mine is on yours."

I shrug, trying to play it as cool as I can while the hot doctor notices just how attractive I find him. "Yes, isn't that how it works for my race? That's what the grandpas told me at least." He nods, quickly letting me go and allowing me to move.

"Yes, Lila, it does, but it's never happened to *me* before. The attraction has never been mutual, so marks have never appeared." He sounds amazed, his normally very factual voice full of wonder.

I settle myself on the bed, and it's in that moment he realizes that I'm entirely naked. He unashamedly peruses my body, his eyes full of a longing heat that's anything but clinical. Shaking his head, the desire disappears as quickly as it appeared, and he's all professional once more.

"Okay, Lila, I'm just going to scan your body. I will stop when I get to the eggs to make sure everything is okay, and then I will go back to the translator to find out what's wrong with that." He explains it all very matter-of-factly, and after all the new information I've had to process, I really appreciate his straightforward way of speaking.

True to his word, he pauses at my stomach, but

then he starts doing something unexpected. Softly, his hands touch me, palpating my lower abdomen, though I don't know what he's looking for. His lips purse at whatever he sees or feels, and my heartbeat increases. Is something wrong?

"It's okay, Lila. Just breathe in and out, everything is fine. There are three healthy, viable eggs in there, and they all have a heartbeat even when they're in stasis. But they are giving off a hormone that is going to make you…" He breaks off like he's not sure how to tell me.

Oh, I'll help him out any time. "Horny, right?"

"Yes, exactly, and you seem to have a high libido anyway. This is going to make it worse."

"It's okay, Link. Caspian explained it all to me. I'm going to give off fuck me vibes. Maybe that's why my mark appeared on you." I can't help the disappointment that's in my voice, and I look away from the gorgeous cyborg. I don't want hormones to have manipulated this man into liking me.

"The marks appeared *before* you were pregnant, Lila. Don't worry about that," he assures me quietly, and when I look up, his eyes have changed back to showing me what he really wants.

"Would you like me to take care of the need now before we continue with the translator? You may be more comfortable, and I heard your mate say that it was okay." He makes the offer just as he explained the steps of his examination. If I couldn't see the truth in his eyes, I might think this was some kind of treatment, simply the concern of a medical professional wanting his patient to be comfortable, but those eyes don't lie.

Well shit, since Caspian gave the go ahead and the Doc is offering so politely... "That would be great, thank you," I answer just as politely even though all I want to do is mount him and ride him like a pony. Save a horse, ride a cyborg!

With a smirk, he walks around to the end of the bed where my feet are. He wraps his hands around my ankles and gently pulls. I slide down the bed until my knees are hanging over the edge, my aching pussy in easy reach. He bends down, his silver hair flopping over his forehead, and sticks out his tongue, running it through my folds.

A moan slips out of my mouth before I can help it. God, I can appreciate a man who goes straight to what he wants.

"You better muffle that noise if you don't want the nurse to stop us again," he cautions, so I grab the pillow from behind me and put it over my face. I'd much rather watch him eat me out, but there's no way I'm going to risk having him stop again.

Unlike the rest of his body, Link's tongue is hot. As it licks a path from my entrance to my clit, I grab his hair without thinking, pulling at the strands.

"Fuck, Link, yes." Thanks to the pillow, my voice is muffled, but he shushes me again.

"Lila, I'll stop," he warns, his voice rumbling against my core. I grit my teeth, not allowing the noises I want to make escape.

He licks and sucks before dragging two fingers

through my lips, swirling them into my wet heat, his tongue skillfully teasing my swollen flesh, before plunging them deep into my swollen pussy. I whimper with pleasure, wanting to be unmuzzled and unfiltered like I normally am. Some girls like to do that quiet thing, and that's great for them, but I'd much rather let it all out. He curves his fingers slightly so that he hits my g-spot with every thrust, and he has me writhing on the bed within minutes. The rising pleasure has my toes curling and my muscles locking up with delicious tension. He skillfully keeps me on the edge for what feels like hours but is probably only minutes. Tears leak from my eyes as my nerves are plundered by exquisite sensation. My chest heaves from exertion, but my ability to receive air is restricted by the pillow over my face. This kind of sensory deprivation only sends my pleasure shooting higher. The thought that anybody could be in the room watching what Link does to me is titillating to the extreme.

I beg him quietly, "Please, Link, I need it."

"Tell me what you need, Lila," he orders quietly but firmly, slowing his thrusting fingers. Another sob escapes my mouth.

"I need to come," I plead, forcing the words past the pillow.

"Good girl," he praises me, and when he does, something happens to his tongue and fingers. They both start to vibrate, and his thrusting speeds up until it's just what I need to tip me over the edge. I can't help myself. I throw my pillow back and scream.

"Fuck!"

CHAPTER TWENTY FOUR

When he comes running into the room to find me, legs splayed and the doc grinning with satisfaction between them, the look on Nurse Ratched's face is priceless. Seriously, Doc has his own crazy skills, and if the pleasure bots are anything like that, it's no wonder Pleasure Bot Industries are one of the richest companies in the galaxy.

After my orgasm, he helps me into a spare pair of scrubs, placing kisses across my shoulder in between telling me what a good girl I was for him. Fuck me, I like this good girl shit. It makes me tingle, but it also makes me feel proud that I pleased him. What's with that?

The horny edge I'd been riding all day has finally eased, and Link runs a diagnostic of my translator. "I set it for Skarrian parameters, and I need to adjust it to cope with being a shifter. Not to mention if you're going to swim in higher pressure atmospheres." He holds up the same thing he used to implant it, but this time it just hovers over the injection site, beeping a few times before it stops

"All done. You should be good now. But if for any reason you end up with other mates who have unusual abilities, I can adjust it for you again."

I jump down from the bed and grab his hand. "Right now, I don't want to talk about potential fictional mates. I'd really like to get to know *you* better. Come on, let's go to dinner."

I drag him out of the medical room, stopping at a frowning Nurse Ratched.

"Link will be off for the rest of the night. Only call him if it's an emergency," I tell him, and he crosses his arms.

"Who died and made you the boss?" he snaps out.

"Well, they haven't died, but her grandpas make her the boss," Link answers for me, and he screws up his face in annoyance.

"That doesn't make her in charge yet." He's determined to fight us on it so I lift my watch and scroll down to William's name, pressing the screen.

"Hi, Lila, how was your swim?" he asks me when he answers.

"It was great, but it messed up my translator. I had the doc fix it, and I'd love to take him to dinner, but his nurse has objections." I smile as said nurse's face pales.

"Well, why is he objecting? You're the boss; you can do what you want." His face pales even more when William's annoyance practically leaks through the communicator.

"I'm not sure that everyone got that memo," I reply wryly.

"Josa, if Lila says Link is taking the night off, then he's taking the damn night off." His voice projects loudly enough for everyone to hear him.

"Of course, sir. I was just worried about what to do if we had an emergency."

"Well, you just call him if you do. Damn man works too freaking hard anyway," he grumbles mostly to himself.

"Have a good night, Lila. We'll see you in the morning for power training again." William hangs up, and we leave Josa quietly fuming.

Link holds my hand all the way back to my room as we ask each other typical first date type questions: family, favorite foods, those kinds of things. I'm dying to ask him more, so much more, but I think those are more like second date questions. I'm also dying to repay the favor from before. My mouth practically waters at the thought of having this man at my mercy, but I have a feeling it might be the other way around. He seems to take pleasure very seriously.

We're still laughing when we get to my room. I push open the door, but I freeze at what I find, my heart sinking to my stomach. Dylan has his arms wrapped around Caspian, and their mouths are fused together.

A sob escapes before I can stop it, and Link's arm immediately wraps around my shoulder as Caspian pushes Dylan away.

"You heard her fucking coming. You planned that,

you cunt," he growls in a voice I haven't heard before. It's not just angry. This is full-on fury. He turns to me.

"I swear, Lila, that was all him. We'd simply been talking, but we could hear the two of you coming down the hallway. Just as you pushed open the door, he lunged at me." Caspian steps toward me and pulls me out of Link's arms. "I swear I would never do something like that to you."

"Did you tell her about us?" Dylan sneers, flopping down on the nearby couch and gesturing between him and Caspian. "Did you tell her we were a thing?"

Hurt stabs at my heart. I'm not stupid; I know that he would have had lovers before me, but I would have thought he would have told me that Dylan was one of them.

Caspian sneers right back at him, the tiniest hint of black creeping into the edges of his iris. "Please, once or twice when I was horny. It was a mutually beneficial arrangement, and you knew it could never become anything. You knew my beast wouldn't allow it to be something real, and it hasn't happened for a while now."

"But I love you!" Dylan yells, bolting up from the couch, and both Link and Caspian snort.

"You sure proved that love by having sexual relations with most people on the ship. Only a few of us said no, and you obsessed about the ones who denied you. I can't even begin to tell you how many times he's propositioned me. It's like it was a challenge that he just had to win. Like that Earth game... What's it called? Pokemon! He had to catch them all." There's no snark in Link's words, just honesty, and that's what makes me believe him. It doesn't sound like he's trying to hurt Dylan. He's sharing his experience as objectively as possible.

Whoa, this just got all soap opera-like. Hello, Jerry Springer. Ready to give me a spot on your show now? I'll take surprise alien egg babies and raise you a slutty dragon with boundary issues! I could sign a multi-episode contract with all the shit that's going on.

"I can't believe you mated her." He looks me up and down in disgust. Gone is the kind, friendly guy that I had been getting to know, replaced with this vicious, jealous twat. "She's nothing, barely even a Skarrian. No powers or anything."

"Skarrian enough to get mating marks, seal that bond, and carry his eggs. How's that for being *nothing*?" I know I'm throwing it in his face, but I've about hit my limit. Tonight was supposed to be relaxing, an opportunity for me to get to know my mate and learn more about another potential partner. I did not sign up to be looked down on and insulted.

"You're pregnant? You let him implant you? You fucking whore!" He lunges for me, but Link and Caspian jump between us, not letting him near me.

"But why?" I cry, wanting to know the answer. "I thought we were friends!"

"Haven't you heard the saying 'keep your friends close but your enemies closer'?" he screams at me, spittle flying from his mouth.

Holy shit, he's flipped his sanity switch. He's breathing smoke through his nose and vibrating.

"Fuck, he's going to shift," Caspian yells, and Link lunges, grabbing Dylan's shoulder and pinching. Dylan's eyes roll back into his head, and he collapses before he can manage to go full fire-breathing dragon on us.

The guys let him drop to the ground, none too gently, just as the door to my suite slams open and my grandpas run in, followed by two armed security guards.

John wraps me in his arms as Eric and William check out Dylan's prone figure before looking at Caspian and Link.

"This your doing, Doc?" Eric asks, gesturing to the unconscious dragon shifter.

"Yes, he was out of control and almost shifted. In his current emotional state, he would have destroyed Lila's room, not to mention I think he would have eaten her." I'm still a little shocked, so I hear his statement even though the words seem to bounce off of me. I definitely can't handle thinking about being eaten right now. Or ever, really. I mean, is NOT becoming one with someone's digestive tract really that much to ask for?

"What just happened?" I still don't understand.

"Dragons can be a little unstable. The need to breed rides them hard, but like Caspian, they need to be compatible with their partners. So it won't happen until they seal a bond. Though there are others, like Dylan here, who choose promiscuity over permanency. He may claim to have loved Caspian, but that was the man. The beast he carries inside of him knows that

Caspian can't reproduce with him and would have never sealed the bond."

"But wasn't Dylan gay? He would have never found a breeding partner?" I ask, feeling confused.

Everyone snorts. "Dylan fucked anything that could be nailed down," William tells me dryly.

I shiver a little bit as I remember the way he looked at me when he was in my room. I got changed in front of him. Damn, was I wrong. I'll never assume again.

"Gay dragons have options. They will usually find a donor dragoness to give them children. They pay very handsomely for it, and some female dragons use this service to set themselves up before they settle down with their own clutch." Link gently rubs my shoulders as he imparts his up-to-date dragon breeding information. I wonder if he brushed up on all of the species on the ship when he realized his kraken knowledge was lacking; he seems like the type who would.

"So dragons only breed with dragons?" I ask as I take the glass of water from Caspian before he sits on my other side. I'm still trying to ignore the fact that the guy I thought was going to be my new bestie just tried to attack me. Me and my babies. I rub a hand across my little bump for comfort. Noticing what I'm doing, Caspian takes my hand, placing a kiss on it before putting it back on my stomach.

"No, like me, if they choose to mate with another species, the mating bite will change them to make it possible for them to breed. Females will be able to lay eggs and incubate them, while males will be able to impregnate those eggs for females to lay." Caspian leans back, pulling me against his chest, while Link keeps hold of the other hand.

I feel myself relaxing as these two provide me with comfort and some distraction.

"Throw him in one of the cells overnight, make sure it's got shifting restrictions on it. We will let him wake up and calm down, and then we will put him on the next flight home. He has no place here in the circus after an attack on our granddaughter." At William's order, the guards pick Dylan up, dragging him out of the room.

"Caspian, you will have to do your show without him. Lucky we only have one stop after Earth before we take our month-long break. We'll put a call out for new dragons or something else to replace him during that time." John's all business now that the threat is over.

"We will let you get back to your dinner now, but I'm sorry, Lila. I know you liked him and had hoped he would be a friend. Drama comes along with running this circus, but I had hoped you wouldn't discover that fact quite so quickly." Eric is sober and serious for a change, and it's weird to see. But it doesn't last. His cheeky grin spreads across his face. "Let's go and let these lovebirds get back to dinner... or whatever." He winks, waves, and waltzes out of the room. John and William both lean down and give me a kiss on the head before they follow him out, calling back with a promise that they'll see me tomorrow.

Then I'm left with my mate, Link, and a sad, sick feeling.

"I just can't believe he did and said all that. It was like he was invaded by the body snatchers. I feel so betrayed. Did he even like me at all?" I shudder and snuggle into Caspian a little more.

Link clears his throat and drops my hand, standing up. "Let's take a raincheck on dinner. I'll leave you to look after your mate." Before he can step away, Caspian leans forward and grabs Doc's arm.

"Get back down there and hug *our* girl. She needs all the affection she can get." At Caspian's urging, Link sits back down and grabs me, hugging me from behind, his body slightly cooler than the one pressed against my front. It's a nice contrast.

I feel warm, comfortable, and happy despite what has just happened, and all that's left for me to do is sigh as I wonder what tomorrow will bring me.

What a fucking adventure.

THE END FOR NOW

GALAXY CIRCUS GLOSSARY

PLANET ICEEN

Lightning Cats

They are a shifter race that has two forms—a bipedal human form and their cat form. Their bipedal form is humanoid in shape, but they are covered in a soft downy fur except for the front of their torso and genital area. They have sharp teeth, big ears, and long tails in this form. Their animal form is similar to a saber-toothed tiger from Earth. They can shoot lightning from their tails, and it can be used for defense and attack.

They are a matriarchal society and live in family groups called streaks. They have alpha, beta, and omega distinctions, but there is always a female alpha who acts as head of the family.

Alphas have a rut and omegas have a heat. Only alpha and omegas can breed with one another, and betas can only breed with their own designation. There are male and female omegas. Both have breeding capabilities, but male omegas are rare. Most are killed once their designation is discovered to prevent competition with females for coveted positions within the streak.

The planet Iceen is a frozen tundra of caves and outcroppings, and the streaks usually have two dwellings—a cave for their animal form, and a dome-like, insulated glass building which they live in with their streaks.

Maxsim (Alpha Lightning Cat)

The leader of the streak of lightning cats that performs in the circus, despite it being a matriarchal society. Maxsim is a dark aqua blue that ombres out to snowy white in the legs, with black, tribal style markings across shoulders, chest, and arms. He has high cheekbones, cat ears, feline eyes, a tail, and fangs, which are bigger when in animal form, as well as a broad chest and well-defined arms. Fur covers his body when in humanoid form, except for a patch across his chest and down to his groin.

Maxsim keeps the rest of the streak safe from an aggressive Natalia.

Natalia (Beta Lightning Cat)

Only female in the group that performs in the circus. She is heir to her matriarchal streak, but is a beta designation. Natalia has pale blue fur all over, with long black hair, high cheekbones, cat ears, feline eyes, a tail, and fangs. She has small breasts, a slender, toned body, and a lean backside and legs. She has naked patch across her breasts and down to groin.

She wants to form a streak with Maxsim, Trace, Fuse, and Sim, but they are alphas and cannot breed with her. She took her omega sister's place, who was supposed to be the one performing with the circus.

Echo (Omega Lightning Cat)

He is a pure white lightning cat, with a smaller frame than Maxsim's, and built much more delicately. His designation is omega, and he has survived because he comes from a rare streak with a male omega. The streak, with help from the warlocks, protected him while growing up. They hid it, and he presents himself to the world as beta. He wants to form a streak with Maxsim, but not Natalia. She discovered he is an omega and keeps trying to kill him.

Other cats in the group
Trace (Alpha Lightning Cat)
Fuse (Alpha Lightning Cat)
Sim (Alpha Lightning Cat)

Yalani

An abominable snowman type creature with shaggy white and gray fur. They are good at blending into their surroundings. It is a hunter-gatherer species that lives in caves on Iceen. Eight to nine feet tall, they are an aggressive species that will attack if they feel threatened. They live solitary lives unless mated and raising a family.

This planet is the birthplace of the human race. The original humans were exploring Skarrians who crashed on Earth, and because they no longer had access to the magical waters, lost all their supernatural abilities.

Skarrians are mostly polyamorous and have attraction marks that show up on both parties' bodies. If attraction wanes on either side, the marks disappear. Skarrians find themselves bonded to others after five rounds of sex, which requires them to orgasm simultaneously. Skarr is basically a sister planet to Earth in that it is made up of ten different land masses surrounded by pink oceans, but it has different species of plants and animals.

When reproducing, all bonded members of the family must participate to produce a child.

Lila Jenson (Liliana Adams)
Orphaned at a young age, she moved from foster

family to foster family, never really fitting in anywhere, though nothing terrible happened to her. One family put her into gymnastic lessons and self-defense courses to keep her out of trouble. She has no real goal in life, but has always thought there must be something more than working in a bar and having the occasional one-night stand.

She is average height, with a curvy figure, long chestnut hair with turquoise streaks, golden skin, and green eyes.

Lila discovered she has grandparents who are still alive, and they invited her to learn their family business.

Currently, she has shown no signs of having Skarrian powers despite an impressive first showing.

John Adams, William Adams, and Eric Adams

Triplet brothers who appear to be in their late forties, they possess chestnut hair, tall, slender builds, and emerald green eyes.

They have been searching for Liliana, also known as Lila, for years, and are thrilled to have finally found her. They are also the CEOs of the Galaxy Circus and guardians of the power orb.

William has a buzz cut and is gruff.

Eric has long hair, which he wears in a man bun, and is the joker and tease in the family.

John has short, tousled hair and is the kind and loving brother, but he is subject to spirals of depression.

Alina and Marcus Adams (Dec.)

Lila's parents moved to Earth in order to raise her in relative safety, but they were killed in a car accident. Alina had blonde hair and green eyes, and Marcus had brown eyes and the same chestnut hair as the grandpas and Lila.

Magenta

She is a performer in the circus. When on Earth, she uses the circus silks, but on other planets, she uses her levitation powers. Magenta has bright pink hair and pale skin. She is mid height with a slim build and light blue, almost gray, eyes. She has been a lifeline for Lila when it comes to all things alien.

Broderick Potter (Bubby)

Captain of the mothership and Marcus Adams' best friend. He has red hair and a red beard with crystal blue eyes. He's rugged and well-built and thrilled to meet Lila.

Phillip and Fiona

They are Lila's twin cousins, but not on the Adams' side of the family.

Fiona has long, curly red hair, brown eyes, and freckles with a tall, slim build.

Phillip's red hair is cropped short, and he has brown eyes and freckles with a tall, slim build.

They oversee the dinosaur act. The dinosaurs were hand raised in the zoo on Skarr.

Captain Lester

Captain Lester is an alternate captain for the mothership and circus pod. He has an abrasive personality and a voice like he smokes two packs of cigarettes a day.

PLANET EARTH

Susie

She is Lila's best friend, with dark, mahogany skin, melted chocolate colored eyes, and black corkscrew curls. She's a nurse and previously lived with Lila.

Mark

Mark is Susie's boyfriend. He has black hair and blue eyes, and works as an emergency room doctor. Mark is also bi.

PLANET CYBERTRONIA

A technologically advanced planet inhabited by life forms that are half organic, half nanobot technology, allowing them to change their features at will. Reproduction occurs through intercourse, but parents program their respective organic matter with the traits and features they wish their babies to have. Once the baby is born, their source code is imprinted on a microchip, which is then deposited into a secret storage facility for safe keeping.

Pleasure Bot Industries is one of the main sources of employment for Cybertronia. They produce lifelike robots for sexual pleasure and are one of the galaxy's most popular purchases. Pleasure Bots are not like cyborgs, in that they are incapable of thoughts, feelings, or responses that have not been programmed into them.

Link (Cyborg)

Link is the ship doctor for the Galaxy Circus and is one of Lila's boyfriends. His skin tone is peach with a shimmer. He has silver hair and eyes. He is built like a swimmer, with long, lean lines, a tapered waist, and broad shoulders, and he is able to change his body parts at will. Cyborgs can't lie.

Josa Spears (Cyborg Nurse)

Josa is the nurse to Link's doctor, but he was hired by Link's mom to spy on him and the circus. He was promised Link's hand in marriage and a share of the Pleasure Bot Industries fortune if he complied. He has the same shimmery skin tone as Link, with metallic green hair and eyes. He has a slender, feminine frame and a dirty attitude.

PLANET VILAX

Vilax is home to a race of blood drinkers, the sanguinistas. Much like Earth's legend of vampires, this race is strong, fast, and has heightened senses. They can fly, and are very hard to kill. Their bodies will regenerate as long as their body parts are close to one another. To kill them, you need to burn both of their hearts. They are a warrior race and one of the fiercest in the galaxy. Military service is mandatory for all Vilaxians.

Vilax only gets five hours of sunlight a day, so while they are not allergic to the sun, they do prefer the dark. Sanguinistas drink blood because their bodies cannot process their own red blood cells. They have a fated mate called a blood rose, but not everyone finds them. They live in family clans, and blood sharing can be a sexual thing, but with children, it isn't.

Saxon (Sanguinista)

Saxon is part of the aerial troupe in the circus. He has magenta-colored eyes and thick, short black hair that's long enough to run your fingers through. His body is muscular and broad, and he has pale skin and fangs.

Hale (Sanguinista)

He is in the same troupe as Saxon and is Saxon's best friend. He has blond hair, teal eyes, and fangs.

Radella (Sanguinista)

Estrella (Sanguinista)

Velorina (Sanguinista)

Xenos (Sanguinista)

Saxon's brother.

Dante (Sanguinista)

Kavita (Sanguinista)

This is the warlocks' home planet. Warlock powers include, but are not limited to, mind manipulation and control, teleporting, and manifestation. Powerful warlocks have harems to feed from because they are psychic feeders who feed from strong emotions. Weaker warlocks and other creatures make up these harems. Weaker warlocks benefit from it, as they are able to feed off the stronger warlock at the same time and get a temporary boost in power. Members of the harem receive a wage and a comfortable position within the warlock's household. Powerful warlocks are able to absorb powers and life force, but it is frowned upon and is only used as a punishment. Warlocks have soul-mates they call intimates. When a warlock finds their intimate, they no longer need a harem to feed from.

Xavier Colest (Crown Prince)

Xavier is one of the most powerful beings in the

galaxy, only second to his parents. He is mostly with the circus because he gets bored easily. He helps with glamour to confuse the humans. He has purple/blue eyes and long indigo hair. His body is lean and muscular, and he has piercings in his ears, nose, and eyebrow. His ears are pointed, and he has lavender-colored skin with silver markings.

Xylene Colest

Queen of the Westalins and Xavier's mother. She was best friends with Alina and Marcus Adams, Lila's parents.

Cronus Colest

King of the Westalins and Xavier's father. He was best friends with Alina and Marcus Adams.

Elyan (Warlock, Head Harem Girl in Xavier's Harem)

Nambra (Warlock, Harem Member)
She has red hair and a voluptuous figure.

Lexus (Warlock, Harem Member)
She has short dark hair and a petite frame.

Ara (Warlock, Harem Member)
Ara has pale pink hair, eyes, and skin.

Jastia (Warlock, Jarem Member)
Jastia possesses buttercup yellow hair, eyes, and skin.

Sinath (Rasque, Harem Member)

The Rasque is a humanoid race that looks like an Earth grasshopper. They have segmented arms and legs with plated body structure. Their penis is covered by plated sections, which retract when manipulated. Once the penis extends, claspers lock the copulating couple together.

Mithus (Milobar, Harem Member)

He has a stingray-shaped head and body, with arms, legs, and a barbed tail. Mithus has two penises, which both have barbs that activate during intercourse, locking them within their partner.

Zanorn (Morpheian, Harem Member)

A race of metamorphs, they are able to take any shape they desire. In natural form, they are like a blank slate with limited features and gray skin.

Topirey (Dionall, Harem Member)

Dionalls are plant creatures with two forms—one is an upright humanoid sentient form, and the other is a stationary plant form which is similar to the Earth's Venus flytrap, only a lot larger and it feeds on flesh. They have leafy foliage on their head and sharp teeth, and are able to grow their body parts at will.

PLANET AQUILIA

Aquilia is seventy-five percent water, and the Aquilians are an aquatic species with three forms—humanoid, mer, and beast form. In beast form, they resemble an Earth dolphin, but are scaled and have sharp teeth. They come in a variety of pastel colors. In half form and on two legs, they retain the pastel colors and cannot glamour. They require a glamour spell if they want to tour Earth. Family groups are called pods. Aquilians rarely leave their home planet, and if they do, they will return once they form a pod so that their young are born in their home waters.

Nikos (Aquilian Prince)

Nikos is one of the performers in the dolphin show in the circus. He is a member of the Aquilian royal family, but not in line to inherit. He is arrogant and horny. He has pastel green skin, and his scales are pastel green and gold. His hair and eyes are metallic gold.

Nixie (Aquilian princess)

Nixie is Nikos's sister and also a performer in the circus. She's friendly and fun and is interested in exploring the galaxy. She does not want to get trapped by being mated on Aquilia. Nixie is also open to trying relationships with other species. Her colors are pastel blue and gold, with metallic gold hair and eyes.

Galaxy Circus Pod Members
Joaquin
Nolani
Marin
Dorado

PLANET RILU

Rilu is a desert-like planet with small green oases dotted across its land surfaces. There are no above ground oceans or seas, but there are large underground ones which provide fresh water for the inhabitants of the planet. At each of the oases, which usually center around a small lake, are wells which provide fresh drinking water for travelers. Some of the larger lakes have permanent villages established for trade. The people of Rilu are nomadic tribes. They raise larnuks and are miners. Under the surface of Rilu are extensive gem mines, and the people of Rilu mine the gems for trade and to feed their larnuks.

Zala (Larnuk Mistress)

Zala is the larnuk mistress for the circus and is in charge of that portion of the show. She has exotic, Middle Eastern looks with darker skin and wavy, pitch-black hair with streaks of color in it from her horses.

Her eyes are a pale blue, almost white, rimmed in kohl, and framed with long black lashes. She is tall and slim, and her body is covered in silvery scars from bonding with her horses. Five appear in the show, but she has more.

Larnuks

These are creatures much like Earth's Pegasus, possessing both wings and a horn. They come in the same colors as the gems that are mined on their planet—emerald, ruby, sapphire, gold, and amethyst. They eat gems and spout fire, and they have sharp, vicious teeth. They are bred and raised by a larnuk mistress or master who will bond with their herd. The larnuk will bite them, and a lock of their hair will turn the same color as the larnuk's. The more streaks a master or mistress has, the more larnuks they control.

Rilax

Rilax are berries that grow in the mines alongside the gems. The berries are used to make rilaxious, a pink alcoholic beverage popular across the galaxy. It is slightly bubbly with a thick, creamy consistency.

PLANET RECCEDEA

A lush, foliage-covered, tropical planet with frozen poles on either end. It is the birthplace of the dinosaurs found in the circus. Many species of dinosaurs that once roamed the Earth continue to survive and thrive on this planet.

Vigolash

Viggy is a red and black tyrannosaurus rex. He was trained from a baby, and acts just like a giant, overgrown golden retriever.

Htead

Htead is a yellow and orange velociraptor, who was also trained from a baby, but is unruly and kind of crazy.

OTHER ALIEN RACES

Unas

A race of highly intelligent, peaceful, powerful beings who created the power orb that the Galaxy Circus protects. The now extinct race had powers that were fueled through sexual energy. They didn't have mates or partners, it was just a free-for-all orgy.

Their war with the Aaz'ax dwindled their numbers until there were only a handful left. Their energy was absorbed into the orb when they turned it over to the Adams brothers. They used the Adams' ancestors' blood to link it to them, and if it leaves their line, anyone remaining will be absorbed too.

The power orb was supposed to be a clean, free source of energy capable of powering planets across the galaxy. It can be used as a weapon of mass destruction, but cannot be destroyed because the galaxy would implode.

Aaz'ax

The leadership of this race was cruel and vicious and wanted to use the orb to conquer other lands. They possessed it momentarily and laid waste to a number of planets, but the Unas were able to take it back. By then, the Aaz'ax weren't doing well. A mysterious illness had taken most of their women, and women of other races wanted nothing to do with the men. Their species has been on the brink of extinction and were finally able to dispose of their tyrannical leadership. Remaining survivors scattered to planets far and wide. The Aaz'ax are distant ancestors of the Vilaxians. Although they do not require blood, they can consume it, but it acts much like alcohol and drugs to a human. They have the ability to glamour, and their natural form is humanoid, but their shoulders and backs are covered in ridges and their body looks like they are covered in thorns. With their green skin and blood-red hair, they resemble a rose.

Telazions (Planet Telaz)

They sold the tech for the iPhone to Steve Jobs.

Nengh

They perform as clowns in the circus. They have detachable limbs and are able to adjust their body's size and mass. They are humanoid in shape, but they are orange with feathery tufts instead of hair. They use a glamour provided by Xavier to appear human when on Earth.

Jelliads

A race of gelatinous amorphic creatures. They are sentient and communicate via telepathy.

Phoeall (fo-all): Warlock for…

Vigolash: Obedient one in Aaz'axian

Sandar worm: native to the planet Westalin, they are large creatures that turn soil over in their paddocks between crops. They eat all organic matter left from past crops, leaving it free for farmers to plant the next crop.

Silax worm: Native to Rilu, it lives in the mines and is a pest. Their secretion kills the rilax berry plant. They are trapped, and their secretions are used to make achom.

Achom: A drink that is like a blend of coffee and chocolate with a chili vodka kick.

GIN: Galaxy Information Network.

Karta monster: A large, kaiju style creature the size of an elephant.

Cirillion: Little bundles of fluff with big eyes.

Lastovian hog: A long pig like creature with six legs, five eyes and a piercing squeal.

Saturn's Rings: A restaurant on the mothership.

Edalaxion Space Station: A space station with dodgy bars and meeting spaces for the dregs of the galaxy.

Celesian Brothel: A popular brothel if you want to have sex with living beings as opposed to sex bots.

Jaxa bird: A bird native to Westalin, it looks like a cross between a peacock and a phoenix. Its tail is a fanned bloom of fire.

Kala mouse: A marsupial found on Westalin.

Coolmy shell: This is a crustacean found in Aquilian waters.

ACKNOWLEDGMENTS

As always Grace and Hope. My throuple members, my author wife and PA, my best bitches. So glad I can feed your tentacle fetishes.

To Jillian and Kerry, the best alpha readers a girl could have, I love you guys.

To my super awesome beta team, your help is as always much appreciated.

To my cover designer Jessica, of Raven Ink Covers. Thank you for making the covers exactly what I envisioned, you nailed it.

My editor Michelle, none of this would be possible without you. Pretty sure Lila is a combination of the craziest parts of you and me.

Thank you to Kirsty Ellis, Belinda McCormack, Elise Parnham, Tanith Rhiannon Helena, and Kelly Paez for your name suggestions through out the book, you guys rock.

This was the first book I ever started writing and I'm so glad you guys finally get to read it. I hope you love Lila as much as I do so I can keep writing her. Until next time happy reading.

Lexie

ALSO BY LEXIE WINSTON

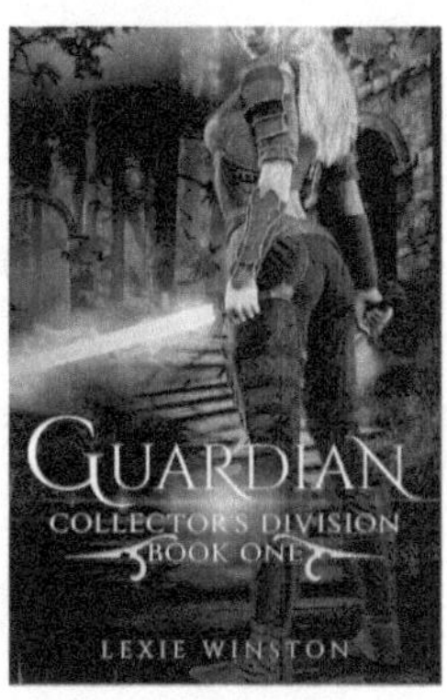

Buy on Amazon

Joining the Collectors Division was my only goal once the orphanage washed their hands of me at the age of twelve.

Unruly and quick to anger, I was taken in by an academy instructor until I was old enough to attend myself. With love and understanding I thrived, and it became my mission to be the best Guardian the Collectors Division had ever seen. I couldn't

wait to run the Gauntlet and join a team.

Little did I know what fate had in store for me.

Guardian is a reverse harem novel and contains MM and FF. Not recommended for those under 18

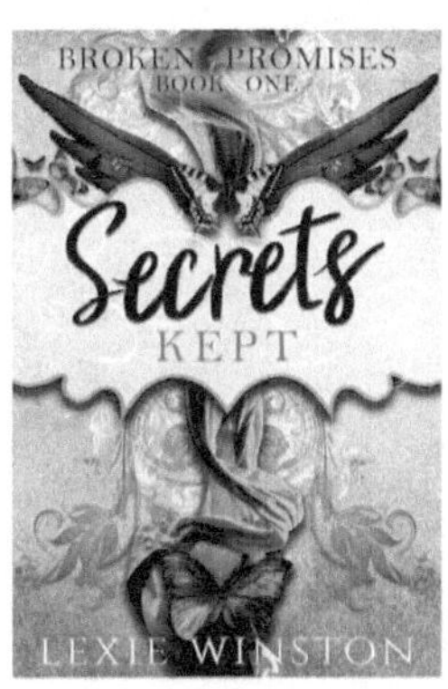

Pre-order on Amazon

I wasn't always like this you know. I used to be one of those girls who was bubbly and people thought sunshine came out of my ass.

That is until my best friend kissed me and then betrayed me with those same lips. I became ridiculed and bullied and my soul slowly died inside until I was a shadow of my former self.

But then my father introduced me and my brother to our family legacy and I became glad of the fractured, broken soul I'd become. In fact, I reveled in it.

We trust no one but each other, blood is always thicker than water. Heaven help those that betray us.

Because we aren't afraid to get our hands dirty....

This book will be dark poly. There will be MM and FF and various combinations. It will contain sexual situations that may make you feel uncomfortable. There will be drugs references and violence. You have been warned